HARMONY DOZEN

First published in Newcastle, Australia by Ryan Berger
(product of Simpl Scribbles), 2021

This edition published 2023

ISBN 9780645297805

Thank you to Reid for beta reading, and your
support throughout the process

Thank you to Emma for your patience and
amazing work on the cover design

PART I

1

HEXAGON WALLS

I knew nothing but pain as my head throbbed against a hard surface. Unable to move, I understood that my body lay sprawled across a tiled floor.

Where am I? My body pulsated with pain and delirium. I raised my eyebrows slightly and allowed my eyes to swivel across the room, cautiously scanning my new surroundings.

I neglected to move, uncertain of the dangers of the foreign environment. My skin regained feeling with the coldness from the tiles seeping into my body, and slowly my sense of touch was joined by vague memories.

A bus. No – a plane. A man in handcuffs. These thoughts didn't make sense, and as an array of vivid yet hazy memories charged into my mind, I realised that my own recollection of myself was clouded. I forced myself to re-establish my own truths: *I'm Tyler. I'm nineteen years old and I run a social media website . . .*

Yes, that's right. I had received a gift from a colleague to travel to the island of Touhere. Memory of the flight over the Pacific came back to me. Why couldn't I remember the landing?

After a few moments, I adjusted my neck to look around the room. It was hexagon-shaped, with concrete walls. A soft white light along the perimeter artificially broadened the space. The room was austere – like a modern prison cell. A toilet and sink were fixed to one of the walls.

As I craned my neck further, I found a lone bed directly behind me covered in a lurid orange doona. On first appearance, the bed seemed far too small for an adult, let alone my lanky limbs. An emerald light cast from above stole my attention, and my eyes were guided to an illuminated sign reading EXIT. Beneath it was merely more wall, no exit visible at all.

I slowly pushed myself to my feet, stumbled towards the bed and slumped onto it. I raced my fingers through my messed hair as I tried to recall detail from the plane. Black dots appeared before me as I clenched my eyes shut to strain my memory.

Turbulence . . . a bald man staring at me aggressively . . . an energetic man on a bus . . .

I sat up, hunched over the bed. My fingertips scraped my chin's stubble in frustration. I looked down at my hands, barely familiar, and slowly began to recognise this body as my own. I turned my hands over slowly, examining them. A silver bracelet – not one I recognised – was secured upon my right wrist. It blinked, two miniature blue circles of light pulsating effortlessly. Beneath it, an intense pricking of my skin irritated me. I knew that I was not wearing this accessory by choice.

As my body became familiar, the bracelet continued to feel foreign. I pried at the silver accessory, but there seemed to be no way to remove it; no form of a release button, notch or clip. It refused to budge.

I absorbed the room in its entirety. The walls felt as if they were gradually closing inward. They radiated a chilled ambiance and, coupled with the tiled floor, made me feel colder with each passing moment. A sense of claustrophobia twisted inside of me. My stomach jerked awkwardly, and my eyes fell upon the sanitary facilities. I had barely made it to the toilet when my stomach contents violently ejected from me.

The toilet flushed my vomit with a hiss, and I lay with my face hanging in the bowl of the toilet, shaking both from the sickness and from the cold floor tiles. My eyes closed, and a scene formed before me.

I was walking in the middle of a line of people towards a wide building encased in mirrors. I was outside. The sun owned the back of my neck, its heat penetrating the exposed skin above my collar. A bald head bobbled before me, attached to a man shorter than me however far more muscular. A linen shirt hung loosely over his broad shoulders, clinging to him as it danced in the wind. Beneath this, a spiralled tattoo slithered upward onto his neck and disappeared behind his ear.

Ahead of him, several other passengers walked silently across the tarmac, accumulating sweat as we headed towards the terminal, which I hoped to be air-conditioned. A large man led the queue, escorted by a uniformed guard who was firmly gripping his bicep. A reflection briefly flickered beneath a thick cloth that hung over the large man's hands. I glimpsed the silver handcuffs that fixed his arms behind his back and only just realised that I had been sitting only few metres from the prisoner on the plane. I recalled the man's ginger crewcut which resembled an army general's.

The people ahead of and behind me were strangers, I knew only myself as we trotted onward towards the terminal. I turned back and watched the plane shrink behind me with a feeling of relief. I'd always loathed flying.

The air on the island felt heavy, and a natural orangey tinge radiated across the tarmac. My shirt now stuck uncomfortably to my back as I turned back towards the front of the queue.

I failed to notice the man stop abruptly before me. My feet stumbled but couldn't prevent me from colliding into his back, knocking his phone from his grasp onto the asphalt.

'What the—?' The man turned curtly. He straightened himself and stared directly into my eyes. I stuttered an apology, which was dismissed by his fierce glare. I caught my own unsteady reflection in his darkened eyes, and a lump in my throat swelled that it ached as I forced a swallow. Despite standing a head shorter than me, I felt his eyes scrutinise me.

With a snort he collected his phone before resuming his place in the conveyor-like formation.

Back in the small room, I pushed myself up from the toilet and stretched my gangly arms high above my head. At least a metre separated the tips of my fingers from the ceiling. Although the bed and toilet were on opposite sides of the room, they were only three metres apart – or two lanky steps. I took those steps towards the bed and paced between the two halves of the room in search of an exit.

Behind my eyes, the image of the bald man lingered – the ferocity of his stare fixed in my mind. Was he somehow responsible for my situation? Why couldn't I remember what had happened after that confrontation? I collapsed onto the bed and strained to remember what happened next. But instead, I decided to revisit the events that led to my encounter on the tarmac.

2

THE RIDDLE

Forty thousand feet above the Pacific Ocean my spine twisted uncomfortably in the cushioned seat. The sight of the vast blue that skimmed beneath the plane caused my stomach to churn inside of me. I hastily shut the screen to my side, blocking the glare that pulsated through the window like blazing breath.

A brochure lay on the vacant seat beside me.

Touhere — Brand new, six-star island resort.

Opening in the summer, this exclusive resort located on a remote island is not one to be missed.

Experience luxury as you can only imagine.

The brochure featured a bamboo villa with a backdrop of palm trees. A shallow tide of clear ocean greeted the villa's entrance. Smaller pictures bordered the brochure, featuring a massage bed, an elegant restaurant setting and a scatter of spiritual symbols.

As the resort had only been open for a few months, I knew only the limited information that the retreat had made public, and a little about the island of Touhere itself. I knew of Touhere's location – a remote island somewhere to the east of New Zealand, previously occupied by indigenous islanders. I had heard that Touhere was purchased by a wealthy businessman who within a few years had redesigned the island to become an elegant retreat limited to the few that could afford its hefty fee. Glancing at the heavily-edited pictures on the brochure, I internally thanked my associate and family friend Chase for recently gifting me the ticket for my nineteenth birthday.

How he'd managed to secure tickets to the exclusive resort was nothing short of a mystery; however, it was known that Chase had connections around the globe. He had been in my life longer than I could recall, and each passing birthday he managed to outdo himself from the previous year. *He's set the bar high for next year*, I thought.

The plane only carried a handful of passengers, each privately tucked away within their own compartment. The moment we had departed Sydney, I had closed the curtain to isolate myself from the other passengers and crew. Within a few hours I would be sipping cocktails on a private beach; I had no desire for human interaction for the next fortnight.

I pulled at my laptop and thrust it onto the adjustable tray before me. Surely I had time to scan through my work emails before our descent. Met by my dishevelled reflection in the screen, I watched

myself blink heavily as the computer loaded.
Darkened circles hung below my eyes, which had
become a staple of my appearance in recent months.
The device loaded and I found an email that had only
come through since I had boarded the flight, titled
Stop reading your emails:

> *Tyler,*
>
> *I hope you enjoy your trip to Touhere. You don't want
> to know how difficult it was to secure your ticket! Investing in
> your start-up has been the highlight of my career, and after all
> the work you have put into your business, you deserve a break.*
>
> *I apologise that I've been uncontactable recently;
> however, we will catch up when you return to discuss the future
> of the business and the direction you want to take.*
>
> *Now, stop checking your emails and enjoy your
> vacation!*
>
> *Regards,*
>
> *Chase*

I thought of Chase and how he had indeed
been absent recently. He and my father were
colleagues turned best friends, and I hadn't seen
either in several months. Their busy work schedule
had always ensured they were travelling for lengthy
periods at a time.

Ignoring Chase's request, I fell into the
kaleidoscope of emails before me, and time slipped
through the clouds. A soft voice announced the
plane's descent and within half an hour I would be
stumbling into the rear of a hostile bald man on a
scorching tarmac.

The taste of dried vomit lingered in the corners of my mouth and my legs quivered with my attempt to stand. I looked up at the sink before me. Twisting the tap produced only a drizzle of water, which I invited to the back of my throat. The stream ceased suddenly, as if the water had run out, and turning the tap brought forth nothing more.

I let out an involuntarily scream of frustration. Sweat gathered above my brow and crept past my temple. My cries of fury transformed into emotional pleas, unanswered.

'Help!' I called at the ceiling. I ran towards the EXIT sign and bashed my closed fists against the wall, turning my hands pink. 'Let me out! Please! Help me!' My voice didn't even echo a response. The sound seemed to absorb into the walls. My wrists burned in agony with each new blow to the concrete wall. My skull leaned into the wall in defeat and I allowed my legs to crumple beneath me.

Hours passed. I continued a cycle of calling for rescue, bashing myself against the concrete, retreating to the floor, and repeating. Ultimately, I found myself on the bed hugging my knees to my chest.

My eyes scanned the tiny chamber. The bed on which I sat occupied most of the space, with the toilet and sink against the wall to my right. The illumination from the EXIT sign overpowered the dim light of the hexagonal perimeter. Nothing more.

Interrupting the silence of my thoughts, the shrill static sound of a speaker penetrated the room. I could locate no visible speaker; it was as if the sound radiated from the walls themselves. No sooner had the static began ringing, it stopped. Then a strangely familiar voice, enthusiastic and triumphant, trailed the static:

> *Welcome, welcome, let's have some fun.*
>
> *Today is Oranga Trials day number one.*
>
> *You're all the contestants, and I am the host.*
>
> *The prize that you seek is well worth the boast.*

At first, I was not convinced that the message was for me. The ecstatic voice seemed to be addressing an audience, but I was the only soul within the room. The owner of the voice was difficult to place, although it seemed eerily familiar. The message continued excitedly:

> *A variety of Trials awaits you ahead,*
>
> *You will use your strength, but you must use your head.*
>
> *Quick instincts will help you, and strength in your heart,*
>
> *Above all, do not let your faith fall apart.*
>
> *Innocence will prevail, this is fate,*
>
> *However, if you fail in the Trials, we will terminate.*

Static rang again, evidently signalling the end of the announcement, and with that my heart sank. The voice haunted me. Who was it that made the announcement, and why did they have a tone of familiarity?

The static evaporated into the cracks of the walls followed only by silence. What felt like an hour passed of generating wild conspiracies about where I was and how I'd got here. My memory stopped on the airport's tarmac, but visions of an aqua-coloured bus flickered before me. And the face of a youthful boy, smiling.

I didn't recognise the boy. I wondered if he was responsible for my capture and what relationship he might have with the bald man. My brain continued to piece together how I had arrived at this point until an abrupt *whoosh* interrupted the silence. A section of the wall beneath the EXIT sign shot upwards, revealing a small space between the bed and toilet; pitch black and ominous.

Curiosity overcame me. My legs slid from the edge of the bed and crept forward towards the opening. The glare of the EXIT sign shone a tinge of green over the dark hole in the wall, inviting me onward. My heart thumped against my chest – either from the excitement of a potential escape or nervousness about what lay beyond. Hesitantly, I allowed myself to edge closer to the threshold of this new environment.

The room beyond was dark, but as I stepped through the opening a light flicked on. My desire to flee the hexagonal pod outweighed the unnerving feeling that squirmed inside me, and with that I took another step forward to investigate further.

It was like stepping into a walk-in wardrobe. The sensored light illuminated a narrow corridor and beyond. To my right was a low wooden bench and over it, a clothes-hanging rack with a quartet of coat hangers. On one hung an orange towel, matching the doona in the adjoining room; on a second an intriguing jumpsuit, silky and black, feeling almost felt like liquid as I allowed it to roll through my fingertips. The only rough texture on the material was an elegant thin orange stripe which ran along one side from the ankle upwards towards the chest until it linked with a thick number 4, matching the gaudy colour of the doona and towel.

It had taken me until now to realise that the clothes I was wearing were not my own. A sense of unfamiliarity came over me as I felt the fitted black track pants and singlet upon my skin. I had never witnessed the exact shade of unattractive orange which the singlet featured as much as I had in the past few hours.

With one step, I moved from the small walkway into a room resembling a bathroom. The walls were tiled, and the ceiling rested as high as it had in the original room. The only artefact in the room beyond the corridor was a shower fixed snugly in the corner of the space. A thunderous *whoosh* caused me to turn: the gap in the wall behind me had closed.

Beneath the foreign clothes, sweat had accumulated and dried since my awakening. The shower invited me into its clutches. I hesitated only a moment before undressing and thrusting myself beneath the lukewarm stream. I struggled at the bracelet again in the shower, but my attempts were short-lived. Instead, I allowed the flow of water to numb my body as my eyes rolled to a close.

3

THE HOST

Showering seemed to clear my mind and I began to grasp the situation around me. I accepted that I was a hostage, but a debate raged in my mind as to whether the people I encountered from the plane were fellow hostages or my captors.

I could not comprehend what my captors gained from my detention. I couldn't recall crossing anybody shady and I offered no financial gain. Perhaps this was an organised terrorist attack performed on an unfortunate, random group of travellers. I finished my shower, dried myself with the provided towel and slipped into the tracksuit that hung in the walkway. It fit my lanky body perfectly.

As I floundered in a tunnel of conspiracy theories, a loud creak from the first room snapped me back to reality. The wall beside me shot up and I slowly propelled myself towards the light projecting from the adjoining room, the hexagonal chamber where I had awoken only hours ago.

I was met by the back of a man sitting facing away from me on a chair in the middle of the room, his hands clenching a clipboard in his lap. A second, empty chair faced him. He did not move as I walked towards him, nor when the gap in the wall secured behind me with a *whoosh*. Light floated from the skirting toward his spectacular face and highlighted his sharp cheekbones and jaw. His familiarity came not from his facial features but from his tight suit, which clung to him as a glove would to a hand. His navy blue outfit almost glistened with the light's touch, and his hair was slicked back neatly so that the tips curled against his neck.

He turned towards me and beamed as I approached him, apparently unfazed by my confusion. 'Hello, Tyler!' he exclaimed.

The greeting was extraordinary; as if he were addressing an audience, although there came no applause. I looked at him, dumbfounded, before he gestured in the direction of the vacant chair.

'Tyler, the saffron contestant, number four,' he began, reading from his clipboard. 'My name is Alexandro. I am – well, I am the host!'

Before I could make sense of his statement, the only logical question that formed in my brain spilled out of me. 'The host? The host of what?'

'Why, the inaugural Oranga Trials, of course! You, Tyler, are one of ten hand-picked contestants for the Trials.' Alexandro was buzzing, his clipboard bouncing eagerly against his knees as he watched me intently. A touch of madness superseded the eagerness in his voice.

In contrast to Alexandro, I remained standing beside the empty chair as a blend of confusion and rage radiated through me. I had not noticed my fists clenching until I noticed Alexandro's eyes divert toward them suspiciously.

'Hand-picked? By who?' I demanded. Hundreds of questions flooded my brain as I stood over the man. Anger overtook confusion, and I felt a vein swell against my temple, its throb growing in ferocity as I glared down at Alexandro.

'Now, Tyler, unfortunately, I cannot provide you with that information yet. But I can answer some other questions you might have. We want you to feel as relaxed as possible going into Trial One.'

Relaxed? Are you kidding? I thought. I swallowed the curse words that tried to escape my lips.

'Get me out of here right now!' I ordered. Without thinking, I approached Alexandro aggressively, my right arm raised, ready to strike.

The events that occurred next happened instantaneously. With the bow of Alexandro's head, I lost all sensation other than the pain that struck my body. I could not identify a source of the pain but felt each of my bones clatter against one another, vibrating violently inside me. Time stopped, yet the vibrations intensified. I could not tell which body part ached the most as my legs, arms, chest and skull felt like one; all on the verge of penetrating my skin.

I collapsed onto the tiles. I thought my bones would shatter beneath me as I fell, but the pain slowly subsided once I found the floor. Each compulsive twitch stabbing me from the inside.

'Aggression won't help you here, my friend,' said Alexandro calmly.

Slowly, I no longer felt the presence of my bones or their vibrations, but I remained on the floor clutching at various parts of my body.

'If you try anything like that again,' he continued, 'I'm afraid that the pain will only be intensified. Now, please, I must insist that you sit up. Let's talk like adults.'

I failed to comprehend how the pain had been generated, or how no visible blemishes were marked upon my body. I had never felt an electric shock, but I imagined the pain I had just experienced surpassed that.

My hands rubbed against my limbs furiously. My insides didn't feel natural; the phantom vibrating of my bones remained. Through gritted teeth, I obeyed the host's request and fell upon the chair opposite him. 'What *was* that?'

'That was your bracelet controlling the situation. I have come to understand that it will generate a shock to your body if you become uncooperative.'

He did little to explain how the event that just unfolded was possible, but more pressing questions needed to be addressed. 'Why am I here? I haven't done anything wrong.'

'Now, that is a question I can answer!' Alexandro grinned. 'Let me have a look here . . .' He glanced over his clipboard, running his bony fingers along the page. Although the clipboard only held a single piece of paper, I got the impression that Alexandro theatricalised his search. I watched impatiently as his eyes darted across the page. 'Ahh, here it is. Tyler Knight . . . a thief.'

Thief? I had stolen nothing more than a paperclip, maybe a couple of grapes from my weekend grocery shop! The accusation stunned me. Before I could ask for clarity, Alexandro continued reading.

'A thief, of a sum of $250,000. Stolen from Mr Chase Iscariot six months ago.'

I met the hazel of Alexandro's eyes as he peered over the clipboard. He had to be referring to Chase's investment. I recalled the exchange six months ago as if it were only last week. Within the blend of emotions that raced through me, a slither of relief came. Perhaps this misunderstanding could be resolved.

'Stolen? No. No, that money was given to me as an investment. There is clearly some confusion. We should call Chase himself and—'

I was cut off by Alexandro with a snappy 'Uh-uh!' He gently raised his hand for silence. I sat with my mouth open as he dropped his hand onto my wrist. 'There has been no confusion, my friend. Mr Iscariot himself informed us of the thievery.' He paused. Alexandro turned his head slightly to meet my eye. His grasp tightened on my wrist. 'If you are truly innocent, my friend, the Trials will decide your fate.'

The following minutes passed in silence. It was difficult to translate my thoughts into words, so instead I remained seated, staring past the host in frustration. Alexandro meanwhile appeared machine-like, as he sat motionless with a fixed, conniving smile, waiting for me to recommence the conversation.

Eventually it was he who broke the silence. 'Tonight, you will be required to attend a feast. All contestants will be present. Let us use this as an opportunity to provide a more thorough explanation of the journey ahead.'

My stomach plummeted into my lap with the comprehension of my situation. I was a hostage, and there were others who must be in similar cells to mine. I wondered if they knew of their wrongdoing before their captivity. How many 'contestants' had Alexandro captured? I turned my head away from Alexandro. *He will go away if I ignore him*, I told myself.

A few more silent minutes passed until Alexandro eventually fulfilled my desire. 'I wish you good luck, Tyler.' He stood and collected his chair.

The sound of another *whoosh* caused me to jump as a new opening appeared, this time opposite the wall that had been exposed earlier. The chamber now disclosed two potential exits, concealed as concrete walls. I wondered if all six walls featured a hidden escape. Within an instant, Alexandro disappeared through the new opening, and when it closed, I was alone again with only my mind to keep me company.

4

THE INVESTMENT

The silence in the room screamed louder than all else. Confusion was the overriding emotion as I tried to dissect the information Alexandro had imparted. Evidently, I was a contestant in the 'Oranga Trials', and I had been accused of thievery. But the host had raised more questions than he had resolved.

Rubbing my arms, I felt debilitated physically. I had never been very active, preferring spreadsheets and computers to sport and the gym. Whatever these Trials were, I was certain that it was in my best interest to avoid them.

As I further strained my brain for answers, I continued to return to one comment Alexandro had made: *If you are truly innocent, my friend, the Trials will decide your fate.* What tests could he have prepared to determine whether I was innocent? How could I prove that I was no thief without Chase's word for it? Alexandro had said that it was Chase who informed him of the theft; how could that be?

Perhaps money was not the motive for my captors. Alexandro failed to mention ransom of any sort. *So, what do they want?*

I lay on my back, spread-eagled on the mattress, and my memory took me to six months ago, only weeks after my high school graduation.

Far from Touhere, I assembled myself upon a comfortable leather lounge in a modern foyer. Grand graphite tiles separated the lounge and reception desk, where a young woman sat busily typing at her computer. She had the straightest teeth I had ever seen, neatly arrayed to produce a radiant smile for each worker who hurriedly brushed past her.

Although making an effort to smile at her distracted co-workers, she failed to notice me as I absorbed myself in my mobile phone as I waited. Across the foyer, two men strolled towards me, engaging excitedly. I slipped my phone into my pocket and straightened up – Chase had arrived.

He was the shorter of the pair and had his hand fixed on the other's shoulder as he laughed exuberantly. The taller man, unknown to me, clapped his colleague on the back before departing through an open door off to one side.

Chase then advanced towards me offering a smile as our eyes locked. Some believed that Chase's smile was permanently etched onto his face. He had olive skin and his beard – along with most of his features – was neat, clean. In all my years of knowing him, I had never seen him appear underdressed or ungroomed. Chase's shirt was tight-fitting, and his rolled-up sleeves exposed large forearms and an expensive golden watch.

'Tyler, me boy!' He clapped me on the back so hard that I almost toppled forward. 'Thanks for coming in today. I have some exciting news for you.'

Chase was beaming at me. With his hand still on my back, he ushered me into an empty office across the foyer. We crossed the woman behind the reception desk who looked up at us as we passed.

'Just going to use this one for a while, darl.' Chase said with a wink. She smiled coyly.

Once inside the office, Chase offered me a chair before seating himself across the large oak table. The room was long, and the desk had almost a dozen chairs around it. Scattered across a whiteboard on the wall behind Chase was an array of unintelligible words and various number combinations.

Chase poured two glasses of water from a pitcher and passed one to me. 'Your father has shown me your designs. I hope that's okay?'

'My designs? Why?' The social media website I had been designing for the past few months was not ready to be shown to anybody. The layout was still sketchy, the coding was completely messy, and I hadn't even come up with an appropriate name. I scrambled for a response. 'I, I don't think—'

'I love it,' Chase said, cutting me off. Three simple words that made my heart tingle with excitement. 'Smarter than the average bear, you are.'

I wondered how my father had seen my notes, but I was too overcome with Chase's words of praise to question this. I had told my father that I was working on a social media website, but his lack of interest hadn't created an opening for me to divulge any more information about it to him.

'Now, as you know, Tyler, I have a wide network of people within the industry. People who are interested in innovation. People who can help you. Tyler, *I* want to help you.'

I nodded, and together we began scrutinising and developing the minimal concept of the site that I had innovated. Within a few hours, it had transformed from an insignificant idea to a spider web of ambitious creation. We created mind maps of business opportunities and contact cards of stakeholders who could support the company. Chase formally offered me $250,000 to be used as an investment; however, it had come with a condition.

'You must promise me not to tell Victor.' He was referring to my father. 'He wouldn't want me investing money, but I can see real potential in you.'

I accepted this without question, and I promised I would return the entire investment with a sizeable return once the company was operational. We spent the remainder of the afternoon in the office, building on my ambitions.

Back in the isolation of the hexagonal chamber, I lay motionless, engulfed by memories of my life outside this cell. I thought of my father and Chase, neither of whom I had seen for an age before my expedition to Touhere and wished to see them both again.

5

AIRPORT TRANSFER

It had been hours since Alexandro's brief, bizarre visit, although it was impossible to know the time as there was no clock, nor any windows in the hexagon. The only concept of time came from the strip of light that illuminated the floor's perimeter. I wasn't sure if my mind was playing tricks on me, but it appeared that the light dulled as the hours passed.

My lower forearm had started to swell slightly, which did little to prevent me from continually pulling at the jewellery clamped around my right wrist. I ran my fingers along the bracelet slowly in an attempt to locate a clue as to orchestrate its removal, but to no avail. Time absconded in my room absently. The minutes felt like hours, hours like weeks.

The desire to explain myself to Alexandro engulfed me. If only I could reason with him without the distraction of 'a series of tests'. If only he could contact my father, or Chase, to explain everything.

The idea of 'Trials' dictating my innocence created a cauldron of anxiety in the pit of my stomach.

Although alone in the room, I sensed an abundance of invisible eyes observing me from a distance. I couldn't shake the feeling of being watched, despite the concrete walls that surely prevented anybody from observing me from the other side. Like a caged animal, I strutted from corner to corner feeling for an escape.

Whoosh.

Where Alexandro had disappeared hours before, the opening appeared again and a dim light shone into the room. The opening resembled the mouth of a monster; what lay beyond was a mystery. I moved forward with caution; the end of the tunnel unseeable. As I approached the gap, I saw two thin strips of white light racing along the skirts of the floor.

The illumination stretched farther than I could see; the two lights curved around a corner and met at a point in the distance. Aside from this minimal lighting at floor level, the tunnel was completely black. With nothing to lose, I stepped into the darkness.

Click, click, click. My feet clapped against the pavement of the tunnel as I moved away from my confinement, comically breaking the uncomfortable silence. I walked aimlessly for a minute before a fuller light became visible in the distance. As I approached this light, I watched it transform into the entrance to a large, open hall. Sounds of soft voices grew stronger as I crept along the tunnel towards it. When I reached the opening, a final backwards glance confirmed that my room had faded from view. Only a string of dull lights twisting along the floor remained.

The hall was simple and elegant. A high glass ceiling gave a view to a picturesque sunset above, projecting a warm orange tinge upon the hall. Ten dark corridors extended out in separate directions from one side of the hall like the assertive limbs of a spider, each numbered from 1 to 10 above their entrance in different colours. I turned to see that I had stumbled from the tunnel labelled 4 coloured in saffron orange.

A series of lamps illuminated the hall further, each affixed between the tunnel entrances. On the opposite side to the tunnels, a grand set of double doors – bright silver, with no visible sign labelling where it led – stood tall. An impressively polished oak table occupied the middle of the hall with ten chairs placed around it. An elegant setting of a plate, goblet and cutlery laid before each chair.

Multiple silver cloches formed the table's centrepiece, each tantalisingly covering a dish like a metallic present, shining as bright as the other tableware. A smaller yet higher table sat between the main table and the double doors.

I observed a variety of other guests, all wearing identical outfits and confused expressions. Their jumpsuits looked like duplicates of the one I wore, although each of us displayed a unique coloured stripe and number. To my right, another man stumbled into the hall, looking as uneasy as I felt.

Scanning the room, I met the eyes of a young boy who had tucked himself in a corner away from the others and was scratching at his elbow. An image of his face, smiling, flashed behind my eyes. I turned away as a memory surfaced. I closed my eyes and instantly I remembered how I had arrived here.

A single sky-blue shuttle bus awaited directly outside the airport's main doors. I recalled the airport process as swift, as only a handful of passengers were passing through the idle terminal. I had kept my distance from the bald man after our encounter, and before I knew it, I was again under the blazing sun walking toward the shuttle bus.

The bus was parked a short walk away and was difficult to miss. Mustard-yellow lettering contrasting against the bus's blue paint announced: AIRPORT TRANSFER. I hastily stowed my bags in the bus's luggage compartment, then made my way up the few steps onto the bus and quickly found an empty seat towards the back, aiming to be as far apart from both the bald man and the prisoner as possible.

Although appearing average at first glance, the shuttle bus featured a large transparent panel which sealed the driver within his own compartment at the front. The polycarbonate panel stretched the whole width of the bus, with an opening that the passengers passed through inconspicuously as they walked past the driver. In my haste to find a seat distanced from the man from the tarmac, I ignored the polycarbonate panel and failed to notice it close as the final passengers made their way through the opening.

'Good afternoon, friends, and welcome to Touhere!' I looked up to find a youthful, well-dressed man with jet-black hair standing beyond the clear panel. I had not yet met this man – but I would come to know him as Alexandro.

Alexandro bounced on his toes eagerly, his suit wrapping him tightly. His eyes glistened when he spoke. I smiled towards him unintentionally.

The bus driver was hidden from view; he had fastened his seatbelt and shifted the bus into gear as Alexandro continued his speech from the front of the bus. 'The trip is a short 40-minute drive to the resort, so please enjoy the beautiful panoramic view and in no time I'm sure you'll all have your feet up, with a drink in hand!'

He laughed spiritedly to himself and turned toward the driver. It appeared that almost all of the passengers had ignored him, some still desperately searching for reception on their smartphones rather than engaging with the blissful views outside the bus. I took the opportunity to observe some of the other guests.

My attention was drawn to a caramel-skinned woman two seats in front of me, fidgeting with her fingernails. The sound of her scratching sent a shiver down my spine, although she gazed absent-mindedly upwards, appearing not to notice her twitching. Across from her sat a chubby man with darker skin than the fidgety woman. My eyes were drawn to a protruding scar slanted across his face, with one end disappearing into his thick brown hairline. The man's cracked lips were slightly swollen, and he looked to have a chunk missing from his right ear.

The bus rocked soothingly as we slowly moved away from the airport terminal; only sections of the ground seemed to have constructed roads. With each slight bump of the bus, I felt a tiny wave of nausea and I was forced to focus my attention out the window as a distraction.

Beautifully coloured birds soared high above the trees elegantly boasting their wingspan which resonated a swirl of vibrant colours. Several native species seemed to survey the bus as we crept through their territory. At one point a flock of sheep ungracefully began to gallop alongside the bus. Each sheep featured thicker wool than ever I had seen before, and broad white horns curved from some of their temples.

I watched admiringly as one particular sheep, smaller than the others, awkwardly attempted to keep up with the flock. The small one gave an irritable call as the bus pulled away, before becoming engulfed by the forest.

'Beautiful . . .'

A boy – barely eighteen – sitting directly in front of me was also peering out of the window. Unsure if he was talking to himself or to me, I leaned forward, ready to converse. The boy was grasping a small book, opened at a page displaying an array of exotic birds with a mixture of printed and handwritten notes scattered in the margins. His wavy brown hair was unkempt, and he had a sprinkle of light freckles across his nose.

'I've never seen birds like these before,' I decided to reply, causing the boy to turn to me and smile shyly. 'I'm Tyler.'

I extended my hand but again wondered if the boy was even talking to me in the first place. He closed the book in his lap and shook my hand softly.

'My name's Sydney, but my friends call me Sid.' He gave a kind smile, his large blue eyes pierced into mine momentarily before directing his view back out the window. Sid was just as skinny as me, although I assumed he was slightly younger.

We had only been travelling for a few minutes before the vehicle jolted to a halt. Most of the passengers kept their attention on their phones, unfazed by the unexpected stopping of the bus. I looked towards the front of the vehicle; only a couple of others – including Sid – began to shuffle in their seats.

I watched as the energetic man who had welcomed us got up slowly from his seat to approach the polycarbonate door. As he stood at the frame of the door, he and I locked eyes. Without breaking eye contact, Alexandro pressed his hand against a small button on his side of the door. I felt my heart drop. I was unaware what the button was for, but I understood that something wasn't right.

Alexandro shifted his eyes from me as he scanned the bus. Nobody had moved; the other passengers remained absorbed in either their devices or distracted by the wildlife past the windows. The man directed a final glance in my direction before raising his arm towards the ceiling and to a smaller red button above the driver's head. His fingers crept towards it. I stood up, hastily bumping knees with the passenger across the aisle. Before the passenger could comment on my interruption, a loud hissing noise commenced inside the passenger compartment.

I tried to scream, but my surroundings drifted away from me . . . I began to fall backwards onto my seat . . . Alexandro's anxious smile filled my view as the world began to shift into a darker shade . . .

6

CRIMINALS, THIEVES AND TRAITORS

Sid wore an expression of terror as he stood trembling in the corner of the hall, his skinny arms wrapped tightly around his torso. His mustard-yellow stripe was as ugly as my orange one, although it appeared to highlight the freckles on his horror-stuck face. I felt an urge to comfort the boy, but before I could move towards him, a large body bounded in my direction, roughly stopping me in my tracks.

The body belonged to the prisoner from the airport. Unfortunately, no guards were at hand to escort him away. He appeared much broader than I remembered. His thick ginger beard formed a point on his chin. He stood close, his colossal frame blocking everything else from view.

'Name?' the man demanded some sort of accent.

'Uh, I'm T– Tyler.'

'Ah, Tyler . . . Tyler.' He repeated my name a few times under his breath. 'Zey call me Mechislav. Why are yew here?'

The accent was Russian. Some of his consonants rolled across his tongue so strongly that I struggled to comprehend him.

'I'm not meant to be here. They've got it wrong about me.'

'Sure zey do. Zey alvays got eet wrong.'

'They do.' I rolled my eyes when I found him looking away momentarily. 'Why are you here, then?'

I wanted to call back the words as soon as they left my lips. But I had gained Mechislav's focus again and his eyes pierced me sharply.

After a moment's pause, he spoke. 'Yew don't vant to know.' He shrugged and strutted towards a woman who had entered the hall beside us.

A burst of air escaped from my lungs once he moved on; I hadn't realised I was holding my breath. This prisoner scared me. I should not have provoked him.

Before I could collect my thoughts, a gentle hand brushed my shoulder and I turned to see a pale face smiling timidly up at me. It was the freckled boy.

'Hullo,' he said. 'Are you the guy from the bus?'

'Yeah. It's Sid, right?'

He nodded. I held out a hand, which he accepted once again. 'Do you know where we are?'

'Not a clue. The last I remember was arriving in Touhere, and the bus on our way to the resort,' I explained.

Sid recalled his own experience since our last exchange, which sounded just like mine. His final memories on the bus were our conversation, and he was also paid a visit by Alexandro after awaking in an unfamiliar room. We discussed at length the interaction we had had with the host. Fortunately for Sid, he had not felt the surge from the bracelet, and his mouth dropped open when I explained the pain it produced.

'Alexandro thinks I'm a thief. But I'm hoping he will appear soon so I can explain the mix-up,' I said.

'He told me I was a traitor.' Sid looked down at his feet. 'He . . . he said that I'm here because treasonous blood flows inside me. But I'm not. I . . . I . . .' Droplets of tears formed in the corner of his eyes.

'What do you think he meant by "traitor"?' I asked eagerly. I could see that the word upset him, but I felt that any information could help me understand who Alexandro was, and why he had taken us as prisoners.

With a whimper, Sid tried to reply but he couldn't construct a sentence.

Beyond him, I watched as a tall woman with beautifully dark skin limped into the room from the tunnel numbered 1. She collapsed against the wall of the tunnel, slumping to her knees. Her jumpsuit hung loosely on her thin body, sagging like an oversized scuba outfit. Her dark, heavy eyes were obvious from a distance.

It appeared as if the woman had not seen daylight in weeks. She looked severely undernourished, evidenced by the thinness and lack of colour in her face. How long she had been imprisoned was difficult to know, but it was clear she had been here much longer than the rest of us.

Sid continued to sob, but my attention was now on this new arrival, and I was not alone. Mechislav immediately broke off a conversation with an elderly Chinese woman. The old woman continued her story, her hands frantically trying to keep up with the words spilling from her mouth but Mechislav was pacing towards the mysterious, ragged-looking woman from tunnel 1. His long strides quickly turned into a jog until he absorbed her limp body in his arms, pulling her upright and shepherding her to a pair of chairs at the centre table.

'. . . But I . . . I haven't wronged anybody . . .' Sid seemed unaware of the events behind him as he held his face in his hands. I decided to comfort him by wrapping my long arm around his shoulders.

The scene was most bizarre. Small huddles of people formed as we waited for something more eventful to occur. I was sure that any food that lay beneath the cloches could not remain warm. I stayed with Sid, and he with me. We reminisced about our shared experiences – our flight to the island, the strangers we had witnessed on the bus and who were now scattered around the room, and our isolation in our hexagonal chambers.

The chatter around the hall grew louder until the grand doors burst open dramatically, and all faces turned to see Alexandro stride in, bouncing on his heels eagerly. The doors closed swiftly behind him. I regretted being too distracted by his entrance to note anything identifiable from the space he had come from.

'Ladies. Gentlemen. Friends. Please take a seat. I'm sure you all are curious for answers!' He clapped his hands together, gestured towards the long table and casually made his way to the smaller table near the doors. It was now obvious that this higher table was reserved for the host.

Sid walked quickly towards the main table, along with some of the others. I stayed still, in shock, observing the room and eyeing Alexandro.

His wide grin lingered in place as he encouraged the stragglers to join by waving his arms invitingly. 'Now, now, friends. Let us sit together, let us converse!'

To one side, an outline of a man with a bald head stood with tightly folded arms. I recognised him as the man I bumped into on the tarmac. Why did that now feel like an eternity ago?

Several seconds passed; the tension was high as several people started to notice both of us still standing in place. Alexandro eyed me curiously, and Mechislav turned away from his companion to focus on me. Uncomfortable with the attention, I made my way to an empty seat between Sid and an aging woman who looked as nervous as I felt. The woman was rocking back and forth, and looked strangely familiar, but I did not recall her from the flight or the transfer bus. Alexandro gave me an encouraging smile, which I ignored, before his eyes moved over towards the bald man.

'My friend . . .' Alexandro smiled. 'This feast cannot start until we are united, and if you do not join the table, well . . .' He raised an eyebrow cockily. 'I know you have already found out the hard way what that bracelet is for.' I involuntarily pulled at my own wrist, as did several others around the table.

The bald man, however, did not move. If anything, he straightened himself to appear taller. The air was heavy with tension, and after a few awkward moments it was Alexandro who moved first. His face dropped slightly and the smile now faded as he turned away from the group and moved his hands together.

Before the bald man could let out an agonising scream, he had dropped to his knees. I'm not sure if the cries of pain came next, or his body twitching horribly on the floor, but they both occurred in quick succession.

The audience watched in horror as the man continued to give yelps of pain, although attempting to suppress his outbursts. I recalled the feeling that he was experiencing, and I did not envy him. His cries extended for several seconds.

The torture stopped, and he lay on his back facing the high ceiling. Only his large chest moved, rising and falling rapidly.

'We will wait. We cannot begin our feast until Tallis joins us,' Alexandro calmly informed the table. Nobody moved.

After a few moments the man now known as Tallis jerked himself on the floor, pulling himself to his knees. When he gathered the strength to stand, he pulled his shoulders back and pointed a finger aggressively at the host.

'Now, friend,' said Alexandro, 'if you were a smart man, you would join the others quietly.'

Suddenly I felt a shuffle from the table as the familiar-looking woman beside me rose from her chair. All eyes watched as she advanced towards Tallis.

'Come now,' she said as she reached him. 'Do not put yourself through any more pain.' The woman appeared nervous. She was far older than the rest of the group, with grey hair tied shabbily in a bun. Her quivering arm rose slowly towards Tallis in a motherly act of comfort. He whipped around and lashed at her arm.

'Don't touch me, old lady!' he spat.

The woman recoiled in fear and clapped her hands to her mouth.

A flurry of angry calls emanated from the table, each directed at one man only. He raised another finger to the group and fell into the remaining empty chair.

Ignoring the ongoing quarrels, Alexandro raised his hands once more and addressed the group. To him, it was as if nothing out of the ordinary had occurred.

'Welcome to the inaugural Oranga Trials!' he exclaimed. 'I understand some of you remain confused as to why you are here, but please remember – we have made no mistakes! Each of you have been selected because at some point in your life you have wronged, and the upcoming Trials are . . . let us say . . . a systematic process of correcting those wrongs.' He paused momentarily. 'Among us are criminals, thieves and traitors.' I flashed a glance at Sid to my left, who bowed his head in embarrassment. 'Some of you have murdered, victimised, or conspired, some have destroyed property that does not belong to you. But friends, let me say this – innocence will prevail.'

A ruckus promptly followed Alexandro's speech. Many of the others around the table threw curse words at him, but he ignored this and pressed on.

'A series of Trials lies ahead of you. To succeed, you will need to find your inner strength, your character, and your wisdom. Some Trials will challenge you physically, others mentally. Some will test your emotional strength and others your intelligence. At the end of each Trial, contestants face termination from the Oranga Trials until there is only one remaining. Upon completion, my friends, one of you will walk out of those doors.' He pointed at the large double doors behind him. 'And back home to your family and friends, knowing in your heart that you are truly innocent.'

An explosion of voices erupted a second time, and some rose from their seats in rage. Opposite me, Tallis spat on the floor in disgust.

'What about those who are terminated?' yelled one man whose jumpsuit featured a dark blue strip.

'How do we know the last of us will survive?' another called out.

Alexandro simply raised two fingers, commanding silence. 'Now, friends, all your questions will be answered, I promise. I suggest you take this time now to eat, mingle and think about your immediate future. I must warn that excessive discord will lead to another . . . "episode".' He nodded towards Tallis, an obvious threat to activate the bracelets.

Reluctantly, each member of the group found their silence. The ones who were standing adjusted themselves back onto their seats and eventually the chaos settled. Alexandro smiled as he suggested that we eat, and eventually some of the guests began to lift the cloches from the serving platters to find a range of appetising-looking dishes. An overwhelming smell filled the room causing my stomach to growl aggressively.

As time was hard to identify, I assumed it had been over twenty-four hours since my last meal – a tomato and cheese sandwich on the plane. In contrast, these platters boasted a range of cuisines, all of which looked and smelled appetising. Pastas, roasted potatoes, fried rice, pizzas and sushi were all on offer. Several pitchers of water were spread along the table.

Although the lids of the platters were removed, nobody served themselves. I exchanged a nervous look with Sid.

At last, Alexandro approached the main table. Plate in hand, he chuckled to himself as he helped himself to a variety of miniature pizzas. 'If we were to poison you, there would be no fun in the Trials,' he said softly.

I watched intently as he retreated to his own table and began eating. The skinny woman, number 1, who sat beside Mechislav, was the first to collect food onto her plate.

Directly opposite me was the aging Asian woman who had a light brown number 5 on her jumpsuit. I watched as she helped herself to several tuna sushi rolls. Noticing me watching her, she introduced herself as Shy and explained that she was a businesswoman from China who had also intended to visit Touhere as a retreat. Throughout the feast, I came to appreciate her company, her warm smile and her openness to the situation.

I told her of the thievery that I was accused of. 'The money was a gift from my father's best friend, Chase.' I explained. Beside her, Mechislav turned from his conversation to focus on me. I ignored him by collecting more rice onto my plate.

'I see,' Shy said simply. She described her journey leading up to her captivity. She admitted that recently, back home in China, she had made a business mistake resulting in large financial loss for her company. Refusing to go into further detail, she confirmed this as the reason Alexandro had given as to why she was chosen for the Oranga Trials. 'Whatever happens will happen. I have accepted my fate. I must pay for my mistake.'

I spent the remainder of my time at the table observing the others. It was largely uneventful after Tallis's stance against Alexandro. I felt as if Mechislav continued to survey me throughout the evening, but I refused to pay him attention.

At one point, a tanned woman with bushy hair climbed under the table to collect her fork, which she had now dropped for the second time. I could not work out if the woman was nervous or simply clumsy. A few minutes later I watched her reaching for the pitcher of water before mistakenly knocking over her goblet, causing a puddle to appear beside her plate. Nobody bothered to clean up the spill, although it did draw a few people's attention. The woman smiled to herself and continued to refill her goblet.

I made an attempt to distinguish each person around the table. I sat between Sid and the familiar-looking elderly woman, who introduced herself as Gloria. My brain ached as I attempted to place where I had seen before. I knew I had never met her prior to this evening. Perhaps I had seen her in a magazine or on television? Others around the table included Shy, Mechislav, Tallis, the dark-skinned woman who remained close to Mechislav, the clumsy woman, the anxious man from the shuttle bus, who continued to shift in his seat as he scoffed forkfuls of pasta in his mouth, and a quiet Asian man. Ten contestants and one host eating uncomfortably in unison.

The Asian man sat beside the clumsy woman, and they stayed together in conversation for the entirety of the feast.

After an hour of eating, drinking and socialising (besides Tallis, who had engaged with nobody) Alexandro rose from his seat and addressed his audience. 'Friends, we have arrived at our feast's conclusion. It is now time to retreat, rest, and prepare for the upcoming Trial.' There was a murmur among the group. I felt the thin hairs stick up on behind my neck – I had momentarily forgotten about the Trials.

'Each of you will now exit through the appropriate tunnels, corresponding to your number. Once returned to your pods, you will find that access to the en suite is limited. I encourage each of you to use it when it is offered.' His lip curled as he continued. 'But now, a riddle upon your exit!

Many Trials test strength,

This you will find.

But unlike the rest,

This one, your mind.

Strong mental force,

Is required now.

As of course,

The weak will bow.'

The room fell silent. Alexandro clapped his hands together and the group dispersed quietly. Lost in my own thoughts, I let my feet drag me like a slave towards the shadowy tunnel under the large orange number 4.

7

GONE

The room was as dark as it was silent. I lay prone on the bed, unmoved since returning to my pod, not even to crawl under the covers. The thin light around the perimeter had all but diminished, setting the mood that it was well past midnight.

It would have been impossible to sleep after the events that had just occurred. The light from the large EXIT sign cast a green pall over me, and the small blinking of the bracelet at my side ticked away the eventless seconds. I stared at the ceiling, the void above me feeling astronomical in the darkness.

My body motionless, but my brain raced faster than ever. I relived the events of the feast, as images of the other contestants jostled in my mind, complete with theories about their trustworthiness. Alexandro's words, 'innocence will prevail', made me wonder which of the other contestants were genuinely guilty.

I memorised their names (the ones I knew), any unique features on their faces, and separated them into two imaginary columns as to whether I liked them or not. Only Sid and Shy fell into the 'likeable' column. I tried to correlate each contestant with their number and the shade of their jumpsuit strip.

I closed my eyes and was met with Mechislav's scrunched face in my brain. His ginger hair casually transformed into the colour of his jumpsuit's feature – bright red – and his face slowly morphed into Tallis's. Tallis fixed his eyes on me and he opened his mouth to speak, but no words came. I could feel myself slip away from reality . . . my eyelids grew heavy . . . I allowed myself to sink into the pillow beneath my head as I drifted into a deep abyss.

In my dream I was in my childhood home. I was nine years old and enjoying the weekend's sunshine. I understood that I had entered a recurring dream once more, but I could do nothing to escape. It was no less a dream than a memory. I was sitting on the wooden boards of a veranda, and a crisp draught brushed my face, knocking over the tower of cards I had created.

My father came onto the veranda through a sliding door. His navy black and gold tie hung loosely around his neck, and his three top buttons were undone. He did not bother to close the door behind him as he collapsed onto a chair beside me. Never had I see him this dysfunctional. His sleeves were rolled up and his shirt was half untucked and in need of an iron. His eyes were swollen and red – had he been crying?

I looked up at the man I admired above all, the strongest man I knew, he who could do no wrong. My father, the colossal figure who whenever I had a problem was there ready with a solution. Our eyes met and with seven simple words, his image changed forever.

'Son, I'm sorry. Your mother is gone.'

Gone. Not dead, gone.

I was now in a field, running at top sprint. How long I'd been running for I had no idea. What I was running to, or from, was a mystery. The field transformed into my childhood bedroom, my sanctuary. Continuous knocks rampaged on my locked door. The echoes lingered, ignored.

I heard my father's call. 'Please, son. It's her funeral.'

Tears streamed down my face. The room filled quickly with my tears, the water rising rapidly. It had reached the surface of my bed. I refused to move and was now prepared to drown, literally, in my own tears.

I woke abruptly. The bed I lay on was as wet as the one in my dream, but it was sweat, not tears, that drenched the covers. I couldn't tell how long I had been unconscious, but the confined space was alight. The illuminated strip felt brighter than ever, and I shoved my face into the pillow to avoid the glare.

I hated that dream. It had been an age since it had disturbed my sleep, but it haunted me as much as it had the first time. *Your mother is gone.* For years I waited for her return. At nine years old, deep down I understood the truth, but I could never accept her fate was reality. She was only 'gone'.

After a few minutes I rose, determined to formulate a plan. I had to escape before the start of the first Trial. I had a one-in-ten chance of being 'terminated' – whatever that meant – but I had no intention of finding out. If Alexandro wouldn't allow me to explain myself, I could not risk attempting to survive a series of challenges against multiple dangerous individuals.

An influx of ideas for escape formed, each as unlikely to succeed as the one before it. Each plan I conjured had faults, but that did not deter me from formulating another, then another.

I had imagined the outcome of brute force, or a wild sprint through the tunnel the next time the opening to the hall presented itself. But where would I go? There seemed to be no place for me to run once through the tunnel, as each corridor led to another's pod. The large double doors seemed logical, although likely to be locked.

The idea of escaping from within the room was quickly diminished as well. There were no noticeable exits apart from the two that Alexandro seemed to control. The ceiling was too high, and the floor tiles too tough to penetrate. With no tools to demolish the concrete walls, that scheme was also squashed. The prominent EXIT sign deluded me. The opening beneath it led to the en suite, hardly an exit of any kind.

And one consideration overrode every plot I conjured: the bracelet would halt me. It continued to blink cockily, and I shuddered at the memory of the immense pain it had caused the day prior. The pain of my bones vibrating inside me was beyond anything I had experienced before. Images of Tallis's brute but helpless body twitching on the floor came into focus.

Deflated, I drew my thoughts towards an escape plan that was less aggressive. I needed to play to my strengths. It was obvious: the only way to escape was to explain the truth, even if Alexandro refused to concede it. I needed to contact my father, or even better, Chase.

If only the truth could be told, Alexandro would have no motive to hold me captive, to force me into the Oranga Trials. These Trials were clearly not designed for me. I recalled Alexandro's comments last night. *Some of you have murdered, victimised, or conspired, some have destroyed property that does not belong to them.*

To the thud of my head colliding with the wall behind me in frustration, the familiar *whoosh* caught my attention. The en suite had presented itself. With a skip in my heart, I entered, hopeful that something in the room might be different, or that Alexandro was waiting beyond, but the chamber was just how I had left it previously.

The hangers featured a fresh set of clothes – black track pants and a hideous orange skivvy, and another jumpsuit identical to the one currently sticking to my sweaty skin. A towel occupied the final hanger. Fresh underwear and socks were folded beneath the sets of clothes. There was no sign of the clothes I'd had on when I arrived on the island.

I felt a movement of air as the wall closed behind me, and I was again trapped in the smaller confinement. With nothing else to accomplish, I stripped in preparation to immerse myself in the lukewarm water of the shower.

8

WOODEN BIRDS

It took a lot of willpower for me to extract myself from the shower's stream. I opted against the jumpsuit and instead decided to slip into the track pants and skivvy. The top was the colour of pumpkin soup, not something I would wear in the outside world.

The outside world.

Staring at the bracelet, its light blinking slowly up at me, I thought of the blinking lights of my workbench in my home far from Touhere. My tools would be collecting dust in my absence. My last woodturning project must have been several weeks before I boarded the flight that brought to me to this hexagonal prison. I'd been investing all my attention in my work with Chase.

I longed for the smell of burning oak, the feeling of accomplishment when adding another wooden bird to my collection. I should have spent time on my hobbies rather than on my work.

As a school-aged boy, I had been drawn to woodwork after my mother's death. An aging teacher had showed me the art, and I often spent hours at a time distracting myself in my childhood garage, aided by the tools my father bought me. I was keen to create all kinds of designs but often found my way back to recreating species of birds. With my father frequently absent across long periods, my growing collection of wooden owls, parrots and penguins became a kind of substitute for a social life.

I pulled the skivvy's sleeves along my lanky arms, the fabric gliding across my skin and covering the blinking light of the bracelet. In the shower, I had made an effort to submerge the bracelet with water in an attempt to drown its mechanics. This failed to have an impact on the jewellery at all; the flicker continued nonchalantly.

Moving through the small walkway towards the main room, I was greeted by a solid grey wall. The opening had not unsealed. In a fit of agitation, I pounded my fist on the wall.

'Come on, open up!'

To my surprise, I received a reply. The speaker crackled, then came Alexandro's animated voice:

'Many Trials test strength,

This you will find.

But unlike the rest,

This one, your mind.

Strong mental force,

Is required now.

As of course,

The weak will bow.'

Alexandro's repetition of the riddle only led me to roll my eyes and slump onto the bench beside me. The isolation was frustrating enough, but the host's neglect of my pleas distressed me more. I needed to explain my innocence before the first Trial commenced.

Rather than decipher the riddle that echoed the walls of the en suite, my brain instead wandered to a potential appeal to Alexandro. How could I claim my innocence in a way he would understand and be willing to listen to? I knew that Alexandro would give me minimal attention, if any, so I quickly orchestrated a short dialogue in my head. *Please Alexandro, just listen to me for thirty seconds. If we can only contact Chase Iscariot . . .*

For a quarter of an hour, I practiced my appeal to Alexandro, ensuring I perfected every line and could blurt every detail out in under a minute. *I have receipts of the $250,000 received as a business investment, Chase will vouch for me . . .*

My thoughts were interrupted by the static reverberations for a second time. Alexandro's voice followed. 'Welcome to the Trial One of the inaugural Oranga Trials. The Trial will commence shortly, within your pod. If you wish to forfeit the Trial, please call "I surrender" aloud. But do this with caution, as the first contestant to surrender will be terminated.' A momentary pause, then: 'You have thirty seconds to proceed to your pod or an automatic forfeit will be initiated. Good luck.'

The air inside the compartment seemed to evaporate and I found myself grasping for desperate breaths. The two rooms were reunited by the opening in the wall, but I sat frozen on the wooden seat. The first Trial had begun, and I couldn't recall any of the riddle's clues. Something about requiring a strong mind?

My heart buffeted my chest wall aggressively. Every muscle in my body begged me to run. But there was nowhere to go. The only way forward was into the pod that held a Trial – my fate sealed within the room. I forced myself to stand and moved towards the opening. Darkness swallowed all corners of the small room; even the skirting light had disappeared. The room's emptiness engulfed me, and I stepped inside.

I was now aware of my own breathing, inhaling far more rapidly than I was exhaling. I made an effort to breathe in through my nose and out of my mouth, but this proved hard to do. My mouth filled with saliva, but I couldn't swallow; it felt as if a tennis ball had formed at the edge of my throat. I wiped the accumulated sweat from my palms onto the track pants in a flurry.

I stepped forward. The gap behind me closed and the room was flooded with light. Now I was sealed inside the main room, but I was not alone. I double backed and felt the full force of the recently secured wall behind me as I found myself staring at the face of an enormous snake.

9

The First Trial

The large, pointed face of a python confronted me from the opposite wall, its long body coiling around from the EXIT sign behind me. The bed had been removed, along with the toilet and sink. The python had brown-orange scales that twisted delicately along the walls.

It's not real, I had to remind myself. The projection was so realistic that I swore its gleaming yellows eyes followed me as I moved cautiously around the room. I turned away, but the python followed. The evil face somehow anticipated which way I turned, sliding across the walls of the room to ensure we maintained eye contact. As it hissed, droplets of liquid spurted onto my face.

I wiped at my forehead, removing the projectile and my own sweat with one wipe. I decided to keep my hands to my face; the snake couldn't follow me through my fingers. The room disappeared around me as I cocooned my head in my hands. I only had a few phobias: heights, flying and – worst of them all – snakes.

Impulsively, my right forearm began to twitch. The twitch became a shake. The bracelet was activating. My wrist tightened and I could feel my fingers numbing as I threw my right hand away from my face while keeping my eyes clenched tight.

A loud *hiss* vibrated across the room; the snake felt close – *it's not real* – more liquid spat onto my face and the back of my left hand, which I kept over my eyes. The moisture was thicker than water, almost milk-like. A shudder radiated down my spine as I pictured the snake's large face in my imagination. The hiss became deafening, and at the same time the bracelet throbbed more and more intensely.

Unable to manage the pain which now radiated up my arm, I cleared my face and examined the backs of my hands, refusing to observe the slithering animal which maintained its predatory circling around me. The moisture was clear, but evidently not water. Could it be real saliva? I wiped the substance on my shirt and paced around the room in an attempt to avoid the evil yellow eyes. The bracelet's throbbing ceased almost immediately.

The image of the snake dominated the space, roaming the walls freely without withdrawing its focus from me. I understood that the image was not real and that I was the only living soul in the room, but the image seemed as authentic as the walls it appeared upon. I refused to meet the snake's eye, instead focusing on its body gliding around me. Its definition was so precise I almost wanted to reach out and touch it, but of course, I kept my hands tucked in the pits of my arms.

The python would occasionally halt its circulation of the room and from behind me, I could hear it spit loudly, resulting in further droplets on the back of my head. The liquid slid down my collar and my body felt like ice. As I closed my eyes again, my imagination went wild; I imagined the snake pulling itself from the wall and swallowing me whole. Beyond my closed eyes I heard the image hiss at me, and the bracelet began to vibrate again.

Then it dawned on me: all I needed to do was to call 'I surrender!' and the hideous snake would disappear. My anxiety would ease. For as long as another contestant forfeited before me, I would be able to escape termination and have the chance to plead my innocence. I wondered if somebody had already forfeited.

As quickly as that idea fabricated, I quickly squashed it. I could not be the first to forfeit. After all, Alexandro never explained what occurred when a contestant was 'terminated'. I made an internal promise that no matter what the snake did, as long as it was not real, I would not forfeit. *They are just images. It can't hurt you.*

My wrist now vibrated as aggressively as the snake hissed, and I was forced to shake my arm in an attempt to reduce the pain. My eyes remained fixed shut, and behind them my imagination recreated the python now wrapping its thick body around my own, suffocating me . . .

I opened my eyes and the pain in my wrist eased. I now understood that Alexandro was forcing me to experience the Trial in its entirety. Covering or closing my eyes would activate the bracelet's vibrations.

The floor shifted beneath me, causing me to reach for a wall for balance. My hand landed on the tail of the snake, which whipped aggressively, its large head swiftly coming to where the tail had been moments ago. The floor shuffled again. Was something moving beneath my feet? Looking down, I found the source of the floor's movement; dozens of snakes slithered along the tiles.

Immediately I darted my eyes upwards. Despite their high quality, the snakes beneath me were merely moving images as well; they could not harm me . . .

The python on the wall circled me recklessly in my peripherals. I felt my fingertips shake against my body. I could not control my chest from thrusting rapidly with each short breath.

After a few moments, I allowed myself to look down. The projections looked as real as the one on the wall, but I reminded myself that they were just that – projections. Feeling ridiculous, I ignored my fears and took a step forward. The floor wobbled as I moved, but I repeatedly told myself that I couldn't be harmed.

The authentic-looking snake on the walls circled me faster, but I remained calm. My breathing slowed and my chest's trembling eased. I looked the snake in the eyes and accepted the spittle on my face when it hissed aggressively. Every minute that passed was an opportunity for one of the others to forfeit, and for me to progress beyond the first Trial.

The snake's face grew larger, its eyes glaring brightly. It felt as if the stiffer I stood, the angrier that made the snake, which filled me with confidence. The large face expanded so that the entire wall was filled by its ugly head. The mouth of the beast opened, and I forced myself to avoid flinching as I stared at the razor-like fangs. Still, it continued to grow until its open mouth filled the wall.

Suddenly the snake was gone and darkness overtook the walls. The floor ceased its sway; the snakes beneath me had vanished. The EXIT sign was the only source of light now.

Is it over?

I imagined Alexandro entering the room and explaining that I had won the Trial. In my imagination, his smile filled his face from ear to ear as we shook hands, telling me that I could now go home, having proved my innocence . . .

But no such luxury occurred.

Light now crept up the walls, beginning to dance in a mesmerising whirlwind of colour. A beautiful shade of pink covered every inch of the walls before becoming crimson, then gold, as the colours morphed magnificently. They settled into a calm blue. The colour filled the walls, the ceiling and the floor tiles, covering every surface other than the EXIT sign which shone steadily.

Soft white patterns swarmed around the room, contrasting wonderfully with the blue. I felt as if I was floating high in the air. Yes, the blue mirrored the sky-blue colour of the heavens above, and the white patterns resembled clouds. A draught brushed against me, gradually growing in intensity.

My feet were fixed to the floor, but here I was, gliding through clouds. I turned to my left and the draught adjusted and the clouds in front of me moved to the side. It was as if I were flying, and in complete control of the journey. Despite my usual fear of flight, the sensation was overwhelming. I didn't want to ever forfeit the Trial if this was the experience.

How could Alexandro think this was a test? I stretched my arms and turned on the spot. As the breeze hit my face, I closed my eyes. I was met by pain shooting up my from my right wrist. Disappointed, I opened my eyes once more.

The feeling of wonder was short-lived, however, as the clouds that drifted side to side halted, and slowly began to glide upwards. The wind had changed its course too, now shooting forcefully from beneath me. My legs felt as if they had turned to jelly, barely supporting the weight of my body.

The breeze had become a gust, and the clouds now flew upwards so fast that the feeling of gliding had evaporated; I was now falling. Far below, a field of green grass raced upwards at me. For a moment, the realistic sensations allowed me to forget that I was in fact standing in the centre of a confined room. To me the images, the wind, the sensation of falling were as authentic as the clothes on my back.

I shouted in fear at the thought of falling helplessly to my death. My screams were swallowed by the sound of the wind around me, it now becoming more forceful the closer to the earth I fell. My throat tightened and my stomach squirmed as the wind attacked my face. My legs quivered, eventually giving way. Unable to distinguish the real floor, my knees hit the tiles with force.

Incapable of standing, I lay motionless on the cold tiles, staring as the images on the walls raced upward. I had been falling for an eternity. My stomach twisted, and I felt the onset of vomiting creep through my throat. Surely another person had called for the end of their Trial within their own pod by now. I pulled myself to my knees as the green field rushed upwards. Faster and faster the ground raced to meet me . . . I flinched in anticipation . . .

A loud *bang* filled the room and all light disappeared, including the EXIT sign. The walls rattled in the darkness. I could only feel the throbbing of my knees against the tiles, and the patter of my heart.

The EXIT sign flickered, sending flashes of emerald past my eyes, and after several seconds it fixed itself onto its normal state. The walls reflected its light, until slowly the perimeter began to morph once more.

10

Mother

I decided not to return to my feet, instead dragging myself against a nearby wall and pulling my knees to my chest. It was difficult to avoid the new swirl of colours upon the wall, watching them blend and intertwine until they casually returned to their natural grey tone. A soft ringing sound met my ears, but of a higher pitch than the static that usually preceded Alexandro's voice.

I wondered if this was a signal to conclude the Trial; however, the ringing did not cease. Rather, it grew sharper as the seconds ticked on. The ringing was now an agonising screech and had grown louder, like nails scratching down a chalkboard. I impulsively stuffed my fingers into my ears, which instantly brought pain that I had only felt once before. I was forced to the floor, my limbs jerking in all directions. I felt my bones rattle against one another beneath my skin. My screams were lost in the screeching that dominated the room. A battle raged between the vibration of my bones and the ringing in my ears. The ache beneath my skin ceased the moment my fingers were impulsively pulled from my ears. I was forced to experience the Trial in its entirety.

I continued to feel the phantom feeling of my bones' rattle, although it was now merely uncomfortable rather than painful. The screeching echoes resumed as I lay across the tiles, rubbing my arms.

I got back on my feet, shaking my head to distract myself from the painful sound. My eyes wanted to squint against it, but I forced them open. No pain was worse than what the bracelet threatened. To divert my attention, I paced the skirting of the room while counting the steps aloud as I went. *One, two, three, four* . . .

The sound lasted almost twenty minutes, and I spent that time trying to create louder sounds and patrolling the borders of the room. The perimeter of the pod was roughly eight metres, if my distracted estimates were accurate.

When the sound eventually ceased, the ringing continued in my ears momentarily, until the room again swirled with a range of colours from sea blue to lilac, and finally a beautiful golden-brown colour filled the walls.

The colours swam exotically, absorbing my attention completely, until an image began to form. A blurred face twisted itself into existence on the wall. It was out of focus, unlike the snake, although I could tell it was a distorted image of a blonde-haired woman. Dark eyebrows shaped themselves on her face and my eyes squinted in an attempt to focus the image.

Moments passed as the face itself grew clearer. A pointed nose, an infectious smile. The face was now clear. I stood facing the woman at eye level. I managed to control the shaking of my fingers against my hip, however the short snappy breaths were less controlled as I gazed into the piercing green eyes of my mother.

She was young, just as in the photos I'd seen of her. But this was more than just an image of my mother's face. After a few seconds her eyes blinked and her fringe swayed slightly.

I understood that she wasn't truly in front of me, but my eyes swelled as I stared at her. The image was now completely focused, watching me as lifelike as the snake had.

Reaching out in anticipation for my mother's warmth, my fingertips met the wall. I wanted to hug her, to feel her protective touch, but I only encountered stern concrete.

The image swayed. Her mouth twisted in a bizarre angle and her lips parted marginally allowing a voice, just a whisper, to escape into the room. 'Tyler . . .' It was a woman's voice, but not my mother's. The lips on the projection tried to move with the sounds but it was poorly orchestrated. The whisper was gentle but foreign.

Although uncomfortable, I refused to divert my eyes from my mother. Again, her mouth slowly moved awkwardly. 'I miss you, Tyler . . .'

'Stop it!' I screamed.

'No . . . Tyler . . . it is me . . .'

'Shut up!' I was angry and offended, but I continued to stare at the wall. 'Shut up right now! Stop it!' I wiped furiously at the tears that had begun to form from my swollen eyes.

'I love you, Tyler . . . Tyler . . . Tyler . . .' The voice carried on in this whisper. I let out another yell in frustration. Defeated, I removed my head away from the image. 'Tyler . . .'

'Stop!' I cried.

She pleaded with me, her voice growing louder to compete with my own.

I couldn't bear to see her face, to have her memory mocked by another's voice. I knew what I had to do to make the image go away. I called, 'I surrender!' and her voice evaporated.

I dropped to the floor, clutching my knees to my chest as I allowed the tears to flow out of me. I failed to notice my mother's image flicker away and the lights return to normal, totally absorbed in my own agony.

I didn't know how long I'd been lying on the floor crying, but it was long enough for Alexandro to sweep into the room with two metallic fold-out chairs. He sat himself cross-legged on one, patiently observing my sobs as I ignored him. I felt his watchful gaze above me and I raised my head to find a look of empathy across his face.

He raised an eyebrow. 'Well done, my friend. Well done . . .' His voice was gentle, but I felt no comfort from his presence. The trauma of the past hour raced through my mind. I visualised the scenes of my mother's mouth opening and closing gracelessly, the large python throwing itself at me and the feeling of falling, falling, falling . . .

Completely composed, Alexandro continued his watch over me despite my lack of response.

My hand trembled its way to my crown. A lump protruded beneath my hair, and I vaguely recalled knocking my head at the start of the Trial.

'How are you feeling?' Alexandro asked.

This time I acknowledged him. 'Wh– Why am I here?'

'My friend, I have already explained this . . .' He raised a single finger gently as I opened my mouth to protest. 'Innocent or not, you are here now. The Trials are happening, and you did well. So well.' He offered a smile.

'Who . . . I mean, did I . . .?' I felt as if I had swallowed an apple whole. I couldn't manage to ask the only question that mattered. It was as if my body refused to let the words escape my mouth for fear of the answer. But Alexandro understood what I longed to know.

'You did wonderfully, Tyler. No, you were not the first one to forfeit. Today is not the day that you are terminated, my friend. All will be clarified shortly. Please join us in the hall – we are celebrating!'

Alexandro swiftly exited through the opening in the wall where my mother's face had been

projected moments earlier. I watched him disappear
into the darkness of the tunnel.

11

SID'S FEAR

After giving myself a few minutes to compose, I slipped behind Alexandro's trail through the opening – which remained open - into the dimly lit tunnel and shuffled towards the hall. There was a bustle of excitement in the hall. Alexandro attempted to make conversation with a woman wearing a garishly purple skivvy who seemed to be ignoring his presence.

My distress and self-pity evaporated in this infectious atmosphere. There was a buzz of accomplishment, the contestants stood in small groups each boasting of their own victory. As my eyes scanned the room to find who remained absent, my view was briefly obstructed by a large mop of brown hair. Underneath, smiling nervously, was Sid – his bulging eyes appeared larger than normal and it looked as if he had also been crying. I wiped at my own face, embarrassed for him to notice that I had spent the past few minutes sobbing uncontrollably.

Sid's hair was dripping wet, along with his jumpsuit, as if he had just stepped inside from the rain. I stared at him quizzically.

'Hello, Tyler. You made it!' he said.

'Yeah, apparently I wasn't the first to give up.'

'A few people still haven't joined us yet,' he explained casually. 'I was getting nervous that you might have been terminated. Alexandro said earlier that someone had already forfeited, so now we're just waiting on the others to finish.'

Sid's concern for me instinctively brought a smile across my face; my heart skipped a beat.

'Oh . . .' I began to observe the other people in the room. The Asian man was standing on the opposite side of the hall, conversing excitedly with the clumsy woman from last night's feast. His jumpsuit had a giant tear along the back, and he appeared to be swaying slightly. Further along the room, the elderly lady sat alone with her head bowed in her hands, seemingly crying. My smile faded in pity for her.

'Who else hasn't come out yet?' I asked, turning to Sid.

'Well, there's three still missing,' he started. 'The first is that large man from last night. Remember the one who was talking to you before I came over?'

I remembered him very well. I explained to Sid that the man's name was Mechislav, and that he had been escorted through the airport in handcuffs. I wondered what they could be showing him in his

room that could possibly scare him into submission.
Before Sid could continue, the air from the hall felt as
if it had escaped momentarily as the audience drew
breath. Silence stole the room with the appearance of
a shadow cast across the tiled floor. Somebody was
entering through one of the tunnels. The shadow
began to shrink dramatically, and a body appeared
beneath the large emerald number 9.

It was Alexandro, who must have slipped
from the hall as I was speaking with Sid. Another
shadow hung over Alexandro as a second presence
followed him from the tunnel. Seemingly unphased,
Tallis strutted to the foot of his tunnel and looked left
to right as he took in his surroundings. He wore a
look of confusion which I realised is how I must have
appeared moments earlier. Once the contestants had
watched the newest survivor enter, the chatter
resumed. My eyes followed Tallis to a chair where he
sat alone.

'Well, there you go,' Sid said. 'That just
leaves Mechislav and Shy.'

'Shy?'

'Yeah, she's the only one not here other than
that Mechislav guy, isn't she?'

I glanced around the hall and he was right. I
was confident in knowing who I would rather have
survive of those two. I nodded slowly in agreement
and after a moment's deliberation, I decided to move
the conversation. 'So, what happened in your room? I
mean . . . did the walls show things?'

Sid went into great length about his
experience. Inside his pod, he'd felt as if he were

submerged under water as all manner of fish surrounded him. A large shark formed itself upon the wall of his pod, and poised to attack him. Then real water rained upon him from all angles. He then went on to explain that he'd had a traumatic experience as a child. At the age of four, he had fallen out of a fishing boat while with his foster family. He detailed the panic he'd felt as he nearly drowned before being rescued by his foster father. 'My memory from that day is vague, but I haven't stepped foot in open water since,' he said. 'You wouldn't find me at an aquarium – I freak out just seeing fish, really. I tried covering my eyes when they appeared on my walls, but this thing kept vibrating.' He pulled at the bracelet on his wrist.

'That happened to me when I closed my eyes too! What else happened on the walls?' I was compelled by his experience and how unique it was and yet similar to my own.

'Nothing.'

'Nothing else?' I probed.

'No. I called to surrender as soon as I was forced to look at the shark, and then it stopped and Alexandro came in. It was either that or go into an anxiety attack.'

'And you weren't the first?'

'Well, I was. I mean, I was the first to come in the hall, at least. But Alexandro told me that somebody forfeited before me. He wouldn't tell me who it was. I've been watching as everyone else has come in here since.'

'And do you believe him?'

'What do you mean?'

'About you being the first to forfeit?'

Sid's face dropped. This was clearly the first time he had considered the possibility that Alexandro might not be genuine. There was a croak in his voice as it dropped to a whisper. 'Would he lie, do you think?'

'Well . . . Didn't he say if we were innocent, we would survive?'

Sid raised his eyebrows attentively.

I felt bad about worrying him further, but I felt the subject needed to be raised. 'Only one of us gets to go home, Sid. One of us.'

Sid's face contorted. His ears grew pink at the tips.

'I only mean to say that if we both believe that we shouldn't be here, then how can it be that "innocence will prevail" if only one of us will be given freedom? And I'm sure we're not the only innocent ones in here.' I flashed a glance sidewards at the elderly lady who sat alone. Her face was still buried in her hands as the shabby-looking woman approached her.

'You're right . . .' Sid took a step back. His eyes swelled slightly, and his ears reddened further. He was staring past me and focused on Alexandro, who rushed out of the large double doors and vanished from the hall.

I felt sick knowing that I had brought anxiety to the only person in the Trials who I felt I could trust. I put my arm around Sid's shoulders to comfort him, and we stood together in silence.

For several minutes we stood like that. I wondered what the other contestants had experienced in their pods. What technological capability did our captors have? My thoughts were interrupted as another pair of shadows cast itself into the hall. Alexandro appeared from the mouth of tunnel number 3. I tried to recollect which contender wore that number, but before I could remember I was distracted by a woman sprinting across the room to meet the figure emerging from behind the host.

It was the shabby-looking woman who Mechislav had comforted last night, and their roles were now reversed as Mechislav emerged from his tunnel. His ginger hair was dishevelled, and his face was white as a ghost. He was welcomed immediately by the woman as she flung her arms around his neck, momentarily unbalancing him.

It was now evident that Shy was the only one missing from the party. Beside me, I could sense Sid shaking as his fate was surely due to be announced in the coming minutes.

I tried not to look at Sid as my mind raced in anxiety for him. Instead, I watched as Mechislav pulled the woman off him and strode to a nearby chair. She shadowed him and pulled a chair up beside him.

Alexandro had relocated himself upon the smaller raised table between the larger table and the double doors. It acted as a podium as he stretched his arms out grandly and he cleared his throat in an attempt to command the group's attention. 'Come now, friends! Please join the table as we celebrate the end of a successful Trial One!'

The triumphant buzz left the room with his announcement. Nobody seemed to want to share their pride of success with Alexandro. As usual, he didn't care to notice the change of mood. He smiled widely and ushered everybody to their seats. I sat beside Sid again and I noticed that all other contestants had kept the identical seating arrangement as the previous feast.

'I wish to congratulate each and every one of you. Everybody sitting here now has passed Trial One with flying colours!' My shoulders relaxed; Sid was safe. 'Trial Two will take place in a few days. But before indulging in that, let us enjoy a meal, a few drinks, and celebrate today's success!'

'What happened to Shy?' the elderly lady asked. Her speech was confident, and although her distress was evident as she shook in her seat, that did not manifest itself in the tone of her voice.

'That is a good question, Gloria,' Alexandro began. 'but not one that I can answer at this point in time. All your questions will be answered shortly. Please – enjoy the feast!' He had dodged the question again, although I hadn't held high hopes of getting an answer from him.

12

THE ALLIANCE

I followed the remaining nine contestants' lead and filled my plate with the warm food from the platters. Presented with options of water, soft drink or cider, I allowed Sid to fill my goblet with a foul-smelling cider, which tasted sweeter than the smell promised.

Although Alexandro dined with the group – albeit from his own raised table – everyone had come to ignore his presence. We learned to cease our conversations while he addressed us – for fear of our bracelets activating, as opposed to respect – before resuming. As he spoke, each person either glared at him with resentment or refused to look at him at all.

As the night continued, I discussed the events of our Trial with the clumsy woman, whose name I learned was Naomi. She sat directly opposite from me and detailed her own experience resembling a severe thunderstorm inside her pod. The walls vibrated, and bright flashes of lightning thrashed around her. Like Sid, Naomi had also had a traumatic experience in her youth which the Trial replicated.

Before I could ask what happened when she was younger, she moved the conversation on. She explained that she had built a friendship with the Asian man, Quyén.

'Nah, never met before we got here,' she said, flicking her fork back and causing a chunk of food to fly across the room, which she didn't seem to notice. 'But we work in the same . . . industry.'

The pause before her final word was noticeable. Quyén, who sat beside her but was facing the other way had made a movement in his chair as she spoke of their relationship and Naomi whimpered quietly before carefully finishing her sentence. I presumed that Quyén had kicked her beneath the table. I decided against asking further questions about their relationship.

Along the table, I observed as small groups formed. The table held two rows of five seats, and I was positioned in the middle of one row. Quyén and Naomi – who sat across from me – had established a relationship based on their shared work history. Mechislav was evidently close with the lady who he had shared an embrace with, who I now knew was called Ruby. Mechislav and Ruby occupied the seats beside Naomi, facing Sid and Gloria respectively. They seemed to have built a relationship with Gloria, and I watched irritably as the three of them questioned Sid thoroughly.

Sid, still seated to my right, was fidgeting as he answered questions about his life outside the confinement of the Oranga Trials. I overheard him give an account of life moving between orphanages and foster homes. He explained that he never knew his parents and had spent most of his eighteen years isolated from the outside world. Mechislav appeared to have invested an interest in Sid's story, asking multiple questions while sharing consistent glances with Ruby. Watching Sid squirm awkwardly in his chair made me feel uncomfortable and I swiftly interjected myself in the conversation.

'So Sid, how do you like the chicken wings?' My attempt to change the conversation was futile, as Mechislav interrupted before Sid had time to answer.

'Ahh, Tyler, ees it?' he asked.

'Yeah' I responded. 'Are you going to tell me why you're here yet?' I was intimidated by the large man, so I was as surprised as the rest of the table when I called him out like this. This man was a criminal, and I was provoking him. I braced for him to lunge over the table and attack me; instead he offered a loud laugh. I caught him exchanging a nod with Ruby. This was the first time I had seen either of them smile.

'No, my boy, zere ees no need to vorry about zat. Ve must focus instead on ze Trials.'

Ruby and Gloria nodded in agreement as Mechislav clenched his fists aggressively.

'Well, we can't all win, can we?' I said. 'Alexandro said only one will get to leave.'

'Right.' His 'R' rolled longer than the rest of the word. 'But ve need to keep on fighting. If ve all vork together, ve can help each ozzer make eet to ze end.'

'So . . . like an alliance?'

'Da!' he exclaimed, then lowered his voice to a whisper. 'Yes. An alliance.'

I looked around the small group we had formed; why was nobody else sceptical of Mechislav's proposal? Four eager faces, including Sid's, beamed at me. I sat speechless.

Ruby spoke. 'There may be a time where we need to team up, Tyler.' Her voice was soft, with an unexpected British accent, which I somehow found reassuring. 'If we know that we five all have each other's back, we give ourselves the best chance of survival.'

I was unsure if it was due to her kind nature, or something else, but the proposition seemed to make more sense when Ruby explained it. If I survive into the final five contestants, I would buy time to formulate my escape. I nodded in agreement.

Our small party spent the next hour discussing our origins and how we all came to be in this situation. Gloria, the oldest of the group, clarified why she appeared familiar. Her husband Winston was Vice President of the United States. He had spent the past few months in the news headlines for reasons I could not recall.

Mechislav explained that his background was in business; a salesman who sold toilet cubicles. When I asked if he'd known Ruby before this week, he rejected the idea with a scowl. Ruby also falsified the idea and refused to detail her back story other than to say she was from London and wasn't sure why she was here. I was unconvinced by both

Mechislav and Ruby, but on the other hand, I felt assured that these people were prepared to help me, so I embraced the company.

As the night progressed, I observed another alliance begin to form around the table. Quyén and Naomi had welcomed the shifty looking man into their group. The large Mexican number 7 was fidgeting in his seat. Mechislav had explained that his name was Hermes.

'Don't trust zem,' Mechislav said, jerking his thumb toward the group. 'Tried talking to zat woman earlier. She doesn't seem right. And zat Quyén, looks like he vill vomit at any second. Suspicious bunch.'

I thought Mechislav had a fair point. Throughout dinner, I noticed that Quyén's plate remained empty, and his face was drained of all colour.

Tallis sat alone. Alexandro attempted to converse with him, but Tallis ignored him until he had finally given up. Alexandro walked off smiling blithely, attempting to join Quyén's conversation. I almost felt sorry for him.

After a long period, Alexandro eventually walked up to his high table and raised his hands dramatically. 'Friends, it is time to retreat. We have eaten, we have conversed – now it is time to go back to our rooms to prepare for the next Trial!' Again, conversations dulled as he spoke.

'But before we go . . .' Alexandro's eyes moved up and down the table to catch each of us individually, then he continued:

'*Sixty minutes, you're bound,*

Escaping is your intent.

Logic, wit; look around,

Last, you must prevent.

Arrive first to eight,

Security you can ensure.

Last, or running late,

Your protection: no more.'

Alexandro insisted that we retreat to our pods immediately and the hall cleared in a couple of minutes. I waved farewell to my group as they moved to their respective tunnels.

I pulled Sid aside and said, 'I don't know about this alliance, Sid. But above all else, you and I stick together, okay?' I fixed both my hands on his shoulders. A smile bigger than I had seen before stretched across his cheeks.

'Thanks,' he whispered as we separated.

Mechislav entered tunnel number 3, directly to my left. Sid – number 6 – was the next person on my right, as tunnel 5 was now vacant, with Shy's termination. I gave Sid a final reassuring smile before stepping into the darkness of tunnel number 4.

13

THE LEVERS

I collapsed onto my bed, which had been returned to its place as if it had never moved. The small toilet and sink were also reinstated on the wall opposite. The opening that led to the shower was exposed, inviting me to wash the sweat off myself in the lukewarm water. Instead, I lay on my back, head resting on my folded arms, reviewing the past twenty-four hours. I had scraped through the first Trial; had even withstood it longer than the majority.

An imaginary anchor fell to the pit of my stomach when I thought about Shy being taken away. Was she still alive? I couldn't help but imagine the worst – perhaps I was fortunate to be lying in my confinement, breathing.

Alexandro's deliberate attempt to avoid answering questions about termination seemed to confirm these fears. Although I had only met Shy briefly, I was fond of her. I replayed our one conversation in my head. She had admitted to making a business mistake, but I refused to accept that as justification for her to die. A shudder raced down my spine at the thought of dying at Alexandro's hands.

I forced myself to refocus my attention on the other major incident from the feast. I had somehow fallen into an alliance with what appeared to be one of the strongest contestants. I knew I could trust Sid, but while the others seemed to be well-disposed towards me, I wondered if I'd really had any option but to join them.

I couldn't help but think of Gloria and how somebody with her status, her high profile, could be abducted. How had our captors managed to lead her to Touhere? And how many American forces were currently searching for her? Perhaps with the resources they had available they would locate her, and in turn save the rest of us. A slither of hope flickered inside me. My new alliance could secure my position through the upcoming Trials.

The next few days passed somewhat uneventfully. I found myself taking notice of the routine of events that unfolded within the pod. The en suite was opened twice daily, and on my return to the pod, a packaged meal was sitting on the bedspread. One evening I decided not to use the en suite's facilities and no meal was provided that night.

The meals were as depressing as the solitude. Flavourless chicken served with a ration of rice was the highlight of the range of dinners. For breakfast one morning, two slices of white bread with cheese lay packaged on my bed. The cheese had an unfamiliar tangy taste. Plastic cutlery was included for only some meals, although they only served to make the meals more difficult to eat so I often disregarded any class and reverted to eating with my hands.

Upon returning to my room from showering on the second evening, I was greeted by a deck of cards on my bed, and a book with *The Metallic Moon* in large silver letters on its cover. The cards' orange backing matched the bedding and clothes.

I spent the empty days quietly playing cards with myself and vowing to decipher Alexandro's riddle. A feeling of regret overcame me whenever I considered his rhyming brainteasers. *Why did I ignore the last riddle?* I asked myself for the hundredth time. I regretted using the minimal preparation time before the last Trial fashioning an imaginary conversation with Alexandro. If I had used my time more wisely, the first riddle could have served as a clue to prepare me of the mental challenge which had lain ahead. I promised myself not to make the same mistake with the second Trial.

Repeating the riddle aloud, I began to decode a few clues as to what to expect in the coming days. *I'll have an hour to complete the Trial*, I told myself. *But what do I need to do?*

The last Trial had tested my mental strength, whereas Alexandro's newest riddle hinted that this one tilted more towards logic and wit. My recent experience of coding and web design gave me comfort that I could possibly outsmart some of the others. To exercise my mental dexterity in preparation, I played Memory with the cards, over and over.

I looked down at my withering body and felt nervous about any upcoming Trials that might require muscle. Even before the few days of isolation, I had little confidence about my performance in any Trials requiring physical strength. But I felt confident in my intellect, and continued to spend chunks of time deciphering Alexandro's riddle. An hour to complete the Trial: this much I knew. And the last to finish would be terminated – as well as anyone who took longer than an hour.

On the fourth morning of isolation, I returned to the room after my shower to discover it had been modified. I had been in the bathroom less than an hour, but in that time three identical maroon levers had been installed, protruding from opposing walls of the pod.

I moved to the closest one and pressed down on it. Immediately, an agonising ringing filled the room unexpectedly forcing my hands over my ears. The lever slowly raised itself back towards its original position, and as it did so the sound diminished. I cocked an eyebrow curiously as I advanced towards the next, which hung beside the sink. This lever produced a sound identical to the first when depressed. The final lever, to the left of the en suite entrance, did the same.

With nothing else to occupy my time, I spent hours experimenting with the levers in an attempt to deliver a new result. I attempted pulling the levers in a variety of sequences, applying different forces and speeds – but each time, the same irksome ring followed. The excitement of my newest toy faded faster than it had arrived.

Time passed agonisingly slowly inside the pod, but I was determined to maintain a strong mindset, constantly reminding myself to cycle through the deck of cards to simulate my mind. The book, however, sat unopened beside my bed. It reminded me of inevitable death. If I decided to read it, here, in this hexagonal prison, then *The Metallic Moon* could be the final book I ever read.

Although I spent the days imagining an escape, I had accepted that it was unlikely. The bracelet had done its job in reminding me that I was a prisoner. I had to play: I had to win the Oranga Trials to survive.

Several hours after the levers appeared in my pod, I discovered an unusual phenomenon while fiddling with them. The familiar eerie ring followed the plunge of any lever, but if I quickly pulled a second lever while the first was still rising back to its original position, a new sound was produced – a sweeter sound, harmonic, almost like a jingle. I leaped in the air at this discovery, laughing with delight as I continued to recreate the harmonic sound using different combinations of levers. The levers were on different walls of the pod, and I found that each lever rose back to its original position after only a handful of seconds, so it was difficult to exercise the required timing, but by the end of the day I had mastered it.

I woke the next morning to find the en suite already open. After rolling restlessly in the bed for a couple of minutes, the blinding light from the room had forced my eyes to waken. Sluggishly, I pulled myself out of bed, stretched, and then dragged my feet towards the shower. The opening in the wall slammed behind me, serving as a reminder that I was confined in the smaller room once more; something that had not occurred since the start of the first Trial. Was this the beginning of the second Trial?

It wasn't until the water began to run cold that I withdrew myself from the shower and moved to dress in the familiar jumpsuit with my trademark saffron 4. The wall did not open, so I sat on the wooden bench and waited. Minutes passed, and my backside grew numb after what felt like an hour.

My brain ran from one theory to the next about what awaited me on the other side of the wall. I spent the time turning the riddle over and over.

Don't worry, nothing in there can harm you, I told myself, remembering the hideous snake coiling around the walls.

I anxiously ran my hands through my hair, now completely dry, reminding myself that I only had to endure an hour of whatever lay beyond the wall. My lower back throbbed with pain, so I stood, and a wave of nausea overcame me. Occasionally I heard ruffling noises on the other side of the wall. They must have removed the bed and toilet again.

I was conscious of my breathing and made an effort to slow it. Then the ring of familiar static raged through the room, followed by Alexandro's voice:

'*Sixty minutes, you're bound,*

Escaping is your intent.

Logic, wit; look around,

Last, you must prevent.

Arrive first to eight,

Security you can ensure.

Last, or running late,

Your protection: no more.'

I nodded as I noted the host's words carefully.

Alexandro continued through the speaker. 'Friends, brute strength will not aid you here. Your mission is simple: escape your pod. Exit through the tunnel and into the hall, where a red buzzer is waiting. Press the buzzer and your Trial will end. The last person to do so will be terminated. Any contestant who does not press the buzzer within the time limit will be terminated.' He was silent for a few moments, then he concluded with a gleeful 'Good luck!'

14

THE HIEROGLYPHS

The wall shot up to the sound of static at the end of Alexandro's announcement. I was faced with a completely transformed view of my pod. The furnishings had been removed once again and replaced with a variety of unique décor. I had one hour to escape, and not a clue where to start.

Where the bed usually stood was an enormous potted fern. A pile of twenty to thirty wooden blocks was heaped in the centre of the room, odd shapes carved into each of them. The EXIT sign remained, hanging above me, although it sat between two other objects fixed to the wall. To the sign's left was a clock, and a wooden, oval-shaped tablet roughly the size of a car tyre to the right. Directly opposite the EXIT sign, above the closed portal to the hall passageway, a large timer had already begun counting down from 01:00:00. Below the timer hung an elegantly framed oil painting – a tropical scene of crystal blue water meeting a sandy shore. Other items in the room included a magnificent bronze statue of a duck wearing a top hat which stood so tall that it loomed over me intimidatingly, and an oak bench; as well as the three maroon levers on the walls which I was already familiar with. The orange deck of cards and *The Metallic Moon* remained on the floor.

I took several moments to carefully scan my surroundings before throwing myself into the challenge. The opening closed noiselessly behind me as I paced the room, examining each of the foreign items. After inspecting the final object, the wooden bench, I glanced up towards the timer: 00:55:21. I had already wasted too much time.

The clock fixed to the wall didn't appear to show the correct time; I noticed the hands remained stationary. Was this a superfluous decoration, or something more? On further examination, I found that each number on the clock had been replaced by a hieroglyph. Strangely, the same hieroglyphs were also replicated on the wooden blocks that were discarded in the middle of the floor. I lowered myself to study the pile of blocks more thoroughly. Their light brown texture was made of the same wood as the bench behind me; elm. I turned a block over in my hand, examining the hieroglyph engraved on it – an image of a staff.

Something twinkled – a brass key was dangling from a short chain on the tablet. The tablet, like the blocks and the bench, was made of elm and a labyrinth was carved into it. The chain which the key dangled on was attached to a manoeuvrable block within the maze. As I carefully moved the block through the labyrinth, the key followed. At the centre of the maze lay an opening for the block, a keyhole beside it. The task became clear: guide the block to the centre so the key could reach its destination.

Several minutes passed as I attempted to lead the key towards its home, although I consistently reached dead ends, often leading me back to the beginning. As time ticked away, my brain became my own enemy. *This isn't the challenge. You're wasting your time*, I thought. I forced myself to concentrate on the task.

Left, down, right, right, up, right, down. Another dead end. Up, right, up, left, down, left – nothing. I threw my head back in frustration and caught a glimpse of the timer; ten minutes had already elapsed. Right, down, left, down, left. So far, the key had remained in the same zone of the labyrinth, but I now found a way to move it into new territory. Down, left, left, up . . . I edged closer to the centre . . . up, right, up, left . . . *click*. I felt a rush of excitement as the block fell securely into the space in the centre, perfectly carved to accommodate it. I had done it. I quickly thrust the key into the keyhole and turned. Beneath the labyrinth, an opening appeared, and a wooden box – the size of a brick – fell from inside onto my readily waiting palms.

I opened the box to find a miniature grey torch. I clicked a button on the base and it produced a dull blue light. Disappointed at my prize, I inspected the torch closely. It appeared to be made of metal, and its sole feature was the button that operated it.

I looked at the ticking timer. *How has a quarter of an hour passed already?* I felt no closer to escaping the room; my only triumph nestled comfortably in my palm. I moved to the wooden bench and examined its features. Four shallow rectangular indents were carved into the top of the bench. I rested the torch in one of the grooves and paced the room in search of another task.

Stepping over the wooden blocks in the centre of the room, I bent down to move them to the side. Curiously, I flipped one over in my hands. On one side the surface was silky smooth, the other featured an engraved drooping flower. The block was surprisingly heavy, and fit into the palm of my hand like a brick. It was of a similar size to the wooden box that had borne the torch moments ago.

There was an obvious link between the broken clock and the wooden bricks: the unique hieroglyphs that replicated on both. I remained, however, no closer to understanding their connection than when the Trial had started. My back was pressed firmly against the wall now as I moved the block between my hands. The engraved flower stared back at me. On the clock, a flower – drooping, just like the one in my hand – rested where the number 7 should be.

To use my time more constructively, I ordered the blocks from 0 to 9, in correlation with the clock's hieroglyphs. A feather represented the number 1 on the clock, an owl correlated to the number 2, and each number had its own image. When the numbers reached double digits, the hieroglyphs multiplied (two feathers for 11, a feather and an owl for 12).

The timer displayed thirty-five minutes remaining by the time I had ordered the blocks in correlation with the clock. I found myself distracted by the abundance of sporadic items in the room. Was everything in here useful, or did some items serve only as a distraction? I wondered if the large statue of the duck would come into play . . .

The realisation slowly began to creep into my mind that escape might not be possible – I may have wasted too much time and I could be within the last hour of my life.

Shaking the idea from my brain, I revisited the wooden bench to collect the torch. It surely must serve some purpose. Its blue light cast across the pod, but this was too dull to be seen on the opposite wall across the brightly lit room. I turned the torch hopefully, shining it on the closest object to me, the wooden box it had arrived in. Nothing happened, and the illumination was barely visible. The box itself was unspectacular, no grooves or symbols on it at all. *This is ridiculous*, I said to myself as I threw the box onto the table.

The box slid ungracefully along the benchtop, eventually being stopped by one of the shallow grooves. An idea sparked: I rotated the box slightly against the indentation. It appeared a perfect fit, but would not squeeze into the groove. I twisted and turned the box for a few seconds before admitting defeat, throwing it on the ground in frustration where it blended with the hieroglyphic blocks.

The timer ticked into the final half an hour as I dropped to the floor with a sudden inspiration. I grabbed the blocks, ignoring the useless wooden box, and discarded them on the benchtop. I slid a block to one of the indentations and it slotted in perfectly. I then inserted four blocks in the four holes at random and waited. Nothing happened. It was simple to remove them as they were slightly taller than the indent was deep, so I rearranged the combination. The room remained as still as ever.

I couldn't spare any more time repositioning the blocks, but I felt certain that the correct combination would yield another clue to my escape. I would come back to the combinations, but now I was focussed on identifying another clue within the room. The lever to my right caught my attention.

If pulling two at the same time produced a jingle, I felt certain that pulling all three could result in a reward. But as I was the only person in the room, the task appeared impossible. My desire to experiment with this idea conflicted with the fear of wasting time I couldn't afford. My stomach turned as I stood in the centre of the room, undecided. I decided that I would spend no more than only a few minutes trying to pull all three levers at once.

I pulled the first lever slowly and dashed towards the next as sharp ringing sounds blasted into my ears. The tempo changed as the second lever was pulled, the harmonic sound now flowing through the room. With a lunge, I dove towards the final lever but the original eerie ringing sounded once more. Too slow. From the floor I watched the final lever gradually rise to its original position. I tried again three more times, unsuccessfully, then collapsed to the tiles and slammed my fist on the floor in frustration.

Alexandro's voice came into my mind. *Brute strength will not aid you here . . .*

I lay helplessly on the floor as the timer ticked down from 00:17:19 . . . 00:17:18 . . . 00:17:17 . . . I looked at the statue. The duck stared at me comically, the oversized top hat tilted to one side.

A new idea sparked, and before it had formed completely, I had jumped to my feet and raced towards the sculpture. It was solid granite, impossible to move by hand despite by heaved attempts.

Brute strength will not aid you here . . .

'I just . . . want . . . to move . . . it!' I said aloud through gritted teeth.

My eyes darted around the room in search of another heavy object. The fern. The plant sat in a corner, undistinguished. The leaves were the colour of lime and I noticed its sweet smell of basil fill the room. How long had it been since I experienced the scent of fresh flora?

I pulled the pot towards the closest lever and cautiously tilted it on its edge. The pot wobbled on its side as I attempted to balance it by gripping the thick stem. With one hand I carefully held the fern, aiming it towards the lever. I prepared mentally: I had only one opportunity to achieve the feat.

I paused for only a moment to envision the route I planned to take, then I allowed the fern's trunk to slip from my grasp and topple over, towards the lever. I darted towards the lever to my left. Behind me I heard the pot smash loudly, drowning the violent ringing sound as it collected the lever on its way to the ground. The commotion was replaced by the merry jingle as I depressed the second lever and lunged myself toward the third. I dived, reaching for the final lever. I felt my fingers wrap around the protruding handle and I pulled.

The music stopped. The room's light vanished.

I was breathing heavily on the cold tiles, in a pit of darkness. The EXIT sign and the red numbers slowly ticking down were the only source of light.

00:14:32 . . .

I felt my way across the room for the torch, cutting my left hand on a shattered fragment of the pot. Warm blood trickled down onto my wrist, but I pushed the pain away and reached for the torch. A beautiful violet-blue shone from the tip of the torch with the push of its base's button. I raised myself from the tiles and played the torchlight across the room. My mouth opened in amazement as the light fell upon five simple words scribbled on the wall above the wooden bench: *When your time is over.*

I read the message multiple times but failed to make sense of the words, although I couldn't help but feel I had fallen one step closer to the end of the Trial. One step closer to escaping. I was exhausted, and felt pulsating pain in my foot as I stepped over the fragments of the pot. I felt blood accumulate beneath the soles of my feet. Using the torch, I swiftly examined the remainder of the room, including the objects, floor and roof – but no other hidden messages revealed themselves.

00:12:00.

I slapped my face in an attempt to focus. I needed more time; one hour was not enough. More time . . .

The clock!

I rushed towards the clock, torch in hand, skipping between the scattered blocks and the pot's shrapnel peppered along the floor. Shining the violet light upon the clock, it took me a few moments to translate the symbols. The small hand was fixed almost exactly in between two images, the large hand pointing directly at the drooping flower. The clock displayed 9:35, but why was it not moving?

Sweat accumulated inside my jumpsuit now, and it stuck against my skin uncomfortably. My mind drifted towards the other participants – were they already in the hall, smiling together in completion of their task? I envisioned Tallis and Mechislav laughing at my stupidity as I was still trapped inside my pod. I shook the images out of my mind and drew my attention back to the Trial.

I needed to decipher the clues I had been given. Four blocks had to be placed in the grooves on the wooden bench. The block's hieroglyphs must signify something, but what? I looked at the hieroglyphs on the clock and suddenly the answer came to me – the four grooves represented a time! *When your time is over.*

In the blue torchlight, I scrambled among the blocks, looking for the hieroglyphs that represented the time of completion. The clock displayed a time of 9:35; with ten minutes remaining in the Trial then the correct formation of blocks must be 0-9-4-5. I rummaged for a cup, a rock, a double diagonal line and a staff – the symbols that represented the numbers according to their position upon the clock.

I thrust the final block – the staff – into the depression and waited with my hands on my hips.

Beads of sweat dropped from my nose onto the bench. I could hear nothing but my own breathing. Nothing happened. I turned to watch the timer change to less than eight minutes. The timer continued to count down, yet the clock stayed the same. The task felt impossible.

My heart beat angrily against the inside of my chest and my breaths grew deeper. I fell to the floor and stared hopelessly at the clock, the torch's violet light illuminating it beautifully. 9:35. This was impossible. The timer against the wall continued to count down, yet the clock remained stationary – the combination would change every minute. My eyesight blurred as the clock's hands appeared to vibrate slightly. *The darkness is playing tricks on you,* I told myself. The clock hadn't moved an inch since the Trial began.

Like a pin dropping, the answer came to me at once.

I scrambled, sending fragments of the pot flying in all directions. I located a new arrangement of blocks quickly and stood over the bench with a new sequence of hieroglyphs and a wild rush of hope. I rearranged the order to 1-0-3-5. It was all so obvious now. Time stopped when the Trial began, as highlighted by the clock's stationary state. *When your time is over.* I had an hour to complete the Trial, and the clock was fixed at 9:35 meaning that my time would be over at 10:35.

No sooner had I placed the last hieroglyph block into its place, than the opening that led to the hall was exposed. Without a second thought, I launched myself into the familiar tunnel, sprinting out of the room away from the riddles, hieroglyphs and labyrinth, and towards the speck of light at the end of the tunnel.

I didn't register the number of people inside the hall when I entered; there could have been three or twelve. Instead, I raced towards a podium perched where Alexandro's table was normally situated. The hall was much dimmer than normal; a magnificent orange tinge cast from the skies above shone through the glass ceiling perfectly onto the podium. A single red buzzer was perched on top of it, awaiting my arrival. With a lunge, I slammed my fist on the buzzer and fell to the floor.

15

BATTLE OF THE BRUTES

Heart pounding violently in my chest, I whipped my neck to absorb my surroundings. A grand timer identical to the one in my room hung above the double doors and ticked, the red numbers counting down slowly. 00:04:21 . . . 00:04:20 . . .

Had I made it? I twisted abruptly on the spot to observe the number of others in the hall. Two groups stood out in opposing areas of the large room. I counted at least five or six bodies before I felt a hand creep onto my back. I flinched, then turned to meet Sid's exhausted, yet horror-struck face.

'Did I . . . ? Has anyone else . . . ?' I blurted.

'You did it, Tyler.'

'But . . . is there . . . anyone –?'

Sid gripped my shoulder firmly, cutting off my breathless stutter. A wide grin began to form across his face, emphasizing his crooked teeth. He appeared genuinely happy to see me and I couldn't resist sharing a smile with him. 'There's still two more to come out,' he said. 'It's over, Tyler. You made it!'

Mechislav and Ruby strolled over to offer their congratulations.

'Vell done, vell done!' Mechislav clapped his large palm on my back, causing me to topple forwards slightly.

Ruby beamed. 'Good job, Tyler!'

'Thanks,' I responded. 'Who still hasn't finished?'

Before my question could be answered, heavy footsteps echoed towards the hall from a nearby tunnel. Mechislav pulled me from the podium and as the members of our alliance retreated to the perimeter of the hall in preparation to observe another contestant's arrival.

At the entrance to tunnel 7, Hermes appeared. His face was sweating profusely, and the light from the skylight highlighted the pink scar across his face. He appeared as intimidating as he had the first time I'd seen him on the shuttle bus. Mechislav flexed awkwardly beside me, and I recalled his words regarding Hermes at the last feast: *'Don't trust zem.'*

Hermes looked around the room, straightened himself and began making his way towards the podium. He glanced momentarily towards the timer which was now into the final two minutes. Without warning, thunderous banging echoed the walls of the hall. Everybody in the room, including Hermes, turned to locate the source of the eruption. Within seconds, the owner of the noise appeared beneath the large, dark green number 9.

Tallis's face was hardly recognisable as he burst into the hall. Hermes only took half a second to understand the threat; he lunged forward towards the podium. The two final contestants understood what needed to be done to ensure their survival.

Hermes' large frame weighed him down as he ran, resembling a hippo awkwardly trying to sprint. He was only a handful of metres from the buzzer; Tallis still multiple strides behind him, albeit accelerating much faster.

In the time it took to take a breath, Tallis had caught up with Hermes, both now in reaching distance of the podium. Before either could reach out, Tallis thrust himself into Hermes' back, propelling him past the podium and onto the ground. But Hermes' quick reflexes allowed him to grab Tallis's arm as he tumbled, so both large bodies toppled in awkward tandem.

Hermes was the first to get to his knees, but his advantage was short-lived as Tallis threw himself on top of him. Ignoring the timer's countdown – 00:00:45 – Tallis sat on Hermes' heaving chest like a lion on his prey. The audience stood within metres of the action, frozen. Nobody moved or spoke as we watched Tallis strike Hermes violently across the face. My blood grew warm with rage with each blow that Tallis landed on his opponent. Mechislav firmed his grip upon my arm when he felt my attempt to pull away.

After several strikes for good measure, Tallis rose. Hermes lay immobile on his backside, blood pouring onto the tiles from his broken nose. As Tallis struck the buzzer, no less firmly than he had Hermes' face, the timer rested. The large red numbers fixed at 00:00:07.

Seemingly unfazed, Tallis wiped the blood from his right hand onto his jumpsuit, made his way to an unoccupied corner of the hall and slumped to the ground. The two small groups huddling together stared silently at Hermes' twitching body. The only sound came from Hermes as he stirred helplessly on the floor, spitting blood.

The large doors swung open and Alexandro glided into the hall with four bulky offsiders. Each of his companions were dressed in dark grey pants and tops, long sleeved and padded. They wore thick helmets atop their broad shoulders, covering their faces. The guards, led by Alexandro, strutted through the crowd to the fallen contestant.

Shaking uncontrollably, Hermes rolled onto his front and attempted to push himself to his feet. It only took a few strides for the helmeted quartet to approach Hermes; two seized him under an arm each while the other two grabbed his flailing legs. I watched, frozen, as he kicked furiously while being dragged back through the main doors and towards the abyss. The sound of the doors closing behind them reverberated in the hall. Alexandro straightened his suit then turned his attention to the rest of us. His groomed face was the only one in the room unfazed by the events that just occurred, perhaps other than Tallis's.

'Congratulations, everyone!' Alexandro exclaimed in his usual ecstatic tone. In his familiar navy blue suit, this evening featuring a golden bowtie, and with both arms raised, he resembled a peacock. His hair maintained its neat composure, distinguishable in contrast to the tattered appearance of us around him.

When Alexandro received no notable response – other than a sarcastic grunt by Mechislav – he continued excitedly. 'Trial Two is now complete, and each of you has now progressed to the next! Now, as your rooms are currently being reset, please help yourself to refreshments. Congratulations, and rest up!'

As if aware that is presence was unwelcome, Alexandro turned on his heel and disappeared quickly through the opening. The doors closed behind him and I was left with the seven remaining souls. Mechislav wrapped his large arm around my shoulders and ushered me towards the table where drinks were laid out. I followed him quietly, my mind still on the events that had just taken place.

My heart rate slowed, my breathing resumed its normal pace and I quickly became aware of the pain in my feet from the fragments of the potted fern that had cut me. I pulled at a piece which had lodged inside the sole of my foot.

'How are you veeling?' Mechislav asked.

'Fine,' I lied.

I couldn't get out of my head the image of a beaten, struggling Hermes being dragged out of the hall towards probable death. It seemed that everyone in the room had swallowed the events in their stride, now sipping drinks and sharing their experiences of the latest Trial. *How are these people okay with what just happened?*

'Here. Have somezing to eat.' I allowed Mechislav to pass me a cinnamon cookie, just to avoid awkwardness. My stomach turned violently. His presence alone was irritating. The idea of an alliance didn't appeal to me; I wanted nothing more but to be alone. I still didn't trust the man any further than I could throw him. I wriggled out of his tense grasp and instead reached for a goblet beside the platter. I managed to ditch the cookie as I took a swig of water from the goblet. I smiled politely at Mechislav and withdrew myself to a quiet corner of the hall.

Tallis had gotten to his feet and helped himself to a handful of biscuits. I observed him with pure hatred. Having just sentenced Hermes to death, he now had the audacity to enjoy snacks only minutes afterwards. I made no attempt to disguise my feelings as my eyes burned through him, daring him to notice me. I wanted to attack him; after all the pain he had caused in here, he deserved to be terminated.

Although I hadn't felt an attachment to Hermes, a wave of grief came over me, as it had for Shy only days before. I wondered if I was only grieving because I understood it was just a matter of time before I suffered the same fate. I had spent so long isolated in my room, longing for social interaction. But as I sat alone now, I savoured every minute that I was unaccompanied.

Before long, Sid joined me. At first I refused to acknowledge him as he quietly sat on the floor beside me. He seemed to understand that I wanted to be alone, although I tacitly accepted his presence. For what seemed like an eternity we sat together, just observing the room.

I broke the silence. 'I don't think I'm participating in the next Trial.'

'What?' Sid looked horrified. He remained facing ahead, so as not to draw any attention to our conversation.

'I mean, I hate it here,' I continued. 'I'm probably going to die here anyway. What's the point?'

'Tyler, the innocent will prevail, remember. And you're innocent.'

'Come on, Sid, you don't believe a thing that monster is saying, do you? There won't even be a "winner".' I rolled my eyes sarcastically. 'We're going to be picked off one by one and I'd rather be put out of my misery.'

'No, you can't think like that. I know we're going to survive this. You can't give up now.'

His positivity did little to motivate me. I thought of Shy, and although depressed, I felt a strange feeling of jealousy knowing that she was now at peace. 'I'm sorry.'

I buried my head deep in the warmth of my hands. Sid had turned away and seemed to be lost in his own thoughts after my declaration.

It won't be long, I told myself. *I will be terminated soon enough, and this can all be over.*

PART II

16

SHY'S SUBSTITUTION

For what felt like an hour I remained in the corner of the hall, my back propped against the wall. The two main groups separated themselves from one another, far from my indolent body. The quiet ambiance was overwhelming, mere whispers carried across the hall like soft waves against the side of a beaten ship. Sid stayed beside me, and occasionally broke our silence to reason with me, but the same reply escaped my lips each time. 'I'm not competing anymore.'

On one side of the hall, Naomi and Quyén had made their way to Tallis, and the three of them were huddled in conversation. I watched as Quyén made erratic hand gestures to Naomi's approval. Tallis appeared disengaged; he would occasionally scratch his bald head before allowing his hands to find his armpits once more.

On the other side, Mechislav, Ruby and Gloria gathered in a triangle of chairs. Their discussion appeared more casual than the other group's, as often I caught a glimpse of Ruby's smile. Every couple of minutes the three of them looked over at Sid and me before resuming their conversation.

'Should we go over to them?' Sid said after some time.

'You go,' I replied under my breath. 'I'll be here.'

My head was still dug into my knees, but out of the corner of my eye I could see that Sid remained with me. With my face hidden, I couldn't resist a smile. Sid was here for me, a true ally, a friend.

The large doors burst open. The sound reverberated around the hall. I looked up. Vision scattered with black dots; my eyes struggled to make out the outline of a figure coming in. The figure was unaccompanied, and wore Shy's light brown jumpsuit, although it appeared that this stocky person was a man.

The chatter ceased and everyone turned to face the intruder. He stood at the doors, shaking. As he limped into the light, I recognised him at once. His face was disfigured by a heavily swollen left eye, but his familiar tanned pigment and clean stubble was instantly recognisable. It was Chase.

Chase collapsed onto the nearest chair dramatically, the room now watching curiously. Before I could think, I found myself on my feet, leaving Sid and racing towards him. Chase looked exhausted, his arms helplessly by his sides and his eyes darting around the room.

'Chase! What are you doing here?'

'Who's that?' He flinched and grabbed at me firmly. I could see his attempts to piece together his surroundings.

'It's me, Tyler.'

'Tyler? Tyler Knight?'

'Yes! What are you doing here, Chase?' I pulled away from his grasp, noticing the severity of his swollen eye. I followed his squinted eyes as they surveyed the hall. They scanned the audience, who were all standing and quizzically watching him in return.

'Where am I?'

Ignoring the other contestants' attention, I propped myself on the chair beside him and explained what I knew of the Trials, the people in the room, and Alexandro. Someone fetched water for him, which he downed in two gulps, but nobody else approached us. I noticed Mechislav staring, his glare burning into Chase's back.

Chase was the closest person to family that I had beside my father. It had been weeks since I had seen anybody beside Alexandro and the other contestants, and I couldn't disguise my emotions as I listened to his story.

Chase had had an adventure of his own since our last meeting, which he related in great detail. 'I was worried when I couldn't contact you after you were supposed to land,' he explained. 'There was no news regarding your flight, so I knew something suspicious was going on when I hadn't heard from you. I began asking questions, but I think the wrong people heard me.'

'Who did you talk to?' I asked.

'Anybody who'd listen. I was pretty vocal about your disappearance, probably too vocal. But I was worried, Tyler. I hadn't heard from you and I knew something wasn't right.'

'Who kidnapped you?' I said snappishly. My appreciation for Chase grew with each element of his story, but I wanted answers, and this was my first opportunity to gain new information.

'I– I don't know. I remember finishing a few tasks at the office. Everybody had left for the evening. I heard footsteps in the distance but thought it was my imagination. Then when I got into the elevator, there were two figures, hooded.' Chase's eyes were clenched, trying to recall every detail. 'That's all I remember, sorry. I woke about an hour ago in a room back there.' He gestured towards the grand doors that separated us from our captors.

Before I could ask what was behind those doors, Chase began to pepper me with questions about my experience. I explained in detail about the pods, the Trials, the bracelets and the two contestants who had been terminated. Despite my best efforts, I couldn't suppress tears as I spoke.

Chase wrapped one of his limp arms around me as I allowed myself to cry. I didn't care that the room was watching; I no longer cared about anything.

'Did they say what they wanted, Tyler? Do you know why you're here?'

I shuffled out of his grasp and looked at him. His eyebrows were raised with concern. My mouth dried, and a weight fell to the pit of my stomach.

Guilt gushed through me before I could conjure the words together. 'Well . . . They said it was because . . . of you.' Refusing to meet his eye, I instead stared directly at his bare feet. They were far cleaner than my own, which continued to drip blood from the previous Trial.

'Me?' he asked under his breath.

'Apparently, you had informed them that I stole your $250,000 investment.'

'No, Tyler . . .'

I could feel him watch me with sympathy. He opened his mouth to explain, but before he could speak, his words were stolen by the cluttering of footsteps around us. Our private discussion was put on hold as the audience of contestants surrounded us – aside from Gloria and Sid who remained together at a distance.

'Vat ze hell are yew doing 'ere?' Mechislav pushed his way between Chase and me, almost knocking me from my chair. He hovered aggressively over Chase.

Chase only needed a moment to register the towering Russian's face, and his demeanour swiftly changed. 'You,' he spat. Chase rose to his feet and stood facing Mechislav, less than an inch separating their noses. They clearly had met before. 'I suspect you are behind this then?'

For a minute they stood silently, sizing up one another. Mechislav's fists remained clenched by his side as Chase, who had seemed to forget I was sitting behind Mechislav, nudged him forcefully in the shoulder.

A third voice entered the argument. 'Are you in the Trials now, too?'

This was the first time I had heard Quyén speak. His unique Southern accent contradicted his Asian appearance. He was now standing alongside the men, looking down at Chase, who was a head shorter than the other two.

Chase ignored Quyén, continuing to stare into Mechislav's rugged face. The room felt heavy, the silence now seemingly louder, more charged, than the chatter of before.

After a few moments without a reply, Quyén burst out a second time. 'This is a joke! We just survived two Trials and now we have more people to compete against? If this man is now one of us – don't ignore me! – this is unacceptable. After everything I've already been through – look at me!'

Infuriated at being ignored, Quyén thrust his arm toward Chase's collar. Before his arm could reach its target, Mechislav and Chase turned towards Quyén, as if triggered simultaneously. Chase blocked Quyén's outstretched arm while Mechislav grasped his other, twisting it awkwardly and pushing him backwards. Caught off guard by this, Quyén stumbled ungracefully onto his backside.

Mechislav and Chase made for a dangerous combination.

I had retreated a few steps towards the back of the crowd, conflicted between joining Sid and staying closer to the scene to protect Chase. Quyén found his feet and withdrew himself from the centre of the ring of people as Chase straightened himself and turned to the group.

'I do not know why I am here,' he announced. 'I don't even know where "here" is!'

Gloria and Sid remained distant to the group. I now longed to be over with them. Chase slumped back into his chair, exhausted. As the contestants began to retreat, I watched Quyén offer relentless curse words under his breath. He appeared depleted; how could one push force a man to be so exhausted? This was the first time I had observed him thoroughly since the first feast. I couldn't recall the swollen blue bags under his eyes back then.

Once the crowd evaporated, Mechislav dug his index finger deep into Chase's chest and leaned towards him closely. He pulled himself to Chase's ear and whispered a prolonged message which I couldn't apprehend before strutting away with Ruby at his side.

17

NAOMI'S THEORY

Though I wanted to join Sid, I pulled up onto the chair beside Chase and watched the groups form once more. Tallis retreated to an isolated location far from everyone else, while Sid and Gloria rejoined our alliance. With Tallis now alone, Quyén and Naomi's group had shrunk. Their group dissolved completely when Quyén retreated into his tunnel. I thought I heard retching sounds come from where he had disappeared to, but it was hard to hear over the rain which had begun to fall on the glass ceiling.

Naomi fidgeted awkwardly for a minute before she dragged her feet towards us, where she then heaved a chair beside Chase and began asking questions about his capture. I tuned out of their conversation, instead sinking deep in my own thoughts. I felt grateful for Chase's presence, but Quyén had a valid point – how could they add a new contestant in if we were supposed to be competing for freedom?

Alexandro's assurance, *the truly innocent will prevail*, replayed in my head. My desire to forfeit the next Trial intensified. The idea of more contestants being brought into the Trials was utterly demotivating. I sensed that others in hall felt the same way.

I knew it would be impossible to convince the other contestants to forfeit with me, to create an absolute alliance of solidarity against our captors. Images of Tallis betraying us and walking away a free man formed inside my head. There was no convincing the others; I had to forfeit alone.

'Quyén and I have mutual connections, including Toby. Toby's my distributor,' I heard Naomi say to Chase. 'Quyén thinks Toby has something to do with us both being here, because he's really well connected, you know?'

'Interesting concept, Naomi. Maybe you're right,' Chase said in monotone. He was looking past her, staring intently at Mechislav, who was leading the discussion in his huddle.

Naomi failed to pick up his lack of interest as she continued her theory. 'You see, Quyén and Toby got into a few fights. They both try to run the drug ring in New York.'

I found Naomi's theory ridiculous. Why would a New York drug dealer want me captive? Or Sid?

'I never intended to work in that industry,' Naomi continued. 'I just hit a bit of bad luck. I mean, the bad luck didn't stop there, as I did accidentally set fire to one of his plantations. But Toby reckons he forgave me, so that's alright . . . Are you sure you haven't met him?'

'Positive.'

'Oh. Well, anyway, I was working one evening – Thursday, I think – wait . . . perhaps it was a Friday? Actually no, definitely Thursday . . .'

Chase shifted his eyes to me. I could feel what he was thinking.

'. . . So there I was, minding my own business and I lit up a cigarette. I mean, it was rule number one: no smoking. But one thing about me is I'm so forgetful, you know?'

Her story dragged for the next few minutes. Chase's interest had failed to ignite. He was still listening to her, but merely contributed occasional nods or perfunctory gasps.

'. . . Next thing I knew, I received an anonymous letter telling me Toby had found out and was on his way to chat to me. I was so scared. I've seen firsthand the things that Toby has done to people who've crossed him; it's never pretty. But the letter was accompanied by a one-way tickct to Touhere, leaving the following morning. The letter said Toby had forgiven me, but now I'm not too sure, because I ended up here. What do you think?'

Chase shrugged, which seemed to satisfy Naomi. She smiled and looked away. I suspected that she'd simply enjoyed retelling her story, regardless of the response.

Naomi's recount finished just as Alexandro theatrically charged into the room through the double doors. The chatter subsided and the attention of the group gravitated to him. The doors swung closed behind him and he took his place on the podium.

Our host was met by immediate outbursts from a handful of people within the hall. Curse words were thrown like daggers towards him, but he appeared not to notice.

Alexandro raised a palm in front of him until it gracefully hung parallel to his shoulder, indicating the order he desired. 'Friends! I have some good news: your pods have been restored to their original state and you may now retreat through your tunnels.' He paused briefly. The eruptions of complaints dulled as the audience took in his words.

Alexandro surveyed room, gauging its atmosphere. 'I understand some of you may have questions regarding our newest contestant, Chase. Now, Chase is indeed a contestant. After strong consideration, it has been decided that he has been substituted into Shy's place, and will serve as contestant number 5.'

'This is a disgrace!' Quyén yelled. He was on his feet, leaning on the wall near his tunnel beside Sid, who had taken a few steps sidewards to remove himself from the attention. Quyén had accumulated stains of vomit down the front of his jumpsuit and his hair was messed, making him look every bit more dishevelled than a short time earlier.

'Quyén, my friend. I understand your frustration; you have worked so hard and achieved so much already.' Alexandro's voice remained as calm as it was when he first explained the Oranga Trials on the first evening. 'Now, Chase has as much right to be here as each one of you. He has created his own destiny, which has led him here, and we must all accept this. In saying that, I can guarantee you all that there will be no further inclusions. The contestants in this hall represent the final nine contestants of the Oranga Trials! It is now time to rest, recover and prepare. The next Trial may be sooner than you may think. Goodnight!' Alexandro clapped his hands together, signalling that our night was at an end. He briskly stepped away from the podium and turned towards the doors.

A small handful of the group made their way to follow him, calling futilely for answers. Alexandro ignored them, and before he reached the door my arm had begun to vibrate viciously. All the others clearly were experiencing the same sensation, as each of us simultaneously grabbed at our wrist. Quyén and Tallis abandoned their efforts to follow the host, and he slipped through the double doors.

I stood up, straightened my jumpsuit and made to approach Sid. I felt horrible that I hadn't spoken to him since Chase's arrival, and I wanted him to know that he still had my support.

Before I could move, Chase grabbed at my shoulder. 'Tyler! So sorry that we couldn't speak for longer.'

'That's okay. We never know how long we have here.'

'Exactly. Now listen to me: you need to keep fighting. You can't give up, okay?'

'Uh, okay.' As he spoke, I watched Sid in my peripherals as he made his way towards his tunnel.

'Tyler, you need to be careful who you trust in here. Mechislav and Ruby, they're not your friends. Your father and I worked with Mechislav. They cannot be trusted.'

'Mechislav knew my father?'

'Yes, and Ruby as well.'

With one eye on Sid, I was mentally pulled towards Chase who had now gained my attention. I needed to be careful who I allowed myself to trust. Until now, I'd had no way of knowing who was trustworthy, but I knew I could rely on my father's judgement.

In the corner of my eye, I saw Sid halt at the mouth of his tunnel. Mechislav had approached him.

'Were Mechislav and my father friends?' I asked Chase.

'There was a time when we were all good friends, Tyler. But Mechislav left, and it's understood he now works for some very powerful, very dangerous people.'

'What do you mean? Who does he work for?'

'We don't have the time right now, but I promise I'll explain everything next time I see you. Until then, keep your head up.'

Chase embraced me warmly. I pulled him close to me; this was the first time since my capture that I'd had anything resembling family to engage with. As my head poked over his shoulder, I saw Mechislav shake Sid's hand firmly. Sid was nodding profusely, as if he was receiving direct orders. By the time Chase had released me, both Sid and Mechislav had withdrawn into their tunnels. I gave Chase a final wave as we entered our adjacent tunnels to head to our pods.

18

CUPS

I was greeted by the smell of ripe pine as I stumbled into the pod. It was unrecognisable, completely transformed from the one I'd fled from hours before. Any evidence of the destroyed fern pot had been removed, although the scent from the fern's soil lingered. The soil had embedded itself into the grooves of the tiles, masking the usual smell of lavender from cleaning chemicals. A sense of nature now filled the small enclosure, the first time in weeks I had experienced any hint of life outside these walls.

The maroon levers had been removed from the walls, along with the other items used for the last Trial. Whoever had been in the pod had also returned the bed, and the toilet and sink were reinstated. I was relieved to find that they had left the deck of cards and *The Metallic Moon*.

The bed remained stiff, as I had left it, and my back cracked against its surface when I lay uncomfortably facing the ceiling. My body longed for rest, but thoughts swam wildly in my head: I had survived another Trial; an old family friend had arrived; Mechislav knew my father.

On top of all this new information, guilt overwhelmed me. I'd failed to thank Sid for his support and wish him luck in the next Trial. I promised myself that despite any interruptions from Mechislav or Chase, I would thank Sid properly at the next feast. He'd been all I had before Chase arrived; I couldn't allow him to continue in the Trials alone.

My body ached for the opportunity to speak with Chase, to ask him the millions of questions that flooded my mind. For the first time in a fortnight, an overwhelming feeling of warmth spread through me as I drifted off to sleep. I had found purpose again, an excuse to survive each day, as it would bring me closer to the next time that I would see Chase.

Perhaps I won't forfeit. I have more answers to discover.

I was met the following morning by a bowl of muesli and a plastic pitcher of milk, reeking as if it had expired. The breakfast rested casually upon the bench inside the en suite, opposite a new jumpsuit, track pants and orange skivvy hanging limply over a hanger. I hadn't changed out of the jumpsuit I'd worn in the previous day's Trial, and the smell of the damp clothes I stripped from my body overpowered the stench of the stale milk opposite me.

Half asleep, I showered then slipped into the provided clothes. Without a mirror in either the en suite or pod, I felt conscious of my messy hair and overgrown stubble, which itched with each passing day. I attempted to flatten my hair although I could feel that this did little to prevent it from sticking awkwardly in all directions.

My stomach grumbled aggressively; I should not have neglected the assortments in the hall yesterday evening. Despite the bad milk, I scoffed the muesli in a few spoonfuls before retreating back to my pod to the *whoosh* of the entrance closing behind me.

I spent the next few hours counting cards mindlessly and thinking about the next Trial. *Why hasn't Alexandro provided a riddle?* I thought. The previous feasts had finished with a rhyme that hinted towards the upcoming Trial, but this time he'd said nothing. I concluded that another meeting must be scheduled before the next Trial, and that he'd provide the riddle then.

Again, a feeling of warmth filled me at the thought of seeing Chase next, when I could learn more about his relationship with Mechislav. I longed to hear his theory as to why I was here. I imagined the thrill on Sid's face when I could tell him that we had a genuine ally.

In contrast to my positive emotions towards Chase and Sid, I found myself hoping for Tallis's termination. I felt some guilt for wishing a horrible outcome on someone I barely knew, but I couldn't help the strong dislike I had for him after his attack on Hermes. I couldn't decide who I disliked more: Tallis or Alexandro. At least Alexandro was evil with a smile. Perhaps that was worse.

The sound of the hole in the wall opening announced lunch. My feet dragged me towards the en suite to find two slices of bread spread with raspberry jam on a paper plate. The bread tasted much fresher than my previous meals, and I enjoyed the taste of the jam after the stale milk and muesli. The entrance remained open and I drifted between the two spaces casually for several minutes before eventually falling onto the bed, picking up the book for the first time.

The cover showed a picture of an artificial moon made from an assortment of metals. Directly in front of the moon, in the centre of the cover, a cardboard rocket ship had been assembled with silver letters shining above reading *The Metallic Moon.* I flicked through the book aimlessly, struggling to find the motivation to read. It appeared to be second-hand, with scribbled graffiti filling several of the pages and several of its corners folded over. The pages had a yellowish tinge and the spine had begun to tatter.

The novel was noticeably modest in length. With the spare time I had available, I could easily finish it within a few hours. But as my body relaxed, I was overcome by a desire to sleep. The book slipped from my outstretched hand as I dozed into the abyss.

My eyes had only been closed for a few moments when I heard the familiar *whoosh* beside me. I had become accustomed to the periodic cycle of access to the en suite. It couldn't be time for dinner yet. I opened my eyes slightly, in anticipation of finding another tragic meal on the bench beyond the hole leading to the en suite. To my surprise, the entrance had not opened.

The sound of it was so distinct now that I was sure that I hadn't misheard it. A flickering light in my peripheral vision made me turn. What had opened was not the way to the en suite, but the tunnel leading to the hall. The light came from the sides of the tunnel into my pod and within seconds I found myself standing at the foot of the passageway, staring wishfully.

Has somebody come to save me? Perplexed, I stepped through the arch and into the darkness, the narrow strip of light along the floor illuminating my passage as usual. But the walk felt longer than normal. I followed the light slowly, listening to the echo of my footsteps as I drew closer to the hall's brightness.

The skylight glowed a calming purple. In the centre of the hall Alexandro stood at the raised table, same smile, same signature navy blue suit hugging him tightly.

Separating me from Alexandro were nine rectangular plastic tables in a row, each uniquely coloured and numbered to correlate to each contestant. I naturally gravitated towards the orange table labelled 4. A triangle of six cups sat against the far side of each of the tables in front of the host.

The shuffling of footsteps scurried on either side of me as the other contestants made their way upon the mats which sat behind their assigned table.

'Come, my friends. Please make your way to your table, I think it's time we ought to have some fun!' Alexandro exclaimed.

The hall felt larger than usual with the absence of the oak table, the usual centrepiece. As the final contestants hesitantly approached the plastic tables, the large silver doors opened violently behind

Alexandro. A posse of large bodies marched into the hall, each dressed identically to the ones who had escorted Hermes the night before.

'Ah, the Scouts have arrived.'

The men looked like soldiers, with no identifying features distinguishing one from another; their dark grey outfits and thick helmets appeared interchangeable. The Scouts lined up to form a barrier in front of Alexandro. One Scout was positioned at the end of each table, facing the contestants.

The Scout directly facing me stood a couple of inches taller than myself, an unusual feeling for me, as I towered above most of the over contestants. His muscular arms were like a bear's, and his legs were like tree trunks. I couldn't see a face behind his helmet, but I had the eerie feeling he was staring directly into my soul.

'Let me introduce you to the Scouts,' said Alexandro. 'I have invited them here this evening for your protection. Now, as the last two weeks have been exhausting, I felt it was time we let our hair down and had some fun!'

I exchanged a sceptical look with Sid, who was shaking, off to my right. Between us stood a relaxed-looking Chase. I felt relieved that he was beside me. Seeing Sid's worried face consumed me with sympathy, and I was impatient for Alexandro to finish talking so I could comfort my friend.

But Quyén cut Alexandro off casually, saying, 'I have no desire to play your games. I'm going back to my room.'

'Quyén, my friend, of course you have every right to not participate. But forfeiting a Trial will result in termination.'

I swivelled sideways towards Chase, who immediately sensed my concern. Discreetly, he moved his hand out from his side and patted the air downwards, to signal: *Stay calm.*

His eyes told me to remain composed and with that, a sensation of confidence came over me. I trusted Chase: he had been a significant mentor to me, and been cool-headed under pressure for as long as I could remember. Tonight would be no exemption.

'Yes, Trial Three commenced the moment you stepped upon those mats,' Alexandro continued.

I glanced down. I was standing on an orange-coloured mat before the table. Several others also looked to the floor.

'This Trial tests your skill in a modified version of a common college party game!'

From the far end of the row of tables I heard Tallis let out a snort of laughter. My blood ran cold at his outburst. A small pocket revealed itself underneath the table on my side, and a second later a single white ping pong ball rolled loosely within it. I looked at the ball blankly.

'Your Trial is as follows: you must pitch your ball directly into one of the six cups on your table without it bouncing on the table first. Once the ball lands in the cup, you must drink whatever the cup contains before taking aim for another. This process will be repeated until you have thrown the ball into each of the six cups and consumed all six liquids. The last to do so will be terminated. Now, my friends, a few rules come with this Trial, so listen closely – they will not be repeated. Firstly, a contestant must only throw a ball at their own cups. Any interference with another contestant will constitute a rule violation. Secondly, you must keep both feet on your mat at all times. This rule will remain in place until the conclusion of the Trial. Finally, when you successfully land a ball, the Scout opposite you will present the cup to you and ensure it is completely drained before you are permitted to attempt any further shots.'

I nodded as I absorbed the information. The rules seemed straightforward: throw the ball in the cups.

'Now, each of you will receive only one warning of a rule violation, and your bracelet will be activated to a medium setting,' Alexandro continued. 'Following your warning, should another rule be violated, instant termination will result.' His smile vanished as he delivered his expectations for the upcoming Trial. 'I am prepared to have multiple terminations this evening.'

Alexandro's expression stayed serious momentarily, then his mouth twisted into a taunting smile. 'But enough about rules – let's have fun!'

19

THE LOSS

Alexandro's laugh reverberated around the room. I caught Chase's eye – he smiled to me approvingly and nodded encouragement. Tallis was squatting excitedly, the most comfortable I had seen him since our arrival. Gloria and Quyén looked stunned. Quyén especially looked dreadful, leaning forward on his table as if struggling to remain upright, the bags under his eyes darker since yesterday.

A suspenseful silence hung in the air as we awaited the next instruction.

'What's in the cups?' Ruby asked.

'Ah ha! Great question, Ruby,' replied Alexandro. 'Although I would hate to ruin the surprise. Let's find out, shall we?'

Nobody moved. Alexandro offered a final glance around the room before commencing a countdown from five.

No sooner had he announced 'Go' than Tallis had thrown his first ball toward his cups. He was celebrating loudly before I had even grabbed at my first ball.

The ball that I collected from the pouch rolled slowly in my palm before I took aim at the formation of cups opposing me. I lobbed the hollow ball at no cup in particular, and it arced past its target and into the Scout's bulky torso before it rolled towards Alexandro, who didn't appear to notice. Almost instantly, another ball appeared in the pouch.

To my left, I looked past Mechislav at Quyén, who appeared to have found his technique. His Scout strutted up to his side, placing a red cup in his hand. Quyén's face scrunched as soon as he raised the cup to his face. Struggling to keep the liquid down, he returned the empty cup to his Scout and turned to his remaining five.

I caught Mechislav's eye as he leaned forward, nodding eagerly for me to hurry.

I nodded back and shifted my attention to the six semi-full cups positioned before me. I felt I had already fallen far behind in this Trial as I heard another cheer towards the end of the tables to my right, perhaps Tallis potting another ball. My second attempt proved to be marginally better than my first: the ball bounced off the rims of two adjoining cups and shot upwards towards the Scout who remained facing me, stiff as a statue. By my fourth attempt, I successfully landed a ball inside a cup in the far corner of the triangle.

My Scout arrived at my side before I had the opportunity to celebrate. The liquid in the cup was as clear as water; looking down on the cup I could see its base through the liquid with ease. From a certain angle the cup appeared to house no contents at all. 'What is it?' I asked the Scout. His helmet was lifeless. I was certain he could hear me beneath it, but he gave no response. After a couple of seconds of silence, I took the cup from his thick black glove and pressed it to my lips. If others had drunk from the cups already, I was certain that whatever this was couldn't be fatal. To the sound of balls bouncing off plastic and the spontaneous cheers and grunts of the other contestants, I pinched my nose and emptied the cup's contents down my throat.

A burning sensation immediately took effect. It was as if the liquid had come from the fountains of hell. Nausea mixed with the burning feeling in my throat, but I refused to allow myself to vomit.

Alexandro had failed to mention the consequence of vomiting in the Trial, but I was not prepared to find out. The ball swivelled between my fingertips inside the empty cup. It repelled my grip like my stomach repelled the contents that I forced myself to digest. I withdrew the ball and placed the cup in the Scout's outstretched glove. I waited for him to return to his place before lining up another shot.

The liquid was already having an effect on me. My vision blurred, and the hall danced around me. Fortunately, my next throw was successful, and the Scout removed another cup from the back row; the arrangement of cups now formed a diamond.

His presence towering over me gave me motivation to quickly consume the liquid in the second cup. I didn't wait to observe the contents, but the milky liquid soothed the burn from the previous one, and it glided down my throat effortlessly. Feeling more confident, I took aim at the diamond in an attempt to catch up to the others. A celebratory bellow, louder than the others, signalled that Tallis had completed the Trial. As the minutes passed, I watched the cups of Mechislav and Chase – who stood on either side of me – diminish as well.

After some time, I eventually landed the ball in the closest cup to me. It bubbled intensely in the grasp of the approaching Scout. A foul smell erupted from this cup, forcing me to gag. The odour made me think of an old carcass, and the dense redness of the liquid did little to convince me otherwise. The cup was uncomfortably warm in my hands.

Don't vomit, I reminded myself. I could feel the muesli and the off milk from my breakfast churn in my stomach. The warm cup shook in my hand close to my face.

'Vat are yew vaiting for?'

Ignoring the Russian giant to my left, I closed my eyes.

I could feel his presence penetrate me from the side. 'Yew need to hurry.'

I swung around to face him, noticing a cup of similar contents in his hands. He offered a smile, exposing his dirty teeth for the first time. The red of the bubbling liquid matched the colour of his skivvy. Stunned, I said nothing as he raised his eyebrows eagerly and gingerly tilted his cup towards me. 'Ve do eet togezzer.'

I gave him a sincere smile as I raised my own in return. 'I – I don't know . . .'

He quickly counted down from three, reached zero and downed his drink. I closed my eyes and allowed the warm substance to trickle between my lips. It felt like a crawling slug – half liquid, half solid – travelling slowly through my insides. I felt my body resist the substance and fought the urge for it to resurface into my mouth.

I opened my eyes. Mechislav smiled at me, his yellow teeth now spotted with stringy red patches of the drink. I ran my tongue over my own teeth self-consciously. I noticed that Mechislav had just drunk from his last cup. At least two contestants had now finished. I spun around quickly to face my remaining three cups.

I grabbed at the ball and returned the empty cup to my Scout's outstretched hand, immediately taking aim at the small triangle of cups opposing me. Optimistically, I hoped the next cup contained water, but knew that was unlikely.

A flash of white as the ball skipped past the cups for the third consecutive time. I impatiently waited for a new ball to arrive in the pouch as I watched Gloria finish another drink at the far end of the tables. Quyén produced a horrific howl to my left; presumably he had consumed something vile.

Hopefully that was something I've already drunk, I thought, hoping for nothing worse than the warm substance I had barely digested.

I hunched over the table for support, forcing my feet to remain on my mat. The pain in my stomach was intensifying.

A new ball arrived in the pouch. I allowed it to fly from my fingertips towards the cups, only missing my target by an inch. The ball rolled helplessly past the Scout's boot. I quickly flicked a glance to my right. Chase and Sid both had fewer cups remaining than me. Naomi jumped in glee simultaneous to her lobbed ball finding the inside her final cup.

The next ball arrived. As I went to collect it, a scream erupted from down the line. Naomi lay on the floor wincing in pain a metre off her mat. Almost all the contestants stopped their Trial to watch the distraction. Only Gloria, at the far end of the line, continued, seemingly unfazed by Naomi's cries.

'Naomi Ark, this is your first rule violation for stepping from your mat,' Alexandro announced over the chaos. 'Your next rule violation will result in termination.'

Tears streak down Naomi's cheek as she lay shivering on the tiled floor. I momentarily felt sympathy for her, but Gloria's persistence reminded me that the Trial remained incomplete. Without allowing any further distracted seconds to pass by, I launched a new ball in the air and watched it land safely in one of the cups. I exclaimed loudly to myself.

The Scout approached me with the cup before some of the other contestants had removed their focus from Naomi. I consumed its contents and thrust it back into the Scout's gloved hand, ignoring the fizzing substance inside my mouth. For a few moments my mouth felt as if it was a cauldron, a furious acid brewing inside it.

Eyes clenched shut, I grasped the table for stability. Ulcers seemed to grow like ivy on the walls of my mouth. I allowed the sensation to dwindle. The acid subsided slowly without the need to swallow, as if the inside of my mouth had absorbed it completely. I opened my eyes and the room span wildly. I felt my legs quiver. I couldn't allow myself to step from the mat.

The pain eased with the subsidence of the bubbling sensation. Only dizziness remained. I took a deep breath for composure. There weren't too many contestants still competing now. I fumbled for the next ball and took aim. With my vision blurred, I watched the ball soar several metres past the cups.

Another scream of pain filled the hall, followed by Alexandro's voice. 'Gloria Robertson, this is your first rule violation for not finishing the contents of your cup. Your next rule violation will result in termination.'

I swayed where I stood; the colours of the table, the cups, the Scout, all blurred into one. I reached for the table again but instead my hand thrust wildly at the air. I heard a call from beside me, but it was indistinct.

I allowed the room's atmosphere to swallow me as I fell.

A new sensation of pain seized my chest. My body was flat against the icy tiles of the floor, the room flashing in and out of focus. My bones rattled inside me so forcefully I expected them to vibrate through my skin and out of my body. I could feel myself screaming in pain, but no sound escaped me.

All I knew was the torture that vibrated through me. After what felt like an eternity, a sound penetrated the pain. A smooth voice, orchestrating peacefulness over the chaos that erupted within my body.

I could not comprehend Alexandro's words exactly, but I understood that he spoke my name then detailed a rule violation. I had slipped from my mat and he had activated my bracelet. I crawled back onto the pad as to avoid a second surge of violent vibrations.

Chase knelt on his own mat and faced me. 'Only two more to go, you can do this!'

I looked up and nodded. I wanted the pain to end, but my right arm continued to twitch involuntarily. Legs like jelly, I stood and reached for a ball once more.

'Focus, Tyler,' Chase urged as my ball bounced off one of the cups. 'So close!'

Chase radiated eagerness and confidence; he must have completed his Trial already. Despite having consumed all six variations of liquids, he seemed as alert and composed as I had ever seen him. This kindled a hope in me: if Chase was coherent and positive, I must have suffered the worst of the liquids already. At the very least, whatever lay ahead of me wouldn't kill me.

'How many contestants are still going?' I asked him.

'Tyler, don't worry about that – focus on what's in front of you.'

My motivation now returning, I grabbed at the ball which lay in the pouch and took aim at the final two cups. With each miss, I collected the ball swiftly and took aim again immediately, allowing no more wasted time between throws. I could hear balls rebounding off cups at a few other tables, indicating that there were still competitors remaining.

With a soft toss, the ball floated in the air, bouncing off one cup onto the other before rolling off the side of the table. Another ball appeared.

Driven by Chase's encouragement, my next throw lobbed graciously into the cup on the right.

Yes! I exclaimed to myself, clenching my fist. I stole the cup from the hands of the Scout before he had arrived directly by my side and swallowed its contents whole. My taste buds had seemingly turned off. All I could feel now was determination to get the ball in the final cup.

I couldn't comprehend the words being shouted on either side of me, but their voices grew louder. It was Mechislav and Chase throwing verbal attacks at one another. Unaware of what was being said, or why, I focussed on the remaining cup.

The Scout took my empty cup with one hand and returned to his post. At least two more contestants were competing against me. I refused to waste time identifying who, instead turning to face the single cup in front of me.

The bickering on either side of me was increasing, and as I waited for a new ball to arrive, I took in snippets of the argument.

'You can't fool me, Mechislav. I know what you're up to.'

'Vatt? You're ze one distracting ze boy!'

I lined up another shot, but the ball fell short, bouncing in front of the cups.

'Tyler is like a son to me, don't talk to me like you know him. He had given up in here before I arrived!'

'And vhere exactly ees "here"?'

'What is that supposed to mean?'

'I know yew're behind zis, Chase!' Mechislav spat.

The ball swivelled between my fingers. Distracted, I sent it an arm's length to the left of the cup, missing the table completely.

'You're crazy! But you've always been a little loopy, haven't you? Now you'll try to convince everyone that I'm the bad guy in all of this?'

'I might be a bit loopy . . . but I know vhat you did to Victor.'

With this comment, my heart dropped. Distracted, I had sent the ball in my hand hurtling past the wall of Scouts and towards the host, who clapped his hands excitedly at nothing in particular.

Both men beside me noticed that the last comment had gained my attention. Silence fell between the three of us.

'Did you say –' I started.

Before I could finish my sentence, Chase had reached across from his mat to grasp my shoulder. 'Tyler, keep going, don't listen to him.'

But the Trials became irrelevant to me. They were discussing my father. How was he involved?

'Aha! I knew zis was his boy!'

I turned to face Mechislav. He looked at me with his deranged eyes, and his head tilted slightly as he examined me.

'What did you say about my father?'

'He is only trying to distract you, Tyler! You need to keep going. We'll talk about it later!' Chase's comments drifted through me as if they were meaningless. Mechislav didn't move; he stared at me in an attempt to communicate through his eyes.

I could hear balls bouncing off cups behind me, but I remained focused on Mechislav. 'What did you mean?!' I screamed.

I heard the celebration of a contestant in the distance.

After a few moments, Mechislav responded slowly. 'Chase ees right, zis can be discussed later.'

I felt my face drop with disappointment. My eyes narrowed on him aggressively.

'Go. Now.' Mechislav persisted.

'No! What did you mean? Do you know my father too?' My voice was raised now, and I noticed Alexandro cock his head towards us. I wondered what the Scouts thought of the situation, or if they remained oblivious to it all.

'Tyler, zhere's not much time –'

'Damn it! Stop distracting him!' Chase interjected. 'Tyler, come on!'

Chase stepped off his mat in an attempt to pull my attention back into the Trial. Almost immediately, he dropped to the ground, clutching his sides and shouting curse words.

My mind flooded with questions. I grabbed at the ball within the pouch and took aim at the final cup. I didn't know who else was still competing, but I no longer cared. I now had motivation to complete it so I could get the answers to the questions that burned in me.

The following throws felt consistently more haphazard as I powered through attempts like a mechanical revolver. The balls missed on either side, too far, and too short, before one finally landed on the cup, circling its rim. It dropped with a silent splash and the Scout approached me with the cup, an orange liquid.

Without celebration, I threw the last cup's contents into my mouth and swallowed. The liquid rattled against my teeth, icy cold, and it took several attempts to swallow it against my body's urge to reject it. Eventually it went down my throat, stabbing my insides fiercely the entire way down.

I tried to compose myself to speak to Chase, however Alexandro's voice filled the hall. 'My friends, this brings a close to Trial Three. Well done! Please remain on your mats until I say. You may still receive a rule violation until notified otherwise.'

The room fell silent. I could not believe that I survived another Trial, I looked around wildly to see who I had beaten.

'Scouts, please remove the terminated.'

In unison, the ensemble of Scouts moved from their posts, heavy footsteps echoing through the hall. They powered past me, and the mustard yellow of Sid's jumpsuit was drowned by the surrounding Scouts within seconds.

'No!' I screamed.

Sid had collapsed on his mat but was hoisted up by two Scouts. I turned to Chase, who was staring at me intensely with widened eyes. He mouthed calmly, 'Do. Not. Move.'

I wanted to run after the Scouts, but my legs disobeyed. All sensation beneath my waist had disappeared. As sudden as the announcement had been, Sid's removal was quicker. He succumbed to the Scouts' force quietly, allowing himself to be withdrawn from the hall with his head bowed. Two Scouts ushered him out and the remaining seven followed.

Sid's body disappeared from view, and I longed for a final glimpse of his piercing blue eyes, but it did not come. The double doors slammed behind the final Scout.

To my side, I watched a grin spread over Quyén's face; he did not appear to care who was terminated as long as it was not him. The room was silent for a few moments after the doors closed, then Alexandro dismissed the remaining contestants from their mats and murmuring broke out between the contestants.

I did not remove myself from my mat, and after thirty seconds the doors opened again. I flashed a glance in anticipation of Sid to return, but a trio of Scouts strutted in the hall with a platter of biscuits and several pitchers of water.

Only eight of us remained. Around me, the usual groups began to form. I refused to step from my mat, instead dropping to my knees with my head in my hands. Chase tried to console me for several minutes, then gave up and focussed his attention on Mechislav, who seemed more than happy to welcome him with debate. I no longer cared about Chase and Mechislav's dispute – I only wanted Sid to return.

20

THE INVITATION

The following days breezed by with oblivion. Isolated hours in my room were spent theorising about what had happened to the terminated contestants, coming to the sickening conclusion that they no longer breathed life. On the third day after Sid's termination, I decided to immerse myself in *The Metallic Moon*, which had lain unread beside my bed since before the second Trial.

The story was of a young boy in outback Australia, and his ambitions to reach the moon. The storyline was original and intriguing, but I found myself drawn to the graffitied markings throughout the book. Abstract phrases were scribbled in pen: *wooden artefacts – head towards, animals in clothes to be ignored*, and *Feathers expire, Cup the bird's injured calf, a broken Leg supported by a Staff.*

I struggled to comprehend meaning from these scribbles. They distracted me from the narrative of the book, and I resigned myself to accepting that they lay between the pages only as a distraction.

I found myself re-reading a lot of pages –
even chapters – as my mind continually drifted away
from the story and towards Sid and the other
terminated contestants. I had only known the boy for
a short period of time, but had felt an urge to protect
him – and I had failed. I replayed his final moments
in the hall in a loop inside my head: his limp body,
the tears, a dispute about my father lashing around
me.

Since our arrival at Touhere, Sid had always
seemed unsettled. Anxiety radiated from him at every
feast in the hall, and his nervousness was evident
whenever he spoke. He had attached himself to me
from the beginning, and I had failed to support him as
soon as Chase entered the Trials. I imagined how
frightened he must have felt in those final moments,
viewing the hall one last time, unsympathetic faces of
the contestants watching his dismissal without
objection. I hated that I had stood with the others,
frozen, observing.

My stomach growled; I hadn't eaten since
before the last Trial. How could I? The anchor in the
pit of my stomach grew heavier at the thought of how
the last Trial had concluded. On the first night after
the Trial, I'd spent the night restlessly vomiting into
the toilet bowl. It was impossible to know if the
sickness was caused by grief, guilt or the copious
amount of unidentified liquids I had consumed. Or a
disastrous combination. By the end of the night, it
seemed that all the food I had consumed since my
arrival had resurfaced inside the toilet bowl.

I had noticed my track pants had loosened
since I had received them, and my cotton shirt now

hung baggily over my bony shoulders. Had there been mirrors inside my pod or en suite, I would have felt self-conscious looking at my withering body.

I had always been skinny, but my muscles had never felt weaker. I found it increasingly difficult to raise myself from the bed as each day passed.

On the morning of the fifth day after Sid's termination, I woke to breakfast waiting for me in the en suite. The lights were brighter than usual this morning; perhaps I had enjoyed a lengthy sleep for the first time that I could remember.

I approached the plastic bowl of breakfast. Perched beside it lay a large envelope, completely black, with handwritten cursive on the front. *Tyler Knight*, it read in silver letters. I opened the envelope to find two pieces of thick paper. I pulled at one, accidently forcing the second to gently float towards the floor. On the back of the card in my hand was a message. I slumped on the bench to read it.

Congratulations on your progression to Trial Four.

Before this Trial commences, we invite you to meet with fellow contestants in a one-on-one setting. Attached is a checkbox with the names of the other contestants beside their seven numbers. You may mark the contestants you wish to meet with, using the pencil provided.

Should you select a contestant who also requests to meet with you, a five-minute meeting will be arranged for this afternoon. If only one, or neither contestant desires to meet, no meeting will be arranged.

You are encouraged to use this opportunity to gain emotional support, discuss strategy or enforce vengeance, or for any other reason you deem fit. Strictly five minutes will be allowed; I encourage you to select your meetings carefully.

I retrieved the fallen attachment from the ground. There were seven vacant squares, and beside them seven coloured numbers and names. My name and number were missing from the list.

I took the pencil, thrust one end between my teeth and considered my options. Who did I want to meet with? As I raced through the options, I reflected on the card's suggested reasons to meet. I had no idea where my alliance with Mechislav, Ruby and Gloria stood now that Chase had arrived. My only true ally beside Chase had just been terminated. I did not know who I could trust now.

Disregarding the alliances, the urge to meet with Mechislav intensified. He had a history with my father. But he was a clear rival to Chase, my only trusted ally. I needed to understand the true nature of Mechislav and Chase's relationship, and how my father was involved. Could Mechislav somehow be responsible for my presence in the Trials? I had to know more. I ticked the boxes beside 3 and 5.

I imagined how my conversation with Mechislav would unfold. The meeting would only be for five minutes; would he spend the entire time insulting Chase? Chase had suggested that he was untrustworthy, and on reflection I thought it would be unwise to side with a complete stranger over a lifelong family friend. I scribbled aggressively at

150

Mechislav's box, obliterating the tick beside his number, and moved down the list.

After considerable mental debate, I decided to also select Ruby and Gloria. I could only hope that I remained in close alliance with them despite Mechislav's ruthlessness. I had no desire to enact vengeance; the only outcome I wanted from the meetings was to gain a deeper knowledge of why I was here.

The idea of being alone with Tallis nauseated me, so his number was merely glanced over. Quyén and Naomi were the only contestants that remained; their alliance was strong, but I had no desire to join them. Each time I encountered Quyén, he seemed less stable and more erratic. I was quite happy to leave his square blank too. I ticked the box beside Naomi's number.

I reviewed my selection. Four meeting requests. Chase and I would meet up for support and to find out how my father was linked to Mechislav. I knew there was more to the story, and Chase had the answers I longed for.

I remained hopeful that Ruby would also choose to meet with me. I wanted to hear her story, uninterrupted by Mechislav, and allow me to judge her genuineness.

Gloria might be fragile and weak, but building an alliance was necessary and I couldn't imagine she held any negativity towards me. I was curious about her story and how her husband could be involved. Perhaps that would help me understand why I was kidnapped.

The fourth person I wished to speak with was Naomi. She had always been nice to me and I felt that she was innocent despite the alliance she had fallen into.

Alexandro's theory that innocence was to prevail remained strong inside me. If this was to be true, I had to understand the stories of all the contestants.

I left the completed card and pencil beside the untouched meal and stepped into the shower. When I returned, both the breakfast and my nominations had disappeared.

The rest of the day I spent on my bed, considering the desired outcomes of each meeting. A hot flush raced over me as I realised there was a possibility that nobody would select me in turn. What if I no longer belonged to any alliance and was once again on my own?

I imagined that Mechislav, Ruby and Gloria might blame me for Sid's termination, considering I betrayed him during his time of need. I began doubting that even Chase would want to meet with me. After all, I did ignore him after Sid's termination. The lights dimmed slowly as the day grew into the evening. Perhaps I was meeting nobody at all.

With my knowledge of the perimeter light's sequence, I assumed it to be late afternoon. Dinner was due within the hour. Time passed, but no dinner arrived. It must have been several hours before a *whoosh* signalled the tunnel's opening, inviting me inside. I turned in my bed in anticipation of Alexandro's entrance, but the room remained still.

With a sigh, I pulled myself up from the bed and escorted myself through the tunnel's entrance. The tunnel carried an unfamiliar eerie feeling as I moved away from my pod. My steps grew heavier, the light from the hall drew closer and I found myself at the mouth of the tunnel facing a small metallic table, featuring nothing but a black rose in a slim glass vase. A tall woman with frizzy hair smiled at me from the opposite end. Ruby.

21

WOMEN'S ADVICE

The single black rose looked as if it had been plucked from a garden only moments earlier. The café-style table was lit by an unknown source, the remainder of the space in darkness. The large timer from the second Trial had been reinstalled above the large double doors, and commenced counting down from five minutes the instant I approached the table. My skinny body fell into the unoccupied seat across from a smiling Ruby.

'Hi, Tyler.'

'How's it going?'

Her smile was as authentic as the fresh rose between us. I looked to the ground as I felt the corners of my lips crack into a smile. She radiated a feeling of comfort I longed for, a maternal presence. Her dark skin glowed in the mysterious light, and she wasted no time in formalities. 'I'm good. How have you been after last week? I know you were close to Sid in here.'

'Uh, yeah – we were. I dunno.' I was lost for words. I hadn't expected her to bring Sid up as abruptly as she had, but somehow I felt comfortable with it.

'It's okay, Tyler. You're allowed to be sad. I was sad when Shy left us.'

'Me too. Do you think they . . .? I mean, Sid and that . . . Do you think that . . .?'

'I don't know where they are. I like to think they're okay. But Tyler, that doesn't matter now.'

'Doesn't matter?' I felt my temper rise, and I met her eyes.

'What matters is you and me,' she went on. 'And Gloria . . . and Mechislav.' She hesitated before mentioning the last name and I noticed her eyes dart away from me before she whispered it. 'We need to stick together if we want to survive. You understand?'

'I guess. But we can't all get out, so what's the point?'

'The point . . .' Ruby leaned in so close that her nose almost brushed the rose. Her voice dropped to a whisper, '. . . is that we stick together to buy time. We will all get out of here, Tyler. Just don't get terminated.' The hint of a wink. Was the light playing tricks on me or did Ruby have a plan?

My heart skipped a beat at the thought of freedom, but my lips remained sealed tightly. I knew she understood what I was thinking, and as a new daunting thought formulated silently in my head, she seemed to have read that as well. 'You need to remove yourself from Chase. He isn't one of us.'

'I won't do that.'

'Tyler, we are all here to protect you from him. Me, Gloria, even Mechislav, we are all on your side. You need to trust us.'

I felt the hope of escaping diminish faster than it arrived. I couldn't believe Ruby thought she could turn me against Chase. This group wasn't to be my saviour, these were the people responsible for my imprisonment. Alexandro had explained at the start of our isolation that each of the contestants had wronged; how could I be so naïve to believe Ruby even for a moment?

'You think you know Chase, but you don't!' I said. 'I don't know why you're all against him; he is a good man. He has always supported me and I'm not going to let a group of *strangers* tell me otherwise!' I turned away. My folded arms served as a barrier between us.

Ruby opened her mouth to respond but was cut off by a loud buzzer. The timer had struck zero. The walls of the open spaces reverberated softly signalling the end of our discussion. Two strangers sitting opposing each other, separated only by the thick tension created between them. Ruby's outstretched hand – a feeble attempt to comfort me – lay ignored upon the table.

'Just think about it,' she said as she got up. Her words drifted with her exit.

I turned away, focussing on Ruby's tunnel. The large number 1 above it glowed a brilliant shade of purple. I continued to stare at the tunnel, then turned back to the table as she passed me so as to avoid her gaze.

The rose, elegant and still, matched the darkness I felt towards Ruby and her group for trying to distance me from Chase. I rubbed my face forcefully to clear my mind.

Removing my hands from my face, I was left with tiny black dots impairing my vision as an elderly figure advanced towards me. Gloria.

She gently pulled the opposite chair out and sat down as the timer behind her readjusted to 00:05:00.

'Hi,' I said softly.

'Hello, Tyler.' We exchanged smiles.

Gloria withdrew a pair of oversized glasses from her pocket and positioned them on her face. The glasses magnified her eyeballs, creating the illusion that they were bulging out of their sockets. Her jumpsuit sat loosely on her shoulders; it appeared to be several sizes too big for her. I immediately took pity on the woman; she must have felt more intimidated in the Trials than I had. Despite her alliance with Mechislav and Ruby, I felt genuine concern for her.

'How are you holding up after the loss of Sydney?'

'I don't want to talk about it.'

'That's okay, dear. I just want to check that you're okay. I want you to know that Sydney was—'

'Did you and Ruby plan this?' I cut her words off like a hot knife. 'To interrogate me over Sid? Are you trying to make me feel vulnerable so I'll team up with you when you escape?'

I hadn't realised that I was now shouting, and Gloria readjusted herself in her seat. Her eyes intensified behind her glasses and she leaned away from me in surprise.

The mention of Sid's name had fuelled the fire inside me. Although I wasn't sure if it was regret, guilt or frustration, I was confident Gloria understood the emotion was strong.

Instead of responding, she sat back in her chair, rubbing her lips. I watched her mind tick over, calculating a response. 'No, my dear. What happened to Sydney is not your fault,' she said softly, before becoming stern. 'Nor is it mine, or Ruby's, or Mechislav's.'

'And I assume you think that Chase is a bad influence, too?'

Gloria lowered her head. I longed for her to react, to yell back at me. I hastily stood and kicked the chair out from behind me. I dropped both hands on the table with more force than intended, causing the vase to topple over. 'Enough about me, what's your story?' I said.

She calmly repositioned the vase in the centre of the table. 'Well, dear, as you may know, my husband is the Vice President of the United States of America. He has been investigating certain suspicious behaviours. I believe that he stuck his nose in places where it wasn't invited, and they got him.'

'Who got him?'

'They call themselves . . .' She leaned in close, as Ruby had done previously, also dropping her voice to a whisper. 'Private Sector Eleven.'

Her voice was so quiet that I only apprehended her words by reading her lips. I began to repeat her, but she quickly raised an index finger to silence me. With the softest of whispers, she continued. 'Private Sector Eleven, or PSE, is an underground organisation who have influence over several governments, including the United States. They contribute to a large amount of corruption throughout the First World.' Her eyes narrowed. I felt my stomach turn awkwardly. The timer behind her had inconveniently reached its final minute.

'Listen, dear. I don't have time to go into detail about them now, but you need to understand that the Oranga Trials are bigger than you think. None of the contestants are here by accident, Tyler. Each of us has been hand-picked by PSE. I am here because of my husband, and Sid was here because of his parents.'

'Sid doesn't know his parents,' I said quickly, trying to pick apart her conspiracy.

'Exactly.' She raised her eyebrows slightly, making her wrinkles squish together.

'I don't think I understand.'

Her warm hands rolled on top of my own. It felt like sandpaper, but her warmth was comforting. I should not have raised my voice at her earlier. 'You don't need to understand. Just know that we are here to help you, dear.'

The timer struck zero and the number 10 above one of the tunnels illuminated in light grey. Gloria rose from her chair, but I grabbed at her hands tightly. 'Why am I here?'

'I am not the one you need to ask, dear.' She removed her thick glasses. Her grey eyes appeared cartoon-like without them. Her expression was as if she had been waiting an eternity for me to ask the question. 'I think you know who really knows the answer to that.'

Gloria did not turn back. Her fragile body was swallowed by the darkness of her tunnel, leaving me with her words repeating in my head like a looped recording.

22

PRIVATE SECTOR ELEVEN

I fumbled in my seat, my mind racing with new information. Despite the rocky start, I felt the last meeting had provided more insight than the first, and I wondered who I could be seeing next. Could it be Naomi, potentially a new ally? Or Chase, who could further theorise with me as to why we were both here.

The story of my captors thickened.

Chase had mentioned that he had been investigating my disappearance before being kidnapped. Had he identified Private Sector Eleven?

The timer in front of me readjusted to 00:05:00. A figure materialised in the depths of one of the tunnels. His strut was unmissable. An eye still swollen; Chase stepped into the light.

'How's it going?' He said encouragingly. The timer had yet to commence ticking down. I was grateful for the few extra moments we had.

'I'm alright'

'Good. I think you did really well last week. I'm proud of you, kiddo.'

I mirrored his smile.

'I thought you were going to give up at one stage, but you hung in there like Christmas lights!' We both laughed, which filled the hall with a warm feeling of ease.

'Thanks for helping me out,' I said.

'That's my job, Tyler. Now, we don't have long, so tell me what's going on inside your head.'

I felt the full weight of my stomach perform a somersault. I could tell that his intent was genuine; he was concerned for me. Since I had entered the Oranga Trials, I'd been torn over deciding on an alliance, or watching people being taken away, and new appreciation of Chase overcame me.

Words spilled out of me automatically. 'Everyone is trying to pit me against someone. I don't know who to trust. I want to go home. I don't understand why I am even in this place, or what I've done to be put here.' I felt like a passenger to my own thoughts. Neither Chase nor I knew what I was going to say next. 'I'm so angry that I failed Sid. It's my fault he's gone.'

To my surprise, Chase smiled. 'Listen, you're doing an exceptional job so far. You've survived three Trials, each presenting unique difficulties. It's not your fault your friend was terminated, okay? This is not the time to trust others, or to form alliances. We must survive on our own abilities. Do not be trapped into a position where you sacrifice your chances of freedom for others.'

Chase spoke sense. Why had I felt compelled to be part of an alliance? I had forgotten what it was like to have somebody genuinely care for my wellbeing. He didn't want me to join any alliance; he only wanted me to feel better inside my head.

I glanced at the timer. It appeared to be stuck. The bright red numbers were fixed at 00:05:00. I saw Chase follow my eyes. I opened my mouth to comment on the timer, but he cut me off before I could speak.

'I've been thinking about what you said last week. You mentioned that Alexandro told you that it was me who nominated you for the Trials.'

'Yeah.'

He ran his fingers against his rough stubble as he pondered his response. 'I think I may know what's happening, why we are all here and how you are involved. I can't be certain but I'm pretty sure I'm close to the answer. Has your father ever told you about Private Sector Eleven?'

Chase didn't lean in as Gloria had. It was the second time this organisation had been mentioned in the space of ten minutes. Curiosity raged inside me like a caged animal, starving. Starving for information.

Chase read my expression. I felt as if he was prepared to provide me with the answers I desired, so I told him what I already knew.

'Interesting . . .' He replied, after I had relayed my conversation with Gloria. He leaned back in his seat. The timer still remained at 05:00:00.

'What do you reckon? Who are PSE?' I said, now leaning forward on the table.

'Okay, Tyler. The government funds a secretive initiative called "Harmony Dozen". Harmony Dozen is divided into twelve sectors, named Private Sector One, Private Sector Two, Three, all the way through to Private Sector Twelve. Each Sector has its unique area of operation. For example, Private Sector Eleven is responsible for controlling the influence of underground organisations.

'Underground organisations?'

'Yes. Like drug traffickers, arms dealers, organised gangs, and others of that nature.'

'PSE ensures that these underground organisations maintain order. They hold professional relationships with them, and strict guidelines are followed by both parties to ensure harmony.'

My mouth had fallen open. Questions flooded my mind, but no words came.

'I know this is a lot to take in, but I feel it's necessary to tell you as I believe Private Sector Eleven has something to do with these Trials.' Chase made no attempt to keep his voice down when he spoke. He glanced confidently around the room briefly before drawing his eyes back to me. The timer had finally begun ticking down.

'How do you know all this?' I asked.

Chase pondered my question for a moment, then answered with one of his own. 'Tyler, what do you think your father and I do for work?'

I felt stupid answering honestly. I had never understood what my father did for work, and I now realised I had been too self-absorbed to really ask. 'I don't know,' I responded.

'Your father and I work for Harmony Dozen.'

I didn't return his smile; my brain was working too hard. 'But I thought you didn't work together anymore,' I ventured. Chase's eyes narrowed, so I elaborated. 'That's what he said a few months ago when you stopped coming around as often.'

'Tyler, we both still work within Harmony Dozen. Your father just moved on from PSE.' He paused, considering his words. 'He transferred to another sector. Different offices, you see?'

'But if you work for PSE, why are you here? And why am I here?'

'Well, I'm not certain, but here's what I do know. Each of the contestants in the Trials is linked to PSE in some way. Quyén is an international drug trafficker; he and I have crossed paths many times. His friend Naomi is in the same business. Mechislav once worked for PSE too, but he left us last year, and it is understood that he is now working against us.'

'Really?'

'Yes, that's how Mechislav and I know each other. It's the reason we don't get along.'

The timer now ticked into three minutes remaining.

'I don't think Mechislav trusts Quyén either, though,' I said. 'He hasn't spoken to him, that I've seen.' As far as it appeared, of the remaining contestants, Mechislav had only engaged with Ruby and Gloria.

'I suppose we don't know who's meeting with who this evening, do we?' Chase said with a cocked eyebrow. 'I believe I have been put here because I was asking questions about your disappearance too loudly in my workplace. There would have been people who knew what was going on and could have overheard me. And you would be here because your father parted ways with Sector Eleven. Perhaps they were disgruntled because he moved on. It's difficult to be certain.'

'I knew my father had something to do with it. I could just feel it. But Alexandro told me when I first arrived that it was because of a stolen $250,000. He said I stole it from you, and you put me in here.'

I could sense that my words affected Chase. With all this new information, of course I didn't believe Alexandro, but I remained curious as to why he had lied.

'Tyler, there's no way that I put you here, or else I wouldn't be here myself.' His face remained blank and expressionless. 'I have never met Alexandro before these Trials, although he is undeniably interesting. As odd as a single sock, I reckon. I don't understand why he lied about the $250,000. Perhaps he wanted you to feel isolated, as if even in the outside world you had nobody to trust?'

'Maybe,' I said.

'You don't believe him, do you?' Chase moved a hand to my shoulder.

'Of course not. I think I'm just confused.'

Chase pulled himself up from his seat and walked over to me. The timer had reached its last minute now. Chase knelt beside me; it felt warm to receive support from a familiar face. 'It'll be okay, kiddo. I know Mechislav wants you in his alliance, but I just don't trust him. I don't want to make you feel like I'm ordering you around, but this is a matter of life and death, Tyler.'

I had no desire to be in an alliance with Mechislav at all. I didn't even want to be in the same room with the man.

'You don't have to worry about that. I'm not interested in their alliance,' I replied.

Chase smiled, exposing his white teeth. Impulsively, I ran my tongue over my furry teeth. I felt jealous that he had maintained his brilliantly white smile throughout isolation.

'Wonderful!' he said. 'Now, are you getting plenty of rest? We don't know when the next Trial will be, but you need to make sure you're getting enough food and rest.'

'I am,' I lied.

For the first time in a week my appetite had returned. Now that I had gained more of an understanding of how I came to be here, I felt a stronger sense of purpose. I wanted to win the Oranga Trials and go home.

The timer struck zero with an audible buzz, and both numbers four and five lit up simultaneously above their respective tunnels. I got to my feet, but Chase pulled me towards him for a tight embrace. For a few moments, we remained silent and close, until he pulled away.

'Good luck, kiddo. I'll speak to you soon.'

'Thanks, Chase.'

I waved as I entered my tunnel. He smiled and nodded casually. Chase's brilliant smile was the last I saw of the hall before the darkness of the tunnel engulfed me.

My pod felt larger than usual when I returned. I no longer wanted to spend my time alone; I wanted to be sitting with Chase, discussing strategy and learning more about Private Sector Eleven. The next Trial couldn't come soon enough.

23

AN UNLIKELY DUO

Over the next days in isolation, I reflected on the conversations with Ruby, Gloria and Chase again and again. My emotions ranged from anger to comfort, but mainly I was devastated to think that I had lived my life blind to who my father might have been. Had I even known him at all? The man I'd looked up to since I was a small child, the man who'd raised me single-handedly after my mother's death – he might not be the man I thought I knew.

Distorted memories of my father replayed in my mind. I closed my eyes and saw him standing at my school gate one afternoon – a rare occasion, as he would normally work late. I'd glimpsed him through the herd of other children and leapt forward into his big, outstretched arms, safe. I remembered his smile, but now I wondered – where was his mind at? While I had spent the day in class, what had he been doing that very same day? Engaging with criminals, or murderers?

I recalled one other occasion when Chase had met me after school and taken me back to my home. He made me dinner, helped me get things ready for the next school day and tucked me into bed. When I asked where my father was, Chase told me he was working late. But I didn't see my father for three days. When he returned, his face was swollen and blue. As a child I had never questioned his life, but now, isolated inside my pod, I began to connect the dots.

As my mind spotlighted each childhood memory, an avalanche of questions followed. I could not comprehend what my father's previous employer, Private Sector Eleven, wanted from me.

I created a mental list of questions to ask Chase when we spoke next. What did my father do for PSE? Was he involved with criminals? If so, how? I tried to convince myself that he had worked in their office, filing paperwork or processing reports, but that did not explain the injuries he often came home with.

The urge to know more consumed me. I wanted to understand the links that Gloria, Sid and Tallis had shared and how they came to be brought into the Trials. Gloria had mentioned that Sid was here because of his parents, although that didn't make much sense either.

The light surrounding the perimeter of the pod continued to dim. I guessed it must be well into the evening. Why hadn't the opening presented itself yet? I got to my feet and cupped handfuls of water onto my face from the sink.

Whoosh. Finally the opening between my pod and the en suite appeared, and I stumbled towards it numbly. The second I stepped through it, the wall closed behind me with a thud. I was trapped inside, just as I had been in the first two Trials. Suddenly, I heard what sounded like a tap turning on. The shower? No.

I looked up in time to see a thick green-grey fog descending from the ceiling. My eyes grew heavy and my muscles weakened. My body was quickly shutting down and I was dropping to the ground…

I woke with a shudder and pulled myself to a sitting position. My face throbbed against the cold surface. Somebody had changed my clothes – I was in the familiar black and orange jumpsuit.

I was no longer in the en suite, instead I woke in a foreign confinement. I dug the base of my palms into my eyes, then opened them again and looked around. The small area of imprisonment quickly came into focus. I was housed in a clear perspex cylinder with my back leaned on the rounded wall behind me.

Outside this cylinder it was dark, but I could make out multiple identical cylinders on either side of my own, forming a semicircle of giant tubes. I stood and cupped my hands to the perspex to gain a better view outside. I counted seven other cylinders that stretched high, disappearing into the darkness above. The semicircle of cylinders curved around a glistening black platform, a stage. Beyond the stage, across from me, were double doors similar to the ones in the hall.

Each of the other cylindrical confinements housed one of the other seven contestants. Ruby stood furthest to my left. Her small fists bashed forcefully against the perspex. Tallis, Quyén and Gloria all remained seated, each with a look of defeat on their face. Even from a distance, I could feel Tallis's anger transmitting from his scrunched-up face, but I looked away with disgust. To my immediate right, I saw Chase's lifeless body, his short limbs sprawled across the circle of floor.

The remaining contestants, on the floor of their cylinders, began to slowly stir as they brought themselves into a realisation of their situation. Ruby had ceased her blows to her cylinder; however, her frustration was still evident, and mirrored Tallis's. To Chase's gradual rise to consciousness, the doors beyond the stage opened loudly and the space was flooded by brightness, followed by a silhouette of a well-dressed man emerging and advancing to the front of the stage.

Alexandro looked as sharp as ever. I met his eyes momentarily but could sense that his mind was elsewhere. In the moment that we connected, he appeared not to recognise me at all. As he raised his hands above his head, the stage below him radiated brightly.

Although the ceiling remained invisible, the room which housed the eight confinements presented itself and I was surprised to realise that it was far smaller than it had seemed. The room was circular, with reflective black walls. The eight cylinders were spaced around one half of the circle, with the stage occupying the other half. The large doors closed behind Alexandro.

Each of the contestants had now pulled themselves to their feet, all attention on the host. Both my hands were pressed against the cool perspex, my breath generating a layer of fog with each exhalation. I wiped it away quickly as Alexandro opened his mouth to speak.

'Friends, welcome to Trial Four! The hardest challenge you have yet to face awaits you on the other side of this door.' He beamed ecstatically and indicated to the doors he had entered from. His piercing eyes whizzed across the room in a failed attempt to connect with somebody sharing in his excitement. 'This challenge is additionally difficult as it requires you to work in pairs.'

I instantly glanced towards Chase, who was instead staring at Alexandro. I noticed other contestants exchanging glances around the room for their closest allies. This was not missed by Alexandro who produced an affected laugh.

'No, no, my friends. Your pairs have already been decided. Based on the results of your previous Trials, each contestant has been ranked. The contestant who currently sits in first place has been paired with the contestant in last place. He or she who finds themselves in second place has been paired with the contestant in second last, and so forth. This way, the teams will be equally matched.'

Muffled complaints arose from the cylinders, but Alexandro ignored the outcry, his voice was clearer than ever as he continued. 'The pairs will be as follows: Mr Quyén Miles and Miss Ruby Rooke;

Miss Naomi Ark and Mrs Gloria Robertson; Mr Mechislav Borodin-Bishop and Mr Chase Iscariot; and finally, Mr Tallis Abernathy and Mr Tyler Knight.'

Alexandro's proclamation would have been drowned by objections from the contestants had their cylinders not been soundproofed. Instead, I watched on as most of the contestants gesticulated animatedly and shouted their muffled cries.

A glance sideways; Mechislav pointed his finger threateningly against the perspex wall towards Chase. Ruby had her head in her hands, seemingly disappointed at being partnered with Quyén, and Naomi was screaming something incomprehensible towards Gloria.

Given a preference, Tallis was the last person I'd have chosen. I wanted to be paired with Chase. I would have settled for Gloria. This was a disaster.

As the contestants vented their frustrations inside their confinements, my mind focused on the task ahead. Although Chase would have been ideal, Tallis presented his own unique strengths. *Above all, his greatest strength is that he does not want to be terminated,* I thought.

'Friends! Friends!' Alexandro announced from the stage. 'Your noise will do little to change your pairings.' But his raised voice was ignored in the general outcry.

Without warning, I was thrown to the ground in agonising pain. My insides rattled dangerously, and I was paralysed in agony. The few moments I lay helpless on the floor felt like an eternity. My eyes

174

were clenched shut and the taste of metal overwhelmed me as blood dripped slowly from my mouth onto the floor. I had bitten my tongue in the instant that the bracelet assaulted my senses.

In the distance I could hear Alexandro's voice, calm, as if nothing had happened. 'Friends, have you not learned? Patience and equanimity will prevail among all else. A clear mind will allow you to advance further than most, so please, I ask that you refrain from outbursts while I speak.'

My eyes opened to see the other contestants pulling themselves up from the ground, most rubbing their bodies.

'Now, the Trial is as follows: each duo will be assigned a mascot, which you must retrieve before returning to this room. The last team to return will be terminated.'

The room was silent. Without thinking, I had pushed myself onto my knees, my eyes fixed upon Alexandro. In front of him, at the forefront of the stage, lay a metallic black box. No larger than a small bar fridge, it blended elegantly with the stage itself. I had not noticed it before. He bent low towards the box, slowly lifting the lid in suspense. Alexandro withdrew from the box a blue wooden circle, about the size of a football.

'A circle. This will be the mascot for Miss Naomi Ark and Mrs Gloria Robertson.' He glanced to them separately before returning the mascot to the box, and withdrawing a golden star also made of wood. 'A star, the mascot for Mr Tallis Abernathy and Mr Tyler Knight'. Our eyes met once more.

Alexandro extracted a blood-red heart for Mechislav and Chase, followed by a green cross for Quyén and Ruby. Despite the difference in shapes, it was impossible to say that any was larger or smaller than another. Once the final mascot was returned to the box, Alexandro closed it and continued.

'A replica of your mascot awaits you beyond these doors. Although there are no official rules governing how you retrieve your mascot, please be aware of the following navigational support: firstly, your bracelet has been fitted with a GPS tracker which has been linked with your mascot. As you travel closer towards your mascot, your bracelet will transmit vibrations that will grow in severity as you near your target. Small pain for great gain, my friends.' A sinister smile stretched across his face as he offered a wink to nobody in particular. 'Secondly, each mascot has been fitted with a compass. The room we currently occupy sits on the south-eastern side of the island. Once you retrieve your mascot, follow your compass directly south-east to return to the finish.'

Alexandro clapped his hands eagerly and commenced rubbing them in anticipation. My underarms filled with sweat as nerves finally overcame me. The idea of competing in a Trial with no rules petrified me.

I remembered what Alexandro had said at the first feast. *Among us are criminals, thieves and traitors . . .*

This line repeated over and over in my head. Then Alexandro's real time voice broke my anxious thoughts. 'Now, to ensure you all do not enter the

Trial at the same time, ninety seconds will separate each duo's departure. Based on the previous Trial's results, it is only fair that as Mr Tallis Brown won the challenge, he and Mr Tyler Knight enter first.'

The claustrophobic cylinder around me vibrated loudly. Without notice, the perspex began to retract into the ground below. I found myself in the open, with Tallis a few metres to my right. His eyes were fixed on the doors, which had opened behind Alexandro.

My ears rang as my body acclimatised to the chilly room. Alexandro beckoned us to the stage, and we went to him obediently. 'Remember, you are seeking the yellow star.'

I turned to lock eyes with Chase, who rested a hand on his perspex wall, a look of concern across his face. He smiled unconvincingly, and I returned it with a silent nod. In my peripherals, I noticed Mechislav staring at me eagerly, but I steadfastly avoided his gaze.

I turned towards the opening, where Tallis had already disappeared into the abyss. My strides grew larger as I rushed to join him beyond the door. The cool air of the outdoors greeted me with such force that I was forced to steady myself as to avoid toppling backwards.

24

THORNS AND RIVERS

I was standing on a scaffold that floated above the depthless ripples of the sea, a hundred metres from the shore. Behind me, the doors closed with force. The doors were attached to a tall silo that towered up from the water. The floating platform was about the size of half a tennis court and was attached to the cylindric structure.

The humid air filled my lungs, and the breeze shuffled the fringe above my eyes. On the beach ahead of me brilliant white sand glistened, with only clear ocean water separating us. Beyond the beach, an expansive jungle stretched as far as I could see, with no manufactured structures in sight; only trees. The view reminded me of the brochure for Touhere on the plane: *Experience luxury as you can only imagine.*

The sun above forced sweat from my brow the moment that I stepped from the silo and the sound of a body crashing through water nearby snapped me back to reality. Tallis had already dismounted from the platform and was taking large stokes through the water towards the shore. I cursed under my breath before joining him in the water.

The feeling of serenity I experienced on the platform was nothing compared to what I experienced beneath the surface of the water. The ocean's mass brushed against my face with each stroke toward the shore. I felt water fill my shoes and had the urge to remove them, however I decided that I may regret this later. Tallis was a much faster swimmer than myself, and I found him already pacing the shoreline when I emerged from the ocean.

'Hey!' I called. 'Are you going to wait up?'

If I hadn't already been aware of Tallis's arrogance, I would have assumed he couldn't hear me. Scratching his bald head, he surveyed the trees that stood as a barrier between the peaceful beachline and the jungle within. He approached one tree at random, looked up at it quizzically, and went back to the beach, where he continued to pace.

Exotic, unidentifiable wildlife sang in harmony with the waves crashing behind me.

For a brief moment I considered running off in one direction without looking back. The feeling of freedom was so pure that I wanted to stay on this island forever. However, Alexandro had mentioned that our bracelets were fixed with a GPS tracker. Considering the pain that I knew the bracelet could produce, I knew it would be foolish to attempt an escape here.

Blazing sun hit the beach and dried my clothes, and beads of sweat began to form above my upper lip.

I went to Tallis and pulled at his shoulder in frustration. 'What are you doing?' I asked him.

Tallis turned so quickly that I jumped backwards. We stood only a foot apart, his dark green eyes piercing into my own, but I stared back blankly, refusing to be intimidated by my teammate. I couldn't sense any fear in his eyes, but I detected something brewing in his head. After a few moments of silence, Tallis turned and refocused his attention on his own agenda, pacing the shore and examining trees at random.

Annoyed that he continued to ignore me, I followed. 'You know that we need to do this task together,' I said. 'You don't have to like me, but you can at least talk to me so we can get this over quickly.'

No response.

'Whatever. I'm going in here. We aren't going to find our mascot by patrolling the beach.' I gestured towards the trees but Tallis continued to walk silently, his strides becoming noticeably longer.

I was tempted to abandon my partner, but after a moment's consideration, I overruled this instinct; we had a better chance of completing the Trial if we didn't separate. I glanced towards the ocean to see two figures emerge from the silo. Chase and Mechislav now stood on the floating platform. I was certain that despite their disagreements, they would work together to complete the Trial. Chase's body disappeared beneath the surface of the water, and I turned to follow Tallis's large footprints in the damp sand.

We trekked in silence for half a kilometre along the shore before Tallis decided to detour into the forest. I followed him, and the temperature dropped more quickly than I had anticipated. I rubbed my arms vigorously. After a few minutes of aimless strolling into the unknown, my teeth began to chatter.

Sunlight disappeared behind the treetops as it struggled to penetrate the thick canopy of branches above. The sound of a large bird's flapping wing thrashed above me. I looked up to see the exotic bird, boasting emerald green and aqua feathers soar deep into the jungle.

With Tallis still a few paces in front of me, I could hear the chatter of various species surrounding us the deeper we ventured. Sounds both high in the trees and scattering below at ground level kept me on high alert, but the animals kept to themselves. I saw no more than a tail fade into bushes in the distance or scuffling of branches above. The wildlife noises grew louder as the tree trunks became thicker the further we ventured inland. But there was no sign of any mascot, or of any other contestants since I'd seen Chase dive from the ocean platform.

Suddenly Tallis grunted.

Something glistened across a slight valley. Tallis pointed firmly at the object, lodged between intertwined vines on a thick tree. Was it a mascot – our mascot? It was impossible to identify; thick thorny bushes growing knee-high separated us from our objective. The valley of thorns was narrow, but high walls of rock on either side ensured that the only way to reach the object was through the pointed weeds.

With no tool to remove the thick thorns that separated us from the mascot, Tallis and I pondered the situation in silence before he eventually took a step forward into the sea of thorns. His shoes provided him little protection, and a thorn penetrated the sole of his shoe.

'Come back. Let's figure out a smarter way through,' I called.

Tallis ignored my request and took another step forward. He suppressed a yelp of pain as his exposed foot met another thorn deeper in the valley. The mascot glistened only about twenty metres ahead of him, its shape hard to identify as it was obstructed by the thick vines that held it in place. As a slither of sunlight came through the canopy, I caught a glimpse of gold on the mascot – or was it red?

'Tallis . . .'

He turned to me, a vein throbbing on his temple, but said nothing. His eyes told me to quit talking. He was clearly in pain; angry but determined.

'You don't need to put yourself through this,' I said. 'We can find another way.'

Tallis turned back, increasing his pace towards the mascot. As the sunlight disappeared behind a tree above, the mascot's reflection faded away.

'Isn't that . . .' I started.

Tallis had also noticed that the mascot boasted a scarlet border. What had reflected the sunlight was the compass that Alexandro had told us each mascot was fitted with. The sight of the compass brought

Alexandro's words into my mind. *As you travel closer towards your mascot, your bracelet will transmit vibrations that will grow in severity as you near your target.* My bracelet remained still. It was evident that the mascot that was now almost within arm's reach of Tallis was not ours.

I cursed under my breath and turned away. I felt lightly sympathetic towards Tallis, who had injured himself to reach the wrong mascot. I now faced a row of bushes, and I noticed them swaying as if moved by a strong wind. But there was no such wind. I stepped towards them curiously, sensing something alive and moving beyond them. As I moved closer to the bushes the trembling subsided. I crept up to half a metre from them; they now lay dormant. Before I could investigate, Tallis cursed loudly behind me.

He was pulling at the heart-shaped mascot with force, and his hands were bleeding. The heart broke free, causing Tallis to stagger back onto the thorns. He screamed loudly, the sound mixing with heavy scuffling behind me as animals fled.

'What are you doing?' I called. 'Our mascot is the star!'

As expected, Tallis ignored me again. He extracted himself from the entanglement of thorns, and came back across the valley, biting his lip the entire way, before collapsing on the ground beside me.

'Thought you'd help the other contestants out by getting their mascot for them?' I asked sarcastically. My patience had run out. I was frustrated with him for delaying our task.

He looked at me harshly, nursing his feet in his hands with the mascot lying beside him. I picked up the heart with one hand; it was heavier than I expected. One side showed a perfectly scarlet heart, with a smear of Tallis's blood across its surface. The other side was inlaid with a round compass, encased in glass, the needle spinning as I turned the mascot in my hands.

I recalled Alexandro's words: *Follow your compass directly south-east.*

'South-east is that way.' I pointed towards the valley Tallis had just crossed. I would have been certain that the direction of the floating scaffold was behind us. But this was not our mascot, and not yet time to identify south-east. Our own could well be located anywhere on this island. Tallis was now standing, his torn jumpsuit exposing open wounds on his legs and feet. He snatched the mascot from my hands.

'Oi!' I hissed.

He snorted. With a swift motion he threw the mascot into the entanglement of thorns. It sank into the tangle. It would be near impossible for anyone to locate it now, and harder still to retrieve. My mouth dropped open. I turned to Tallis, aggressively, but he cut me off before I could speak.

'Go get it.' He mumbled.

After a moment of fierce eye contact, Tallis turned back in the direction we'd come from. I stayed, my eyes on the thorns. That was Chase's mascot; I couldn't leave it hidden beneath the thorns, impossible to find. Tallis disappeared through the trees, leaving a bloody trail of footprints behind him.

I stood for a minute, contemplating whether to extract the wooden heart or not. I eventually decided that I should find my own mascot first, then come back to collect this one. I also decided that I could not continue to travel with Tallis. His lack of teamwork made the task infuriatingly difficult. Perhaps we would be successful in locating the mascot individually.

Taking an alternative route, away from the bloody footprints, I ventured into the unknown. After several minutes, the thick-trunked trees gave way to thinner palm trees. The heavy bushes I pushed my way through became thinner and the ground around me opened up, allowing me to see further ahead. Occasionally I was startled by what sounded like aggravated voices behind me, but no matter how quickly I turned, I never caught a glimpse anything that might have made them. I wondered whether my ears were playing tricks on me.

Eventually, my progress was halted as I arrived at the foot of a cliff so high that I was forced to crane my neck uncomfortably to locate the top. Thick vines wrapped and weaved the entire way up the cliff, inviting me to climb, but I veered left and continued along the cliff's base.

How long have I been wandering the jungle? An hour? Two hours?

I began contemplating where the other contestants were on the island and how they were faring. *Are they working cooperatively, or have*

As I pushed onward, my bracelet finally began to vibrate lightly. Alexandro had told us this would happen as we neared our mascot, and for the first time in the Trial, I knew I was heading in the right direction.

I became aware of the sound of flowing water. I followed it steadily, the sound of a river growing louder with each step. The river came into view. Moss covered every boulder on its sides.

Shaking from fatigue, I collapsed onto some boulders beside the river, throwing my arms into the water. The flow through my fingers felt magical. I took off my shoes and immersed my legs in the water, closing my eyes to enjoy the feeling. Sounds of nature overwhelmed my senses. The birds sang louder, and leaves rustled in the wind.

After a few moments, I pulled myself up and knelt to splash water on my face.

I still had a job to do.

In a tranquil pool between boulders, an unfamiliar reflection gazed back at me. It was my own – but it seemed to have aged an eternity. Patchy stubble across my cheeks merged into a thicker beard along my chin and neck. Beneath the hair, my cheeks had thinned, now almost skeletal. My blonde hair was long and unkempt, falling on either side of my face like curtains.

As I observed my hollow face, something more interesting stole my attention a little way off beneath the water's surface. Swaying in the ripples, a

186

solid object faced up directly towards me. The deep blue circle-shaped mascot lay a metre or so below. I flicked my wrist aggressively, as the constant vibration from the bracelet now tingled the bones in my forearm. I wondered how much more severe the vibrations would be if this mascot was my own.

Did Tallis have the right idea to discard the other contestants' mascots? Should I dive in to retrieve this mascot for myself? It was Naomi and Gloria's. What would they do if they located my star-shaped mascot? Then Alexandro's voice echoed in my head: *Innocence will prevail.* I banished the negative thoughts and chose to ignore their mascot, in the hope that they would do the same if they stumbled across my star-shaped one.

Sounds of shuffling came from the other side of the river. The bushes parted as something large made its way in my direction. Was this the sound that had been following me for hours?

I got to my feet quickly and took cover behind a tree. Barking voices accompanied the movements across the water.

'Oww!'

'C'mon, it's this way.'

'No, it's not – we have to go back that way!'

Two female voices. One of them distinctively more excited than the other.

'You're wrong – oww! The pain is worse now – oww! Trust me. It has to be!'

With a stumble, Gloria appeared on the bank across the river, looking dishevelled and miserable. 'It must be in here!' She pointed towards the river.

Behind her, Naomi gingerly limped out from the undergrowth, holding her right arm in pain and shaking. The women stared at one another for several seconds. It was obvious that the pain was transmitting from their bracelets as they stood only metres from their circular mascot.

Naomi quickly diverted her attention from Gloria and toward the river. Gloria had collapsed on the ground, her aging body shaking uncontrollably, like a paper bag trembling in the wind.

Naomi carefully stepped into the water, her head bowed, letting out occasional cries of pain. Her right forearm visibly vibrated as she unknowingly edged closer towards her prize.

I stayed concealed, leaning around the tree trunk just enough to watch her attempt to locate her mascot.

Among us are criminals, thieves and traitors

. . .

As she approached the spot where I knew her mascot lay, a new set of voices approached on the opposite bank.

'Naomi!'

The voice was deep and aggressive. Naomi, now almost on top of her mascot, turned quickly and slipped backward into the water. I was sure that she had landed on top of it. Quyén had appeared at the opening of trees that she and Gloria had emerged from only moments before, with Ruby close on his heels. Ruby saw Gloria and knelt beside her curled-up body.

'Hey, Quyén,' Naomi called from the water.

The bottom of her hair was now drenched, along with her clothes. Without pulling herself up, she glanced towards her ally, who was holding himself up against a tree.

Quyén was sweating profusely. It was much cooler in the jungle, especially by the riverbank – I wondered how flushed he must have felt in the warmth on the beach.

'Have you found your mascot?' he panted.

'We're close, I think. My bracelet hasn't stopped vibrating since we got near this river, I think it's under the water here somewhere.'

'It's not,' Quyén said, his voice barely audible. He held one hand to his face in agony, seemingly seconds away from fainting.

Naomi looked at him quizzically, her right arm shaking uncontrollably in the water. Quyén turned to face Ruby, who had her sole attention focussed on Gloria, then he stumbled into the river beside Naomi.

I turned quickly, fixing my back upon the tree. Having Gloria and Naomi catch me eavesdropping was one thing, but I couldn't risk Quyén catching sight of me watching him. Ensuring my body was hidden, I pulled my head up, and strained to hear what was being said in the river.

'Listen, don't tell anybody else this, but Alexandro lied to us,' Quyén began. 'Your bracelet vibrates the *further you are* from your Mascot, not the closer.'

'Are you sure?' Naomi didn't seem convinced.

'Positive.'

I heard a slide of a zipper, then Naomi let out a gasp, which was hushed by Quyén.

'You got your mascot already?' she asked.

Nobody said anything for a while. My heart dropped to hear that one group had already located their mascot, and another stood practically on top of their own.

Staring at the forest before me, I was stunned to glimpse a man-made object fixed to a tree to my right. Hidden among leaves, a lensed dome swivelled. A camera.

How many cameras hidden among the trees had I been oblivious to? Alexandro had eyes in the sky. The feeling of hope drained from me faster than from Naomi, who had interrupted my thoughts with a dejected acceptance of Quyén's news.

'So, our mascot isn't here at all?'

'No, Naomi. If your arm is in that much distress, you couldn't be further from where you need to be.' I knew he was lying.

Splashes of water gradually moved further away. Overcome by temptation, I peered around the trunk to watch Naomi and Quyén join the others on the opposite bank.

Gloria had now risen to her feet and was leaning on Ruby. These two were also whispering between themselves.

Naomi looked befuddled, defeated. Still in visible pain, she began looking around at her surroundings. 'I just thought . . .'

'Naomi, believe me or don't, I don't mind,' said Quyén. 'But you'd better get going because you don't have much time.'

Naomi nodded.

I backed away from the river and slipped into the undergrowth; the ruckus of the two teams farewelling one another allowed me to slip away unnoticed.

25

THE STAR

It had been over an hour since I'd watched Quyén at the riverbank. He and Ruby could be back at the beach already. I knew Quyén was lying, but I wondered how long it would take the pair of women to realise. Despite the competitive urge circulating through my body, remorse singed my heart at the thought of Naomi and Gloria's cruelled chances of finding their mascot.

I wondered whether Ruby had been in on the lie as well. Despite radiating a more genuine energy than Quyén, she was still untrustworthy. She could have sent Gloria to her death knowingly.

The bracelet on my wrist had recently begun vibrating more aggressive than it had near the river. Confident that the bracelet was indicating the right direction, I pressed onward.

With no direct path to follow, I often wondered which direction I was walking. After passing yet another stream of water, I contemplated whether I was walking in circles and each new stream

I encountered was in fact the same one – it was difficult to be certain. Part of me wished that I had kept Chase's mascot so that I could use its compass as a guide.

A solid thicket caused me to alter my course to the right, and immediately my bracelet rang more strongly. There was no pain, but the feeling of an itch under my skin became increasingly uncomfortable. The ground was tangled with loose vines and weeds, forcing my knees higher with each step to avoid tripping.

The trees thinned, and the vibration upon my wrist transformed from uncomfortable into painful with each step. I shook my arm to remove the feeling, distracting me enough for my foot to get caught on a grounded vine, pulling me down with force.

The mossy earth was surprisingly soft, and I took time to rest there. The earth tattooed the balls of my hands with green stains.

Behind me, distant voices erupted. I couldn't understand what was being said, but bushes now rattled mere metres away from me.

I sat silently, bowing my head to listen harder.

A deep voice bellowed, 'Leave, then!' Another voice hushed the first. I was unsure how many people were there, but there was certainly an interaction, a disagreement.

I called, 'Who's there?'

My voice echoed for a second before it was engulfed in the sounds of the wildlife. I called again, to no response. I pulled myself to my feet and set off into the thick bushes, in the direction of the argument.

Sharp leaves pierced my face and hands as I wildly ripped the bush out of my way in search of the owners of the voices.

'Come back!' I yelled, my wrist now vibrating harder than ever. I screamed in pain as I pushed further and further into the field of bushes. I toppled forward, my feet staggering beneath me until I eventually tumbled out the other side. I found myself in a clearing.

Tall, thin trees formed a perfect circle around grass, and an array of obscure boulders lay in the middle. There was nobody in sight; I had missed the opportunity to find the people I had heard, but instead discovering a tranquil scene before me. The sound of leaves blowing peacefully in the wind calmed me, and the breeze brushed my fringe. If it weren't for my left arm searing in pain, I would have felt at peace.

With one step into the clearing, the pain in my arm filtered towards my torso and I dropped to my knees. My insides pulsated and I cried aloud in pain. A flock of blue and green birds scattered from the trees, startled by my shout. The birds disappeared, but I caught sight of one tree on the opposite side of the clearing swaying.

I pulled myself to my feet, my arm limp and quivering. Through gritted teeth and squinted eyes, I spotted a body in a familiar black jumpsuit high in the tree. The dark green line down the jumpsuit blended with the tree's leaves. Tallis.

Although still angry with my partner, I couldn't help but be impressed with how high he had climbed. My bracelet had utterly debilitated me; he had somehow managed to climb the tree while presumably experiencing comparable pain.

A yellow star, matching the one Alexandro had shown us earlier, sat perched on a branch only slightly beyond Tallis's reach. I raced to the base of the tree, ignoring the steadily increasing pain spreading throughout my body.

'Hey!' I called. Tallis glanced down at me. His face was drained of all colour. His eyes were swollen as if he had been crying, and he was visibly shaking causing the branch he was balancing on to wobble. One of his arms was fixed to the trunk of the tree, whilst another was slightly outstretched toward the mascot. We stared at one another for a few moments, then I focused my attention on the star-shaped mascot. His eyes remained fixed upon me.

'C'mon, Tallis. It's just there!' I pointed towards the star. He was frozen in place. He hadn't moved since he focused upon me.

'I – I—' he stuttered.

For a few moments we were both frozen; I was unsure what I could do to help.

Then I called, 'I'm coming up.' My fear of heights outweighed the pain from the bracelet. I grasped onto the highest branch I could reach and heaved myself upwards.

'No!' Tallis shouted. He had snapped out of his frozen state and was wiping his eyes with his free hand. He looked at me fiercely. 'Stay.'

Remaining slightly just off the ground, I nodded once to Tallis, and then again at the golden star. Tallis turned his head and reached towards the mascot. His fingertips grazed the nearest point of the star, pulling his body away from the tree trunk. He gave a frustrated curse, loosened his grip on the trunk and made a lunge towards our prize.

Tallis's body dropped. His hand skimmed the mascot, causing it to reshuffle in its place as his loose grip on the tree gave way. He crashed through a thin branch below him before landing firmly on the next one below. More birds scattered from the heights of the trees as he screamed loudly. He turned, so that he hugged the thick tree trunk whilst his legs straddled the branch below him.

'Are you okay?' I yelled. Leaves and twigs fell onto my face. Tallis grunted loudly, his way of acknowledging my concern, and pulled himself to a stand. I was impressed that the branch at his feet supported his weight, and I eventually lowered myself to the ground, accepting that I would not be climbing the tree. My relief was balanced by the anxiety of watching Tallis struggle upwards to the Mascot.

Like an agile gorilla, Tallis scaled the tree, climbing higher with each manoeuvre until he was almost level to where he had been when I found him. I had been forced to the ground by the pain, barely able to keep my eyes open to watch the scene unfolding above. But I had to keep watch; I couldn't allow Tallis to complete the Trial alone.

I surveyed the branches around the ones he clung to. He made an attempt to climb onto a branch to his right, but I called instinctively. 'Not that one!'

He stopped and looked down at me. He had one hand on the branch, unable to see the large crack that ran underneath its base.

'It won't hold you; look!'

Tallis lowered himself and looked at the branch, then nodded silently.

The loud snap of a breaking branch startled me, and I dodged away from the tree in anticipation of impact from above. I heard the snap again. Tallis was violently whacking at the thick branch I warned him about, eventually breaking it from the trunk.

'What – are – you – doing?' I called through gritted teeth.

With his new tool, Tallis was taking aim at the mascot, now only slightly above him and an arm's length away.

With a large swing, the branch pushed the mascot from its nook, and sent it plummeting to the ground. I jumped to my feet and steadied myself. The star landed gracefully in my outstretched hands. Instant liberation filled my body. The ringing inside me had stopped. The mascot sat safely in my hands and I collapsed onto the ground, free of pain.

I lay motionless on my back, eyes closed, in the cool of the sunset. After a time, I opened my eyes to Tallis sitting beside me, his head in his hands. The colour had returned to his face, though his eyes remained swollen. I wanted to ask if he was okay but decided against it, assuming I would only receive the usual grunt in response.

I turned the star over in my hands, examining the sharp edges and the chipped paint on the points. The glass-covered compass on the back indicated our final destination. South-east was directly through the tree line to our right.

I tossed the star gently to Tallis, who caught it with one hand. With a quick examination, he turned his gaze to the direction of the tree line. Together, we got to our feet and began our journey back to the shore.

The setting sun cast dark shadows over our path. The vibrant birds had disappeared as sounds of night wildlife took over. Occasionally I would catch sight of a crowd of bats watching me from the trees. I was aware of countless pairs of eyes observing us, and cautiously walked closer to Tallis.

Tallis continued his silent treatment, apparently too proud to communicate. I didn't mind, as it allowed me to focus on following the path without distraction. Our pace picked up as the ground slowly transformed from grass to sand, and the smell of the ocean flooded my senses. I could now hear waves crashing – we were almost there.

Night fell quicker than I anticipated. Tallis and I were now swallowed by darkness, but a foreign light source shone in the distance. It became clearer as the trees thinned: a floating platform a hundred metres out to sea shone strongly as we came out onto the beach.

Tallis removed his shoes and discarded them. I mimicked him and felt my feet sink into the wet sand. The waves crashed harder, and for a moment I considered staying on the beach for a while, enjoying the ambiance which I had not felt for weeks.

Tallis, however, had thrown himself into the water, one hand clutching the mascot, and with long strides was making his way to the platform. I followed instinctively. The water was much colder than earlier, but with the motivation of finishing the Trial, I trailed Tallis through the water.

I caught sight of silvery, shining fish swimming peacefully beneath me. Their scales reflective from the floating platform's light which was now casting over me. Swimming together in a school, the fish reminded me of my friends outside of Touhere. I missed my life outside of the Trials. The fish appeared to have not a care in the world, swimming wherever they desired – not guided by a compass or a set of Trials.

By the time I reached the platform, Tallis had already got to the door on the far side. It closed behind him as I pulled myself up out of the water.

'Nice working with you,' I muttered sarcastically under my breath.

I ran my hands through my wet hair, tucking it behind my ears. Glancing back at the beach, I could make out two figures launching themselves into the water. It was impossible to tell who they were in the darkness. I turned away and followed Tallis's wet footprints towards the door.

I was greeted immediately by Alexandro's open arms. Beside him stood Tallis, clutching our mascot. The eight cylinders at the back of the room were empty except for two – Quyén and Ruby sat facing away from each other in their respective confinements.

'Mr Knight and Mr Abernathy! Well done!' Alexandro exclaimed. I was unsure why he announced our arrival so exuberantly; I was certain that neither Quyén nor Ruby cared. He placed both his hands on my shoulders and squeezed. 'You are the second group back with your mascot.' He held out his hand towards Tallis, who handed over the star. 'And thus, you are safe from termination. Congratulations!'

Neither Tallis nor I acknowledged his blessings. We exchanged brief eye contact, recognising that despite our differences with each other, we were on the same side in the end: against Alexandro. The silence hung in the room awkwardly for a moment before the host guided us to our respective cylinders. 'Please find inside your compartment a cup of warm tea and some biscuits. Make yourself comfortable as we await our final guests.'

Inside my cylinder was indeed a small cup of tea, and a handful of plain biscuits on a plastic tray. The round walls shot up around me as soon as I stepped inside my circle. On the floor lay a thin brown blanket, which I immediately threw over my shivering body. The blanket absorbed all the water from my skin and clothes, quickly becoming useless, but I kept it wrapped around me tightly.

My mind switched to the other contestants. Had Chase and Mechislav found the mascot that Tallis had discarded beneath the thicket of thorns; had Naomi and Gloria realised that Quyén had sent them in the wrong direction and returned to the river to locate their own mascot? Like a knife in my heart, I realised that I had broken my promise to myself to retrieve Chase's mascot from the thorns. I berated myself for this neglect.

I awaited the return of the silhouetted figures I'd seen start their crossing from the shore, who I knew would be scurrying through the doors at any moment. The teacup I clenched only faintly kept me warm with each nervously passing second. I closed my eyes and hoped that Chase would be the next face to enter. I couldn't imagine moving on in the Trials without him. Losing Sid had been hard enough, but to lose the only other ally I had would be more demotivating than I could handle.

Beyond the doors, scuffling took place on the scaffold. With this, Alexandro straightened himself up and moved towards the doors. He adjusted his silky tie and patted his hair down, shaping it to perfection. I rolled my eyes at him and focussed completely on the doors.

'Please, Chase. Please, please, please,' I repeated under my breath.

The doors opened abruptly, and two men walked in confidently with chests thrust out and heads held high. My chest warmed itself more than the tea was capable of. Mechislav was notably bleeding from beside his right eye and nose; it trickled down his face. His nose was crooked, appearing broken. Beside him, Chase's jumpsuit had a long slash down the middle, barely gripping onto his body. His entire left shoulder was exposed and bleeding. He also sported a black eye. It was unclear who had won the fight.

'Mr Borodin-Bishop and Mr Iscariot: well done!' Alexandro announced, mimicking the welcome he had given Tallis and me minutes earlier. He continued with the same speech as both Mechislav and Chase's eyes darted around the room. I made eye contact with Chase who nodded to me promisingly, a smirk creeping onto his face. I smiled back.

Escorted to his cylinder, Chase collapsed on the floor, scoffed down his tea and winked at me. We were both safe. I still had a friend in the Trials, and I closed my eyes to gain some long-awaited rest.

'Friends! Congratulations again, you have all progressed through Trial Four.' Alexandro stood on the rectangular stage, facing the remaining six contestants. 'Unfortunately for Miss Naomi Ark and Mrs Gloria Robertson, they have been terminated and will no longer take part in the Oranga Trials.'

I momentarily pitied them both. Although glad that I had progressed again and had increased my chances of survival, I felt guilty that they had been fooled by Quyén. I could have told them that they were near their mascot; they could still be alive if not for my selfishness.

'You will each return to your pods to await Trial Five. Congratulations once more!' Alexandro raised his hands theatrically, and with this the sound of familiar hissing commenced in my cylinder. My body numbed and my head grew heavy. I leant back on the perspex wall, closed my eyes and allowed the incoming gas to overwhelm me.

PART IIII

26

SIX SURVIVORS

The few days that followed the fourth Trial seemed to blend and overlap like never before. I often woke when the lights were dimmed to their lowest level and drifted in and out of sleep irritably.

My mind no longer raced between conspiracy theories, or ways to escape captivity. Instead, my drowsy thoughts remained on the contestants who had been terminated and on how much time remained until I shared their fate. How many deaths could I have prevented?

I spent each evening yearning for the survival of the terminated contestants, hopeful that they were sent back out into civilisation with financial compensation – wishful optimism to stop my brain spinning into the abyss. Thoughts of life in the outside world kept my insides from boiling.

My appetite dissipated alongside my motivation. Plates of meals appeared and vanished, neglected, in between my periods of sleep. My limbs grew heavier than lead, and my stomach felt hollower with each day. The reflection that had looked back at me in the river haunted my dreams; I had barely recognised myself.

Lying on my back, I examined the grooves in the ceiling. Small holes and swivelling lines blended brilliantly like an indigenous artwork.

The familiar static noise rang, followed closely by Alexandro's voice. He offered his congratulations and invited the remaining six contestants to a feast.

I thought of those remaining contestants and tried to imagine who I could trust besides Chase. Trust during the Oranga Trials had never been as important as it had been in the forest. Naomi had been terminated because she put her trust in the wrong person, and Gloria was also lost as a result. The lack of trust between me and Tallis almost cost us our survival, and the more thought I put into it, the more I accepted that I would likely have been terminated had Quyén not tricked Naomi.

The opening to the hall revealed itself. I dragged myself from the bed, splashed water from the sink onto my face and prepared to meet with the remaining five.

The space appeared larger than ever as fewer bodies stumbled into the hall. Only six chairs accompanied the long centre table, and the high table was again occupied by Alexandro. His outstretched arms welcomed us.

Mechislav and Ruby stood in a corner together, conversing hurriedly. Ruby's hands danced faster than her lips. As I stepped from my tunnel,

Ruby nudged Mechislav on the shoulder and he cocked his head sternly to watch me enter. The corner of his mouth cracked as he examined me sharply. He then slowly turned back to Ruby and continued to gossip.

Tallis stood alone, arms tightly crossed, head bowed. He stood only fractionally out of his tunnel, giving the impression that he would rather remain isolated in his pod than mix with the other contestants.

Quyén was also unaccompanied, a lone figure seated at the table with his head hanging back over the chair. He looked defeated. I wanted to approach him, to confront him for his treason, but opted to leave him. He looked like his own worst enemy, drowning in his own sweat. Receiving his own natural justice.

Uninterested in both Tallis and Quyén, I scanned the room for Chase, a notable absentee. Immediately I considered the worst. Had he tried to escape and got himself terminated? I shuffled on my feet, unsure where to place myself. Eventually I moved to a corner away from everyone else, with my head bowed – not unlike Tallis.

I flicked my eyes up occasionally to observe the goings-on in the room. Mechislav and Ruby now conversed in a whisper.

Alexandro fiddled with a gadget on his wrist. I narrowed my eyes and realised that he too was wearing a bracelet that seemed to be like the ones we contestants wore. He was concentrating harder than I had seen him before; his natural smile replaced by an expression of attentiveness.

I looked at my own bracelet. I couldn't recall Alexandro wearing one previously. Why would he fit himself with one of our bracelets? Perhaps it had belonged to a previous contestant, I wondered if he wore it as a sign of triumph.

Alexandro's distraction was only momentary; the next time I glanced up he had hidden his bracelet beneath his sleeve and was once again beaming vacantly at the room. I avoided his eyes, afraid that that could be perceived as an invitation for conversation.

Ruby had made her way to Quyén and begun talking to him animatedly, which he ignored. He fidgeted in his seat, unable to sit still as Ruby hounded him.

I was concerned that Mechislav would make his way over to me now that his companion had abandoned him, but he stood alone. Convinced that he would eventually gravitate towards me, I turned my back to ensure he understood my lack of interest.

Ruby had abandoned attempts at conversation with Quyén, instead making her way confidently towards Tallis. With folded arms and a cocky snort at her arrival, he appeared as inviting as last night's dinner.

Time dragged on, and Chase's absence turned from notable to concerning. My heart sank into fear for his wellbeing.

As I watched Tallis also ignore Ruby's approaches, I wondered how the previous challenge would have transpired if I'd had a different partner. Tallis's refusal to communicate had made the challenge difficult, but I wondered how I would have fared with Naomi. Or Mechislav.

I would have loved to be partnered up with Chase. His intelligence and strength would have guided me to the mascot quickly, and I'd have learned more about PSE during our time in the forest. Surprisingly, Tallis and I managed to complete the task before Chase and Mechislav. I imagined how much time the pair must have wasted with their disagreements.

As I fantasised about having been partnered with Chase, I wondered how Sid would have survived the Trial. I thought of him quivering behind whoever he was partnered with. He would not have been the most helpful partner in the forest, but I still would have preferred to have him by my side than Tallis.

My thoughts were cut off by a rusty yell across the hall.

'You!' Mechislav's outburst echoed loudly against the high walls.

Silence followed; every face now turned towards Mechislav. He was staring down a tunnel from which a figure began to slowly emerge. Chase appeared at the mouth of the tunnel, his blackened eye now badly swollen and a bandage around his shoulder visible beneath his shirt.

Chase refused to acknowledge the outburst; he moved to the centre of the room with his chin high. Mechislav made a beeline for him. 'How *convenient*. Vhat vas zee hold up, Chase?'

'Pardon?' Chase replied calmly.

'Took your time to make eet here. Vhere vere you?'

'Where was I?' he repeated. 'Where do you think?'

The exchange stole the attention of the room. Even Tallis had raised his head to watch the spectacle, although Alexandro appeared dazed by the events.

'I zink I have a pretty good idea, Chase,' Mechislav replied. One hand now gripped Chase's collar, his eyes burning through his rival with fury.

Chase's lack of interest in the situation enraged Mechislav further, and he began pushing Chase backwards into the nearby table, where Alexandro sat. Alexandro jolted slightly in his seat and began looking anxiously at the skylight above.

Chase, meanwhile, looked back into his opponent's eyes calmly, without a word. I wanted to inject myself, to pull Mechislav from Chase and pound on his large torso. Instead, I watched on with the group.

'I should have ended you yeers ago vhen I had zee chance. You ees a slimy git, and now you 'ave bought zee boys into zis!'

Chase's eyes flickered slightly but remained composed, although now standing on the tips of his toes to keep his feet from escaping the ground as Mechislav's grip tightened. 'I don't think I underst—' Chase started.

Before he could finish, Mechislav released him and fell to his knees in agony. I watched as the pain of his bracelet overwhelmed Mechislav. Seconds later, Chase fell back onto the table screaming in pain himself. The crowd watched, enthralled. Even Alexandro could have been mistaken for a contestant as he stood inches away from the scene, watching helplessly.

As quickly as it had started, their pain subsided. Both Chase and Mechislav gingerly rose to their feet and straightened their outfits. With a sinister look in his eye, Mechislav turned and left Chase panting to himself.

A cold energy swelled in the room after this confrontation.

'Come, friends. Let's enjoy our meal.' Alexandro announced as several Scouts entered the hall and placed a variety of dishes on the centred table. His feeble attempts to lighten the room only served to create a tenser environment, however my stomach growled at the smell of the incoming food.

We each found our seats and I quickly helped myself to a serving of chicken drumsticks and mashed potato, while struggling to decipher Mechislav's comment: *'brought the boys into this'*.

During the feast, the only sounds were the scraping of plates and chewing of food. Alexandro had discarded attempts at conversation now, and almost all the contestants were too focused on their meal to engage with each other. Occasionally Ruby whispered something under her breath to Mechislav and he would grunt approvingly. One time, Quyén leaned in to Tallis and asked about his experience in the jungle, but Tallis's silent response only intensified the tension.

Chase sat beside me. Attempting to be subtle, I whispered towards him, 'How are you?'

After a moment he turned his head slightly towards me and mouthed, 'Fine.' His half-hearted attempt at a smile did little to convince me.

After a few moments I tried again. 'So . . . how did you find your mascot?'

'What do you mean?' he replied softly.

'I know your mascot was hidden. How did you find it?'

Some of the others were listening in. Mechislav and Ruby looked up in unison at my comment about the mascot, and from the corner of my eye I could see Mechislav smirk.

Chase brushed off my question with his hand and forced more chicken into his mouth. I had a feeling he continued to feed himself to avoid answering questions, so I dropped my attempts at communicating with him and restocked my plate again.

As the skylight above us turned a darker shade of purple, the plates emptied. My stomach felt fuller than it had in weeks.

Alexandro stood to address the group. 'Thank you, friends. A delicious meal. I must say that I am so proud of each and every one of you survivors. I feel as if only yesterday this great hall was full. Now only six remain.'

Survivors? Alexandro had never used that term for us before. I felt a large lump in my throat, and swallowed. I looked to Chase, but it seemed as if nobody else at the table had noticed Alexandro's choice of words.

'Friends, I leave you with this:

Two options lie ahead,

A difficult or easy route.

It must be said,

Do not back out.

The situation dire,

Not far to strive.

Resist your desire,

And you will survive.'

Alexandro beamed at his silent guests.

Resist your desire, and you will survive. There was that word again – *survive.* My mind stayed on Alexandro's final couplet as the table cleared and Alexandro ushered us back to our tunnels.

There were no farewells after the feast, each contestant evidently distracted by the upcoming Trial. I dwelt on the description of us as 'survivors'; it seemed to confirm my theory as to the fate of Sid and the other terminated contestants.

I opened my eyes, and once again I was lying in my bed, staring above at the odd shapes in the ceiling. The last few hours had breezed by without my knowing and despite my guilt about not farewelling Chase, I drifted off to sleep with Alexandro's voice repeating in my head.

And you will survive . . . will survive . . . survive . . . survive . . .

27

Control Room

It felt like months since I had last experienced freedom. The opportunity to shower when I desired or eat whatever I wanted had been missing for so long that I had become accustomed to this new life. The hexagonal walls of my pod became so familiar that I almost forgot what my bedroom at home looked like. The distant memories of my life outside confinement felt like a mirage, an impossibility I could barely believe.

My internal clock told me it was past midnight, but sleep eluded me. I focussed on the cards that I held loosely in my hands. The deck of cards had become my closest companion between opportunities to be with Chase, and as I shuffled them, I felt a stronger connection to them than to anything else.

It had only been a few hours since the last feast, but the time away from the other contestants was already more enjoyable.

The familiar yet fainter sound of a *whoosh* forced me to jump. I had become accustomed to the sound, so why did it seem so distant? I stood in the dark and crept towards the wall to my right, which had so often opened for access.

But neither of the entrances were open. Had I imagined the sound? I pressed my ear against the wall which blocked the tunnel, listening for any sign of movement. After a few moments of silence, another *whoosh* sounded in the distance. My heart skipped. I pressed the side of my face tightly against the wall.

Nothing unusual had ever happened in my pod that didn't lead to the start of a Trial. I felt I had a head start on anyone who had not heard the sounds. Perhaps the other contestants were asleep, and I could begin the next Trial with an advantage.

I raced to the sink and splashed water on my face. Reciting the last riddle aloud, I paced the small area in my pod. 'Two options lie ahead, a difficult or easy route . . .' I rubbed my eyes vigorously. '. . . Resist your desire, and you will survive.'

Whatever lies before me, I must take the difficult path, I told myself. I imagined a fork in the road, with two options. The more desirable path would lead to a more difficult Trial, I thought.

Before my imagination would carry me any further, a third *whoosh* came. This time it came from directly behind me. I spun around and was greeted by the darkness of the hallway. It appeared more ominous than usual; no lights illuminated the sides and the hall itself was obscured by the blackness between us.

Stepping forward into the emptiness of the walkway, I felt more alone than usual. The opening behind me did not close as it had so often done. Every few steps I would turn to see the light of my pod shrinking behind me until it disappeared, swallowed by the darkness.

The hall ahead of me was still out of view. I rested my hand against the cold wall and used the stone surface as a guide forward, taking each step more cautiously than the last. After what felt like a lifetime, I stepped into the open space of the hall. I looked up at the skylight. Stars scattered across the dark sky like droplets of white paint on a black canvas; providing the only source of illumination in the hall.

I stood alone in the centre of the hall for a few moments. It felt emptier than ever with all the furniture removed. I found myself staring towards Chase's tunnel. At any moment he would step out and we could venture forward together.

If only Sid was still here, I thought. We could be nervous together.

Nobody joined me.

I glanced around at the other hallways going off in various directions, but I was truly alone. Why had nobody joined me? Was everyone still asleep? Could I complete the next Trial before the others had even woken?

I inched onward. Staring back at me like idolised sculptures were the large double doors, appearing far darker than normal. Perhaps I had never really appreciated them. For the first time I noticed the grooves forming large squares on the doors. I went to them. They were the only aspect of the hall that invited me to interact.

I pushed them lightly, and to my surprise they swung open as if they were my own front door.

Heart racing faster than ever, I stepped through the doors.

I entered a room smaller than my pod. Rich mahogany floorboards matched the large wooden doors; however, the ceiling was much lower than in the hall and there was no sky light. Directly in front of me lay another wooden door. Claustrophobia set in as the doors closed softly behind me. With a couple of strides I reached the next wooden door. It was far less elegant than its predecessor. I pushed my way through.

Nothing prepared me for what lay beyond. I was in a brightly lit corridor, resembling a hospital. I had no sense of direction beyond the confines of my pod and the hall. Perhaps I would get to the circular room with cylindrical pods if I continued onwards.

My eyeballs ached and the dazzling influx of light forced them shut. I opened them with a painful squint and stepped forward into the corridor. The large tiles appeared cleaner than those in my pod, and the white walls extended as far as I could see, with several frosted-glass doors along each side.

The area was deserted and there was no sign that anybody had ever set foot here. Each footstep clicked loudly against the tiles, masking the heave of my breathing. The fine hairs on my neck and forearms stood up as I ventured along the cold corridor.

On each door a golden plaque was affixed beneath its frosted glass. I had to walk up to within inches of the closest door to read the small writing engraved upon the plaque:

TRANSITION ROOM

I tried the door. It was locked. I ventured further forward along the corridor, reading the plaque fixed to each locked door as I passed.

HOLDING POD #03

PREP ROOM

HOLDING POD #04

I passed ten doors, each of which was secured and labelled, until I reached the end of the corridor. In front of me was not a wall, but a final door – unlabelled – which swung open invitingly as I approached it. Beyond it were two corridors which forked diagonally left and right; a large sign fixed to the wall between them.

CONTROL & OPERATIONS (left)
SANCTUM (right)

I stood beneath the sign; both of the presented options were as curious as the other.

I turned, with the eerie feeling that I was being followed. Nobody presented themselves behind me, so I turned back to the sign. Which was the more difficult choice? Alexandro's riddle replayed in my mind.

Two options lie ahead, a difficult or easy route . . .

Resist your desire, and you will survive.

To venture towards something labelled Sanctum seemed to be the obvious choice for an easier Trial. So I went left.

I shuffled down a corridor identical to the one I just strolled through. The long walls featured only a few locked doors, each unmarked. After a minute of silent walking, I came to the end where a dark frame presented itself.

Another door, singular but as large as the set of double doors in the hall, and with tinted windows. A plaque above the frame read CONTROL ROOM. I gave a long exhale and pushed. To my surprise, the heavy door inched open with a creak.

The room was curved, a perfect semicircle. A large keyboard with knobs, buttons and flashing lights ran around the entire curved wall. It ran neatly beneath two dozen screens, which flickered between projections brightly. The room had no lights, but the entire space was lit up by the screens.

The door struggled to open any more than to just allow me to squeeze through. Something was blocking it from behind. With one hand holding the door open, I bent down to feel for the large object behind it.

My heart skipped a beat and I loosened my grip on the door as I fell backwards outside the Control Room. The door slammed loudly in front of me and echoed down the corridor. I had touched a body. I pulled myself up – was it dead?

I had barely registered what I had felt and seen, but now I replayed it: the path of the door had been blocked by the body's lifeless head. I couldn't shake the feeling that I should not be here; I shouldn't even be outside my pod. I certainly couldn't be caught here.

My body warned me to run away, to retreat back to my pod, but instead I placed my hand on the door again. I pushed on it, and it was once again met by the body on the floor.

I now squeezed myself between the frame and door and allowed it to close behind me. For the first time in weeks, I was grateful for all the weight I had lost, allowing me to slip through the slight gap somewhat comfortably.

The body of a short man lay lifeless in the doorway. He wore tight black pants and a black collared shirt. Embroidered on the front of his shirt was his printed name: Ian. Beside Ian was another body; this one sported a shaved head and wore an identical outfit to his partner. I couldn't see the name, as this body lay face down.

I gently kicked Ian's shoulder, flinching in anticipation of him waking. Neither of the bodies showed any sign of movement. I wondered whether this was part of the Trial. Why had nobody else joined me?

I swivelled around to examine the control board. The keyboard looked almost festive with its multi-coloured lights blinking erratically. Numbers labelled various buttons and knobs along the panel, too complicated to take in on first viewing.

The screens above flickered. Each screen presented a collage of camera angles. I quickly realised that I had a complete view over the entire complex. After a few seconds, each screen would transition to show a different camera angle, and most of the screens merely displayed static. As each new camera angle displayed a new area of the premise, I noticed that each angle was labelled.

I caught a glimpse of an image labelled Pod 4. A bird's-eye view of my own pod presented itself. The bed unmade, and the opening to the hallway visible – a live view of my quarters. The image flicked to a deserted hallway. I skimmed over the other images to locate the other pods, to find who remained in their confinement and who had joined me in the Trial.

Each contestant's pod was virtually identical to my own, the only distinguishable difference was the colour of their bedspread – which mimicked the colour that represented them within the Trials. I could make out similar objects, such as a deck of cards and a book in each pod.

Tallis lay peacefully in his bed, his mouth wide open and one long leg hanging over the frame. Quyén paced irritably inside his pod. His copy of *The Metallic Moon* was destroyed, its pages spread out over the entire room. Unlike my own, neither Tallis nor Quyén's pods currently had access to the hall.

I scanned the cameras for Chase; I wanted to know he was safe. After a few seconds I found the image displaying Pod 5. It was unoccupied. His light brown coloured bed was made perfectly, and there was no sign of a deck of cards or a book in the space.

My heart gave a leap; for the first time tonight I felt accompanied. Chase was on his way.

How long he had been in the Trial I could not know, but I felt confident that he would appear in the Control Room at any moment. As I continued scanning the camera angles, I found images of unfamiliar rooms. Views of narrow hallways and empty rooms with labels that read Holding Pods and Interview Rooms intrigued me. Eventually my eyes fell on an image that flickered so quickly it was difficult to make out what I was seeing.

The image was labelled Research Facility. Every few seconds I would find the same distorted image and examine it briefly before it disappeared. Rows of metallic beds were lined in straight rows like a morgue. Most of the beds were accompanied by a body lying face up, immobile, with wires and tubes inserted in various parts of their bodies. The image was black and white and it was difficult to discern the granular details. Were the bodies alive?

It was impossible to observe the room for any more than a few seconds before the image flicked to another. When I found it again on another screen, it quickly disappeared once more. There had to be a way to pause these screens. I scrutinised the brightly lit control board.

I was instantly distracted by a row of buttons with a label above reading Pod Exits. My eyes lit up more than the panel itself. Three rows of ten buttons lined up beneath the label, each of the ten columns clearly representing each pod. Some of the buttons shone green; most were red.

Each room seemingly featured three exit options but as far as I knew, my pod only offered two: the one I had taken this evening, leading me to the hall and the other giving access to the en suite. Curiosity sparked in me – what was the third opening? I ran my fingers over the buttons, tempted to begin pressing at random. My index finger hovered over the forest of buttons, and I watched the cameras in anticipation of where the final exit led.

Then a sound behind me caused me to turn. I was no longer alone.

28

AN UNEXPECTED RETURN

The roar of footsteps approaching the room broke my concentration. Multiple pairs of feet grew louder. I stared at the darkened door, expecting them to burst open.

'We don't have time, Ralph,' a woman pleaded. Her voice cracked nervously.

'How else will we know where they went?' replied the other.

I scanned the room for a place to hide. There was no exit other than the door the strangers stood beyond. I slid into the shadows, careful to avoid the two bodies.

'Philly said it was heading into Quadrant B,' the woman said. 'There's no way they can escape once in there.'

'C'mon, let's just see if we can catch a glimpse from the cameras. Ian won't mind.'

The door creaked as they pushed on it. A slither of light from the corridor shone into the Control Room. I clasped my hand to my mouth in desperation to drown my loud breaths.

'What the—?' Ralph began as the door hit the unconscious Ian. The body remained lifeless as ever; I was convinced he was dead.

Before Ralph could investigate the blockage, a third voice came from the hallway. 'Ralph! Cara!' It was a woman's voice, authoritative.

The door shut again with a thump.

'Ms Delacour,' they both replied in unison.

'What are you doing down here? Don't you know it's all hands on deck trying to locate the missing subject?'

'Yes, ma'am,' Ralph spouted. 'I – I just thought we could see if Ian—'

'I'm sure if Ian had seen anything, he would have reported it.'

'Yes, ma'am. Of course, ma'am.'

I looked down at Ian. He had a large bruise above his eyebrow and dried blood on the side of his face. I pushed myself as far back against the wall as the room allowed. If the people beyond the door were to enter, I would surely be blamed for attacking the two men.

'Then get a move on!' the authoritative woman barked. 'Ralph, head to Quadrant B – my sources say the subject was seen heading towards the clinical trial rooms. Cara, come with me. We have to wake Alexandro and give him his serum. He may need to make an announcement to the contestants if this gets out of hand.'

'Yes, ma'am,' they repeated.

Footsteps scuffled away from the door and I lowered my hands from my face as I relaxed my body. The three voices had left the vicinity, leaving me alone with a barrage of thoughts. My hands now trembled at my side in realisation that this endeavour might not be part of the Trial at all. On the screens, the other contestants remained isolated inside their pods – other than Chase.

No, I was here by mistake.

I longed for Chase to accompany me, to perhaps shed light on why my pod had opened and why he had also resigned from his own.

A few moments passed, and I heard no further noises. Too frightened to open the door yet, I instead shifted my attention back to the control panel. I concluded that I should investigate this room further before I returned to the safety of my pod. Eleven silver dials gleamed on one side of the panel, each numbered individually. They were each set to 0. I found myself running my fingers over the dial labelled 4. I turned it cautiously, passing 1 and towards 2.

My hand began to shake; for the first time I could visualise how nervous I was. Unknowingly adjusting something, perhaps in my pod, I continued to rotate it towards 3. My hand trembled faster the moment the arrow on the dial reached the number 3 and I instantly understood what I was controlling.

I spun the dial back to 0, and the involuntary vibrations along my wrist slowed to a stop. Perhaps Alexandro was not responsible for controlling the bracelets after all. He was always near the contestants when the bracelets were activated, far from the Control Room. I immediately felt less sympathy for the people who lay lifeless behind me. They had been the ones inflicting the pain through the bracelets.

Before I could experiment any further, an image caught my eye. Bodies in uniforms – similar to the ones worn by the Scouts – ran across several screens, some with handguns, and others holding some other, unidentifiable arsenal. The pods and the hall remained still, but the unfamiliar rooms were in chaos. The Research Facility filled with people who crept between the beds in formation, lowering themselves to look beneath each one.

The door behind me moved, and I jumped instinctively. With nowhere to hide, I slumped backwards onto the control panel, anticipating the worst. The door pushed forward towards me. Ian did not budge, once again butted by the door.

A tall woman slipped through the gap, allowing the door to close behind her. She wore a loose white gown, and her grey hair fell over her face like a nest of entangled twigs. I recognised her immediately.

Gloria's eyes lit up with surprise at the sight of me. 'Tyler?'

She stepped over the body as if it was no more than an inconvenience.

'Gloria!'

She nodded, brushing her messed hair from her forehead. It wasn't just her dishevelled appearance that was different. She stood confidently, as I had never seen her before.

'What are *you* doing here?' she whispered. She looked around the small room suspiciously. I tried to respond but no words came.

'You need to go back right now,' she said. 'I don't know why . . . or how . . . where's Mechislav?'

My brain was racing at a million miles an hour; the urge to retreat to my pod grew greater than ever, followed by an influx of questions. With a leap of excitement, I recognised Gloria's presence as significant. She stood before me, living, breathing: this meant the other terminated contestants might still be alive.

Ignoring her question, I raised my own. 'Where's Sid?'

Gloria frowned and narrowed her eyes at me. After a moment, she pushed past me, muttering to herself. Her attention was on the control board. She watched the monitors above as she fiddled with various dials and buttons. I opened my mouth to ask again but she cut me off.

'Tyler, I'm sorry. I know this must be confusing.' Still focusing on the controls, she pressed a button and multiple screens blackened. 'But you need to trust me. Go back to your pod and wait for further instructions. You should not be here.'

She turned to look at me, and I could see fear in her eyes.

'But . . . the Trial?' I asked.

'What Trial?

'This one?' I said hesitantly.

'This is not a Trial, Tyler! I must have accidentally opened your door instead of Mechislav's.'

'*You* let me out?'

'So amateur of me. I may have just ruined this whole thing!'

'Why are you trying to open Mechislav's pod?' I asked.

'Tyler, please go back. The hall is empty; you won't be seen if you leave now. Trust me.' She was pointing to the cameras displaying the deserted corridors. I wanted to know more. Questions about Sid, Mechislav and her intentions all flooded to my brain. But time was against me. I could only ask one.

'Where is Sid?'

'Tyler! Go! I have to shut your pod's door manually, so you need to leave now.' She was pleading with me.

Time defeated me. She had made a valid point. If this was not a genuine Trial, I couldn't be caught away from my pod. I had felt the vibration of my bracelet when set to 3 as uncomfortable. I did not want to experience it at full force.

I pulled on the door, hitting Ian once more. Gloria was furiously pressing buttons and turning dials.

'Gloria . . . is Sid –?'

'Go!' she barked, without diverting her gaze from the screens.

Conflicted, I allowed the door to slam behind me and ran. I raced away from the Control Room, navigating the white corridors into the darkened hall. Every door opened for me with ease, as if I was meant to be back in the sanctuary of my pod. Looking at the ten tunnels which forked from the hall, I thought of Tallis and the other sleeping contestants, unaware of the crisis unfolding around them.

The guards I had overheard were concerned about a 'subject' that had escaped. Unsure if they were referring to Gloria or me, I sprinted through my familiar tunnel towards the dim light of my pod.

The second that I re-entered my confinement, I threw myself on the bed as the opening slammed shut behind me with a *whoosh*.

29

THE TEMPTATION

I didn't sleep at all for the rest of that night. Unlike Quyén, who I recalled pacing in his pod, I lay like a plank of wood; still. My restless eyes refused to drift, instead staring up, whilst my mind raced. I anticipated Alexandro's appearance in my pod at any moment with an interrogation about my expedition.

Time steadily ticked towards morning. The emerald glow of the EXIT sign was eventually joined by a faint illumination of the pod's perimeter.

Occasionally I imagined sounds beyond my walls. Unconfirmed blasts of doors opening in the distance, or scuffling of footsteps. Each time my ears fastened onto the noises, they vanished, and I convinced myself that my tired brain was playing tricks on my mind.

My mind wandered back to the Control Room.

A camera hidden beyond the grooves of the ceiling recorded me, and somebody further within the

Control Room monitored everything. I presumed that the Scouts had already removed the two unconscious bodies and a full investigation was underway to locate their attacker. I was certain my escape would have been recorded. Above all, I felt relieved that I had managed to retreat to my pod undetected.

What of Gloria? I wanted to believe she was innocent, but her disregard for Ian and his counterpart convinced me that she had been aware of their fate before I discovered them.

The lighting around the perimeter of the floor brightened, signalling that the opportunity to sleep had now lapsed. It was morning already. I rolled onto my side to face the wall, feeling the cold stone radiate against the tip of my nose.

Sharp static penetrated my ears, lasting longer than normal, but eventually broken by Alexandro's familiar voice. 'Friends! Good morning!'

I rolled onto my stomach and allowed my head to sink deep into the pillow. As if underwater, the host's words were muffled causing me to catch only intermittent sections of his speech. Through the feathers of the pillow, I heard him announce the upcoming Trial, Trial Five, was in preparation. He then repeated the riddle from the previous feast.

He paused. I wondered if he was aware of last night's adventure.

I accepted his announcement as confirmation that my experience overnight was not part of the Trial. I had managed to escape from my pod only to foolishly return myself voluntarily. I lifted my head from my pillow by an inch.

'The Trial will begin momentarily. There is no need to shower or get changed; you will be completing this Trial from within your own quarters.' I propped myself up on my knees anxiously. There was no sign of any new instruments within the pod.

As if he were announcing what was on the menu for breakfast, Alexandro confirmed the commencement of another Trial.

'Shortly, I will ask you to stand beneath the EXIT sign with your back and both hands against the wall. The Trial will require you to maintain both hands against the wall at all times. Should you remove either one, or both of your hands, you will forfeit the Trial. The first to forfeit will be terminated.

'Contestants will not be notified when their opponents have forfeited, so willpower will be your biggest strength in this Trial.' He paused again.

'Now, friends, I ask that you position yourself beneath the EXIT sign with your back and both hands behind you against the wall. The Trial will commence in ten seconds. Nine. Eight . . .' As Alexandro counted down, I shuffled to the designated spot, where so often the opening to the en suite was exposed.

'Five. Four . . .'

I placed my hands against the wall like an obedient pawn.

'Three. Two. One . . . Trial Five has now commenced. Remember, the first to withdraw a hand from the wall will be terminated.'

Alexandro's voice faded away and I was left again in silence, both hands pressed against the stone surface behind my back. I imagined the view from the Control Room: six pods with each of the contestants standing like soldiers in formation.

Minutes passed and nothing occurred. My left hand became annoyingly itchy, but I resisted the urge to scratch it. The more my brain focussed on my hands, the stronger the urge to itch became. Surely this was not the desire I had to resist . . .

In front of me, the entrance to the hallway opened with a *whoosh*. My eyes flicked up, anticipating company. Seconds ticked by, with my hands fixed to the wall behind me, but nobody appeared. Had Gloria reopened my pod door? Was she again inviting me to escape?

I considered the outcome if I was to run towards freedom. I saw myself running through the opening and into an empty hall. I wondered if the double doors would again be unlocked if I pushed through, or if I would be trapped in the hall and punished for trying to escape.

I decided against the temptation of leaving my pod. It was safer to stay in my confinement while uncertain of what lay beyond.

After a few minutes, footsteps echoed from the hallway to break the silence. A metallic rattle accompanied the feet, all growing louder the closer it approached. The noises stopped at the foot of the opening. Two long shadows cast into my pod from the tunnel, towering along the tiles up to my feet.

A third rectangular shadow grew as it crept past the opening, the shape coming into definition as it came closer. The shadow rattled loudly. The shape transformed into a trolley; a trio of shelves tiered above metallic wheels.

On the highest shelf of the trolley, an abundance of sweets was tastefully laid out. An aroma of freshly baked brownies, pastries and cakes filled the room. My mouth salivated instantaneously, and my last meal was forgotten. It had been months since I had tasted anything sweet. The strong scent of the brownies tempted me most. I could taste the chocolate already, far more delicious than the two slices of stale bread I expected for breakfast. Alexandro knew about my fear of snakes and heights, he knew of my mother, and somehow, he even recognised my sweet tooth.

Despite the temptation, I jerked my head away from the trolley. My stomach growled angrily. The long shadows of the Scouts over the trolley reminded me that withdrawal from the wall would lead to termination.

Termination. I had no idea what that meant any more. If Gloria was still alive, and roaming beyond the pods, then termination did not equal death. I no longer felt afraid about what occurred after termination. No longer did my fear of the unknown outweigh my curiosity.

I wanted to see Sid. I was determined to know if he was okay and to accompany him wherever he may be. I still felt guilt that I had not been there for him in his final days of the Trial. I owed my friend an apology.

Before a second thought could take hold in my brain, I pushed myself forward and the wall fell away from my fingertips. I stood in the centre of the pod with both hands trembling loosely at my side.

I made a movement forward towards the trolley but as I did, a couple of things happened at once.

No sooner had I withdrawn myself from the stone, the trolley flew out of the opening like a slingshot and the door slammed behind it. Light in the pod evaporated with the trolley's exit; now only the familiar illumination of the green sign above me cast its dull light. I fumbled my way towards the bed for security.

'Forfeit!' Alexandro's voice echoed into the room. 'Mr Tyler Knight, you have lasted three minutes and forty-one seconds.'

I remained where I stood, staring at the darkness where the closed entrance to the hallway should be. I awaited its opening and the arrival of several Scouts to escort me towards the unknown. I wondered how many would come in. As I stood in the centre of the pod, I no longer felt scared. I was ready to embrace what lay beyond the Trials.

Minutes passed, but nobody came. I felt my legs twitch as they grew tired, my weak calves forced to stand for longer than anticipated. The room was stained in emerald from the EXIT sign behind me and my eyes slowly adjusted to the dimness of my pod. I accepted that the Trial continued throughout the other pods and that Alexandro must be waiting for its conclusion before withdrawing me.

I slumped forwards onto the bed. The adrenaline drained from my body and was replaced with anxiety about my decision to forfeit. The longer Alexandro took to come and get me, the more I regretted what I had done.

And there was guilt: I felt I had let Chase down. I imagined his anger towards Alexandro as he learned of my fate, and his disappointment in me. He would assume that I could not resist a platter of sweets for a few minutes, without understanding my true struggle.

I buried my face in my hands, now feeling a pain in my stomach, which rumbled aggressively. I should at least have tried to collect a brownie from the trolley.

My body sank into the mattress as the minutes passed mindlessly. The room's glow intensified after what felt like an hour. Through squinted eyes behind my fingers, I waited for Alexandro to appear. Instead, his voice sounded loudly. 'Congratulations, friends! For you have completed Trial Five!'

Surely this was a mistake. Why had nobody come to collect me from my pod?

'It is with great regret that I inform you that the first contestant to forfeit the Trial, and therefore be terminated from the Oranga Trials is . . .' My heart pounded faster than ever. I could almost feel it in my throat. I was now sitting up in the bed.

'Mr Quyén Miles.'

A cool sensation coursed through my veins as my heart relaxed slightly. Relief. Alexandro continued his speech, but I did not take it in. I collapsed backwards, feeling that I had cheated death.

'. . . only five remain . . .'

I instantly regretted my decision to forfeit the Trial. I only needed to survive a handful more and I could get out. Now that I only had four remaining opponents I should focus on completing the Trials.

'. . . the next Trial features no desires . . .'

But what would happen to Sid if I won the Oranga Trials? What would happen to Chase and the others who would be terminated?

'. . . there is no time for a riddle. . .'

My mind span wildly, conflicted between fighting on and forfeiting. I was convinced that either decision would lead to the same outcome.

'. . . no upcoming feast . . .'

I was amazed that Alexandro's speech continued to ramble. I shook my head to refocus, forcing myself to tune in to what Alexandro was saying.

'Friends, you have three hours. Trial Six will commence tonight.'

30

THE VIEWING ROOM

The en suite opening was exposed loudly, drawing my attention away from the shock of Alexandro's message. Annoyed with myself for not listening to his speech more closely, I tried to piece together what I had missed.

I would be participating in another Trial by the day's end, and could find myself in the quartet of remaining contestants should I avoid termination once more.

I ventured into the cool space of the en suite. It provided a familiar chill as the opening closed behind me.

Clothes removed, I stepped into the cascade awaiting me. The moment the water hit my skin my brain suppressed all meaningful thoughts. Staring ahead, I watched my wet hand fixed to the tiled wall. Droplets raced from my fingertips towards the point of my elbow, their last moments of individuality before plummeting to the pool below and disappearing in the cascade.

Both mind and muscles eased in the lukewarm stream of the shower. I only realised that I had been sweating when the salty taste dripped past my lips. One at a time my muscles relaxed to the penetration of the shower's pressure. At this moment, all I wanted was to stay exactly where I stood.

But I remained torn between my desires. To compete, or to resist?

The decision loomed; I knew I had to wholeheartedly follow whichever path I decided on. If I were to resist the next Trial, I had to commit to finding Sid. If I decided to compete, I would need to win the Trials.

I strained to consider my most notable strengths, but nothing came to mind. For each area of strength I considered, another contestant seemed superior to me. Physically, Tallis was clearly stronger; Ruby more calculating. Chase boasted more resilience than anyone I knew, and Mechislav was more meticulous. What did I bring to the table?

My confidence drained with the puddle of water at my feet. Then, with a jolt of confidence, a thought emerged: I did not need to be best at any given Trial; I only needed to be better than at least one other to avoid termination.

I may not be the strongest contestant, however I should outlast Ruby in any strength-orientated Trial as she appeared to grow weaker with each passing day. She is more calculated, yes, but I felt that I am at least cleverer than Tallis. Despite my respect for Chase, I know I pay more attention to detail than him and should outlast him in any Trial that requires wit.

And although I am not the most level-headed of all of us, Mechislav is far more volatile than me.

I repeated these thoughts as a whisper, masked by the sound of the running water.

I am not the physically weakest. I am not the least intelligent. I am not the least calculated. I am not the most unstable.

My decision seemed clearer now, but a tinge of guilt remained. I would compete in the Trials until to their end, which meant that for me to survive, Chase would ultimately be terminated.

He would do the same, I reminded myself. *He is doing the same.*

But he wasn't. Chase had always been there for me since he arrived in the Trials. I could not shake the memory of his encouraging smile from the cylindrical tubes. That felt like an eternity ago. I recalled Chase's theatrical argument with Mechislav on either side of me throughout the third Trial. Each step of the way, he was looking out for me.

I decided that I needed to speak with Chase. Together we could orchestrate a scheme for survival. I wouldn't have made it this far without him; I couldn't continue on my own. It was vital that we both survived the upcoming Trial.

I was brought back to my senses by a loud blast outside the shower, beyond the walls of the en suite. The source must have come from a room outside my pod. I had now seen behind the curtain; occupied rooms beyond my pod breathed life. The sound could have been routine for the Scouts; possibly the slam of a door, or construction works.

Wrinkles on my fingertips indicated that I had stood in the shower for an age. The water ran cold, but I remained standing, watching the race of droplets down my forearm. I had allowed my mind to wander once more. It was time to get out.

The moment my foot found the external tiles outside the shower, an unusual light caught the corner of my eye.

A new opening to my left was exposed. Pod Opening 3.

I groped for my towel and dried myself without taking my eyes off the opening beside the shower, concerned it would disappear if I looked away. Had the next Trial begun? I recalled last night's experience, fooled into believing I was participating in a Trial when in fact I'd had an opportunity to escape. I couldn't make the same mistake again, but I also couldn't treat this opportunity as anything less than a Trial.

The tunnel, quite similar to the one that wound in the opposite direction, greeted me like an old friend. The walls were stone, but there were no strips of light running along the base of the walls, no bright light to guide me.

I dressed quickly, my skin still damp against the jumpsuit and my hair thick with water. I pushed my fringe from my eyes and made my way through the opening.

I was forced into a crouch as I entered the tunnel. My neck bent downwards to prevent my head from scraping the rocky ceiling. Only one person could pass through this cavity at any one time as it seemed to grow smaller the further I ventured along it. It guided me through bends to the right, and further on to the left, zigzagging away from my pod. If I could manage to rotate and look back, the en suite would surely now be hidden from view.

A yellow light glowed ahead, brightening with each step. I continued to weave snakelike along, my knees bent, and my neck hunched, until a large space grew into view. I had to take several uncomfortable lunges across the uneven terrain before I emerged into a room unfamiliar to any that I had recognised from the cameras in the Control Room.

The room gleamed golden, with light glittering from a magnificent chandelier that hung from the centre of the ceiling. It hovered above a single armchair, isolated like a cynosure. Its thick leather skin invited me to rest, but I turned instead to observe the curious room. The walls were bare, and the ceiling was raised as high as the one in the hall. Opposite me, beyond the chair, was a white door.

The room's openness was a blessing, allowing me to stretch out after the minutes of crouching awkwardly. Looking back at the tunnel; it was pitch black.

Above the tunnel entrance, a screen was mounted. An unmade bed, a deck of cards strewn across the tiles. The familiar orange tinge of the room confirmed that I was staring at my own quarters. A shudder ran down my spine.

My stomach squirmed at the thought of an unknown observer, staring at my every movement since my arrival at Touhere – watching as I fled from

an artificial snake, scrambled over broken ceramics in
the darkness, and collapsed in my own tears.

Shifting away from the screen, I decided to
continue onward.

I approached the white door. It was my only
option. Pausing, I fixated on Alexandro's previous
message to recall any clues ahead of the Trial. I was
frustrated that he hadn't provided a riddle before the
tunnel opened. My brain clicked; a realisation
formulated.

Alexandro had always announced the start of
a Trial. He had announced the commencement of the
Trials that began in the en suite. He had also
announced the start of the surprise Trial, despite it
being sprung upon the contestants.

This was not a Trial.

My neck pulsated aggressively beneath the
collar of my jumpsuit. Wild theories as to the source
of my tunnel's opening circulated, from Gloria to
Alexandro. Knowing that I would not learn the truth
by staying in this room, I grasped the doorhandle.

Once committed to pass through the door, I
knew I had to act carefully and silently. I could not be
detected and would have to locate Gloria before
anyone from PSE found me.

Cautiously, I cracked the door open a fraction,
just enough to peer through it. The area beyond the
door was no room or hallway, but a foyer, an airy
atrium space. Dozens of people scurried; men and
women of all ages, some in uniforms I recognised,
others in casual clothing.

While closed, the door had masked the sounds, but now it was ajar there was a hubbub of scattered calls and hurried footsteps. An alarm rang through the foyer, albeit dulled by the bustle of the workers.

Large marble tiles stretched across the atrium floor. The ceiling rose out of view, a spiral staircase at the far end of the foyer indicating that the building was several stories high. The perimeter of glass walls allowed an influx of natural light into the room. Beyond the panes, trees outside swayed in the breeze, which somehow allowed the smell of invigorated flora to meet me for the first time since the Trial in the forest.

A man with grey hair in a guard uniform raced up the spiral staircase while shouting into a small walkie-talkie. Closer to me, two women stood at an elegant desk, their hair pinned back identically, both wearing matching blue uniforms with a dark red stripe down the sides. They were in animated discussion.

There was a sense of chaos, or at least panic in the room. Were they reacting to the loud blast I'd heard earlier? Unnoticed, I adjusted the door further to take in more of the surroundings.

Along the wall on either side of me was a row of doors identical to one I clutched. Swinging my head out of the doorway, I noticed they were labelled and numbered. Looking up at my own door, I read: Viewing Room 4.

A new blast echoed from above, this time far louder than the one I heard from the shower. The room shook slightly causing me to topple forwards into the foyer. My hand slipped from the door and it closed behind me. Chunks of rubble showered from the ceiling, sending the workers scrambling like ants in rain. I watched in awe as glass rained down, falling onto the two women behind the desk.

High-pitched screams filled the room as a mass of people descended the staircase and filled the foyer. The chaos allowed me to remain unnoticed and something urged me to venture onward. If Viewing Room 4 provided a tunnel to my en suite, I decided to shift along the wall to locate Viewing Room 5, where Chase could be. He was the only person I was confident I could trust, and he had to be beyond that door.

With my back fixed firmly against the wall, I stepped across towards Chase's Viewing Room. Noises overhead grew louder as more glass shattered and poured onto the people below. Colossal glass doors leading past the foyer and outside had now been opened as workers scurried towards the exit, hugging their briefcases and other personal items. I was tempted to bow my head and join them, but I knew I couldn't leave Chase behind.

I approached the door and fiddled for the handle, but there was no doorknob, no handle to open. Instead, a blinking device to the side of the door indicated that an electronic key was required to open it.

I kept my head down, chin cushioned into my sternum as I pushed inward to the foyer.

Without a plan, I allowed my senses to determine my course. Each step demanded caution, but my bowed head made it difficult to forge a path.

Footsteps behind me grew louder, and before I could turn, I was greeted by a force between my shoulder blades.

My elbow buckled as it connected with the hard tiles, and my back was hit a second time as I sprawled on the ground. I closed my eyes in anticipation of another blow.

Papers were thrown in all directions, a walkie-talkie skidded across the tiles before me. My initial fear that I was under attack dissipated as I turned to face a woman who lay beside me. 'So sorry, I – I –' she stuttered.

The woman was middle-aged, her orange hair was as dishevelled as her belongings scattered around us. She reached for her glasses in a panic, her trembling fingers making it difficult to fix them to her face.

Our collision appeared accidental; perhaps she was not one of my captors. I took the opportunity to gather information. 'What's going on?' I asked, attempting to avoid eye contact.

'I – we don't know . . .' The woman stammered.

She mustn't be important, I thought.

Before I could pull myself up from the ground, a projection on a screen above the concierge desk caught my eye. It was my own face, smiling down over the foyer. I brought my hand to my face instinctively, feeling the rough bush of my beard, which was absent from the face above. The face that smiled down was clean-shaven, his hair groomed neatly behind the ears, his white teeth glistening like Alexandro's.

That was not the same face I'd seen in the reflection in the river.

A collection of similarly unnerving faces beamed down at the foyer from the screen. The other contestants. Each of their names and correlated numbers were highlighted in their unique colour above them. Some had large red crosses across them – the terminated contestants. The remaining faces had a range of ever-changing numbers beneath them in bold green.

The woman who fell onto me had disappeared, but her walkie-talkie remained and I scrambled in an attempt to collect it. As I reached for it, one of the hurrying bystanders collided with the device and it shot across the room.

Frustrated, I pulled myself up and examined the projections more closely to try to decipher the numbers that flickered and adjusted rapidly. Two figures appeared beneath each contestant: one was a monetary value which steadily increased; the other was stationary. Looking at my own face, the caption read:

Contestant 4: Tyler Knight

$1,342,500

@4.25

The room shook with intensity as another explosion blasted several storeys above me. The building vibrated. Through the chaos I thought I heard my name. I glanced around the foyer for approaching Scouts but saw only the scramble of people. Nobody had seemed to notice me at all.

'Tyler!' The voice was louder this time, and higher-pitched. It didn't sound like a cry of attack, but of rescue.

The door labelled Viewing Room 1, a few metres away, was slightly ajar. Ruby's face, sweating and flushed, poked from behind it. She called my name again.

Leaving the walkie-talkie, I darted to Ruby. She was not my first choice for a companion, but the company of any contestant was better than nothing at this point. She opened the door a little more and I threw myself into her room, with the door closing quickly behind me. I collapsed onto the armchair in the centre of the room.

Her Viewing Room was identical to my own, the only difference being that the monitor here was shattered. Ruby stood with her back to the door, staring past me expressionless. I could see her mind ticking.

'What's happening?' I asked.

Ruby continued to look past beyond me. I turned to see what fixated her. With a jolt, I stood: we were not alone. Standing in the mouth of the darkened tunnel, with his hands in his pockets, was Tallis. He stood on the shattered glass of the monitor as if it was a welcome mat. I turned back to Ruby. 'What's going on?'

'I think they're here,' she said, a nervous smile finally providing her face with emotion.

'Who's here?' I asked impatiently.

She looked away from Tallis and into my eyes. She took a step in my direction but was thrown forward by a force. Another explosion from above. The three of us fell to the floor.

The slam of Tallis's head against the wall behind him was somehow louder than the blast. Blood quickly began pouring from his temple. I caught his watery eye for a brief moment before he turned away.

'We need to go!' I shouted as I pulled myself up and made for the foyer. Ruby was already on her feet, meeting me at the exit. She pushed her body against the door to prevent it from opening.

'No,' she said. We stared at one another briefly. 'We can't leave him here.'

Together, we turned to face Tallis, who was now crouched in an attempt to stand. He looked up at us, tears now evident in his swollen eyes. Ruby was right. Despite our differences, Tallis was no longer the enemy.

'Come on, we need to make it to the roof,' Ruby said as she made her way towards Tallis, pulling him up by his large arm. His heavy body pushed Ruby sideways, but she was stronger than she appeared and maintained her composure. I hurried to them and wrapped Tallis's other arm over my neck.

'They will be waiting for us.' She said.

Together, Ruby and I heaved Tallis's enormous body towards the door. He tried to help by scrambling his feet along the floor, which only made the task more difficult, however neither Ruby nor I said anything.

'Who is waiting for us?' I asked abruptly. 'What's on the roof?'

Thousands of questions flooded my mind and I wanted to stop to ask them all.

Ruby continued onward silently until we reached the door. 'Tyler, I promise that everything will be explained, but right now we need to get to the roof.'

I understood she was telling the truth, and that she could be trusted. I no longer had an urge to uncover the mysteries of our captors. My only priority was escape. Ruby swung the door open, and thick dust filled my lungs. With Tallis's large body between us, we stepped into the foyer.

31

THE FINAL CHASE

The dust was so thick that I could barely manage to see further than a few metres. It penetrated my eyes and mouth easily, since both my arms held Tallis's frame. Through the dust, mechanical sounds boomed several levels above us. The chaos in the foyer moments earlier was now no more; now only a trio of souls moved across the tiles.

Stepping over unconscious bodies, we dragged Tallis towards the spiral staircase, eventually resting him against a large marble pillar. 'I'm okay,' He insisted, which we both ignored.

I sensed Ruby calculating our next move. She looked from Tallis's bloody face to my own, seemingly taking on a parental role.

'You!' A call echoed through the haze.

Across the foyer, behind the reception's desk, stood a man in a Scout uniform. He pointed in our direction and raised his walkie-talkie device to his helmet.

'Let's go!' Ruby called, pulling Tallis by the arm up the stairs.

I threw myself under his other arm and followed without hesitation. We attacked the stairs two at a time, and behind us, I heard the Scout's footsteps grow louder. Our several-metre advantage allowed us to topple onto the first landing before the Scout had approached the foot of the stairs. I was already out of breath. My hands gripped my knees for support as I drew heavy breaths of dust.

Abruptly, Tallis freed himself from our grasp and limped towards a corridor. Ruby and I paused momentarily, then she turned to follow him while I remained struggling for air. Dust on the walls of my throat prevented me from calling after her. The Scout's feet sounded on the metal of the stairs below.

Ruby had almost caught up to Tallis as he pulled further away, his hobbling strides reaching a fork in the corridor. Despite my urge to follow, my mind spun, the Scout's footsteps banging louder with each step he took. Ruby had now caught Tallis and threw herself under one of his arms in support.

'Wait!' I called.

Ruby craned her neck, a look of urgency onto her face. Her final words found me as she disappeared around a corner. 'Meet us on the roof!'

I could not afford to waste any time at the top of the stairs; the Scout would reach me any second. I attacked the next flight of stairs with vigour, without looking back. My lanky legs skipped several steps with each stride and my mind spun with the spiralling upward course.

The Scout's presence was lost once I approached the fifth and final landing. Perhaps he had opted to follow Ruby and Tallis's trail or had given up the chase altogether. The stairs had run out, but I remained indoors with the rooftop still seeming to be some floors above. I pressed myself against a nearby pillar, drawing fresh air into my lungs. The dust swirled several floors beneath me.

A surge of anger swelled as I recalled Tallis limping away on the lower level. He and Ruby had abandoned me. She should have allowed him to flee so she and I could get to the roof together.

The ginger-coloured dust crept up the staircase, the foyer floor now hidden beneath it. A row of floor-to-ceiling windows ran along the entire wall beside me. The air outside was clear, and treetops stretched as far as I could see. Through the carpet of trees, a dirt road twisted like a shoestring towards a hilltop. There were no other man-made features in sight, other than the debris which continued to rain from the top of the building.

Looking left and right, I decided to venture down random corridors in search of a ladder or stairwell. For minutes I wandered along the weaving hallways but found no avenue upwards. In my erratic attempts at opening doors, the few unlocked ones revealed only deserted offices or meeting rooms. When I made it back to the spiral staircase, I was adamant that I could travel no higher.

Perhaps Ruby shouldn't be trusted, I thought. I considered giving up trying to reach the roof and instead moving back to ground level to escape outside. Before I could decide on my next step, a friendly voice found me.

'Tyler, there you are.'

I turned quickly, almost toppling, to find Chase standing at the end of the hallway. He no longer had on the matching jumpsuit of the contestants, instead wearing grey pants, which wrapped around his thick legs like a tree cloaked in foil, and a white polo shirt. The shirt was stained in patches of scarlet and brown like an abstract canvas. I stood with my back against the pillar, perplexed, as he advanced towards me with outstretched arms.

'Don't mind the outfit,' he laughed, noticing my sceptical expression. 'I stole it from one of the bodies on the ground. Thought it would be easier to blend in.'

'Where have you been?'

'Looking for you! Come on, we need to get out of here before the place collapses.' His poise immediately calmed my nerves. My heart rate slowed, and I allowed him to escort me towards the stairs with his hand between my shoulder blades.

'Wait,' I said. 'Ruby – Ruby said we need to get to the roof.'

'Ruby?'

'Yeah, she's with Tallis. We were chased, but we need to get to the roof.' I realised I had begun shaking again.

'You know where Ruby is?' he asked, stopping in his tracks.

I nodded.

'Where is she?'

Before I could elaborate, he guided me to in the direction of an opened room. 'What do you think is going on?' I asked.

The determination in his eyes gave me confidence, but also confused me. Ignoring my question, he escorted me into the empty room, closing the door behind him.

A wooden desk was surrounded by three black office chairs, two of which were lying on their side. The desk was bare except for some ruffled papers. An array of scattered stationery lay on the carpet around the desk, including a computer monitor and binder folders. The room trembled as another noise was heard overhead, this time it sounded as if someone was drilling.

Chase leaned against the door frame. 'Take a seat and tell me everything you remember about Ruby's whereabouts.'

I sat and relayed my adventure after leaving my en suite, feeling guilty that I had accompanied Ruby and Tallis, despite Chase's clear dislike for them. He listened coolly. I finished by telling him of the Scout who had followed us up the stairs, and how I had been searching for a way to the roof.

On my last word, Chase withdrew a device from his back pocket. I was unaware of how he had obtained the walkie-talkie, but I didn't ask as he lifted it to his mouth.

'This is Chase. I have located Tyler and have him secured in Snider's office. Ruby and Tallis were last seen on the first floor. Tallis has a severe head injury, possibly concussed.'

Bewildered, I stared at him. I opened my mouth to ask the obvious, but he spoke before I could.

'It's okay,' he said, tucking the walkie-talkie away behind him. 'Let's talk.'

32

THE TRUTH

Another explosion sounded overhead, and the room shook. We both steadied ourselves throughout the tremble, and then I adjusted my feet quickly.

'We need to go,' I said, finding the brown of his eye.

Chase no longer looked at me with compassion; instead, a fire brewed behind his gaze. 'We're not going anywhere,' he replied. 'It's time you were told the truth.'

My feet cemented themselves to the ground. Part of me wanted to run past him into the thickness of the dust, to evade all reasoning and responsibility. A more determined part of me fought this urge. I waited for Chase to continue.

'The building is under attack by an uprising who plan to take down PSE. They call themselves "the Defiance" and they've discovered the secret of Touhere and are now attempting to rescue the contestants. Several helicopters have landed on the roof to extract each contestant from the island. We have to stay here. We have to stay hidden, Tyler.'

'What? No, we need to get to the roof!' I stepped towards him, determined to find my rescuers. Maintaining eye contact, he withdrew a spherical silver device from his front pocket. I stopped inches from him, staring at it.

Our noses were separated only by a slither of delicately floating debris; the light from the window behind me sliced through the dust onto the device's surface. It glistened in his hand, and his thumb hovered above a circular dial.

'Stop, Tyler,' he breathed. 'Go back to the chair, sit down and listen.'

Chase's face remained expressionless. I lunged my foot forward, wanting to bypass him, but before it found the ground, Chase had pressed his thumb on the dial.

My bracelet vibrated with such aggression that I did not feel the floor meet me as I hit it. I felt a scream escape me, but I could hear nothing, or see nothing. All I knew was the pain beneath my skin. My bones burned with each intense rattle and my ribs felt like they were clapping together like drumsticks.

It felt like an age, writhing on the carpet in pain. The bones in my legs felt as if they were splitting apart beneath my skin.

Then the pain stopped.

I could not find the motivation to lift myself from my ground. I allowed my face to remain attached to the carpet. I felt the dust from the floor meet my lungs with each breath.

'Nicolai is on his way now to explain everything,' Chase said from above me.

Still quivering, I managed a stuttered reply. 'Nicolai?'

'Yes, Nicholai is the Chairperson of PSE. The man responsible for the Oranga Trials.'

'But . . . Alexandro?'

'No, not that idiot!' he spat. 'Alexandro is as useless as a chocolate firefighter.'

I didn't know what he meant by that, but I suspected that Chase had more to say, so I decided to not respond.

'Nicolai is the man who has organised the Oranga Trials. The Scouts follow his command, and he also controls Alexandro. It is he who brought you here, is he who brought all the contestants here.' Chase spoke of the contestants as if he were not one of us. He held the spherical device tightly in front of him, as a reminder that he controlled me.

I fumbled my way across the carpet towards the window to create as much distance between us as possible.

'Each contestant was brought to Touhere because they have wronged the friends or colleagues of Nicolai in one way or another. Quyén and Naomi have both crossed a very dangerous narcotics dealer who happens to be a close associate of Nicolai. Shy also disappointed a major business associate of

Nicolai, while Hermes found himself in considerable debt to another of Nicolai's friends.'

'I don't understand.' I was now backed against the wall. 'What does Nicolai want with me? You told me I was here because my father left PSE.'

'You, Tyler, have been caught up in a war. Your father did leave Private Sector Eleven, but he did not transfer to another Sector. He left us and joined the Defiance that is plotting to destroy us.'

'But I thought –'

'Yes, your father and I worked together for many years at PSE, but something changed. I love your father like a brother, but he grew weak. He began questioning what PSE stands for, what we accomplish. He decided to leave, and on his departure he took our secrets, our legacies. Six months ago, your father teamed up with that oaf Mechislav and recruited a team of others in an attempt to destroy what we have built. We had managed to capture Ruby, and then Mechislav, but Victor eluded us, so we instead duped you into to coming to the island.'

'You brought me here? It was you?'

My brain couldn't keep up. I heard his words, but I could not comprehend how the man I had trusted through the Trials was responsible for my capture.

'I like you, Tyler. I always have. But this is far bigger than friendship. Haven't you wondered why you haven't seen your father the past few months? He's been in hiding, like a coward, and he left you to fight his battles.'

'You're lying!'

'It's true. At PSE we have built relationships with some of the most dangerous underground organisations across the world. We keep the peace to ensure the general public is not threatened. However, your father and his allies want to destroy that. They want the world to see the darkness that we hide from them.'

Nobody spoke for several seconds. The only sounds were the mechanical noises from above, shifting in and out of my ear's focus. My body transitioned into flight or fight; I was conflicted between both. But Chase held the advantage in the palm of his hand. The device made it impossible for me to do either.

I had never seen Chase display such passion as he towered over me, a rare thrill glistening in his eyes. There was no way out of this room other than the door he guarded. My heart beat aggressively in my chest. Did it know that it only had limited beats remaining, and wants to get its final ones in before the end?

With all hope of evading him gone, I decided that the only resource I had to gain was knowledge. 'If you are working with PSE, then why were you in the Trials with us?'

'Because of you, Tyler,' he replied casually, 'The Oranga Trials are much larger than they appear. Demand for certain markets was raised, and bookmakers were arranged to create such markets for the Trials.'

'You mean, people were betting on us?'

'Of course. And once you began discussing your agenda to stop engaging in the Trials, we knew we needed to act. If your plans to orchestrate a mass non-compliance within the Trials were successful, we would have to void millions of dollars in stakes. I was put into the Trials to calm you, to ensure you remained competitive in each challenge. But Mechislav was onto me; he and I have a long history and he saw right through my act. He knew I was involved in the delivery of the Trials and did everything he could to help you survive.'

'Mechislav? He hasn't helped me at all,' I said quickly.

'Is that what you think? Do you really think you would have survived in the forest if he hadn't insisted on following you for its duration? Regardless of how much I fought him, he was determined to ensure you found your mascot before us!'

I recalled the sounds that had followed me throughout the jungle and how they eventually led me to Tallis and our mascot. If Chase was telling the truth and they had been following me, then that explained how they had located their own hidden mascot – I had led them straight to it. 'That was him?'

'Yes. He would have gotten himself terminated if it meant keeping you in the Trials! And he would have, if it wasn't for Quyén sabotaging Naomi.'

'I don't understand. Why did you continue to motivate me if you wanted me terminated?'

'Don't you see, Tyler? It was all to get you to trust me over the others. It didn't matter if you were eliminated in the first Trial or the last – we would never allow you to return to the outside world. Don't tell me you believe that "innocence will prevail" nonsense!'

Loud footsteps trampled beyond the door. People were now on the fifth floor with us. Unsure if they were friend or foe, I pulled myself up off the carpet to face whatever came.

'Your fate is sealed, Tyler. I truly am sorry.'

My blood felt as if it were boiling beneath my skin. I wanted to attack Chase for everything he had said. The pain from the bracelet was nothing compared to what I felt at this moment. I was conflicted about who had my best intentions at heart. I was unsure of my father's regard; I only hoped that he still breathed life somewhere.

I focussed all of my blame on Chase. I clenched my fists by my side, ready to strike.

Then the door burst open, collecting Chase abruptly and propelling him towards me. I managed to step out of his path, allowing him to collide heavily with the wall behind me. Mechislav erupted into the room, a man on a mission, stepping past me without acknowledgement. He threw his large frame onto Chase.

The men scrabbled on the floor, exchanging blows. Mechislav landed an aggressive hook into Chase's side, his ribs cracking deafeningly from the force. Chase managed to reverse Mechislav onto his back and sat on his chest, attacking him with multiple punches.

'Tyler, go!' Mechislav called from the floor. 'Get to zee roof!'

His face, already bruised, had a determined expression. Chase turned to me but Mechislav grabbed at him to ensure my path to the door was free. I stood frozen in place; I didn't want to leave Mechislav with Chase.

'Go!' he yelled again. With this distraction, Chase struck Mechislav on his temple with force, silencing his victim.

Both of Chase's hands were fixed firmly around Mechislav's neck. The Russian's face swelled, its colour changing from pink to purple.

I wanted to help, but my feet wouldn't allow it. Why couldn't I move? A surge of memories flashed past. I recalled standing motionless earlier, as disaster occurred in front of my eyes. I did nothing when Hermes was beaten by Tallis, and again when Mechislav and Chase fought in the hall after the forest Trial. I stood silently and allowed Sid to be taken after his loss in the Trials. I could not continue to allow myself to stand by while others got hurt.

I lunged at a plank of debris that lay in a pile on the floor beside me. I was unsure if it was from the ceiling or elsewhere, but it was heavy in my grasp.

I swung the wooden plank, meeting Chase at the base of his skull. It smashed into shrapnel in my hands, my only weapon now destroyed. Chase collapsed onto the floor beside Mechislav, whose face now became pale white. Chase's eyes rolled backwards, his unconscious body now helpless in the dust.

33

THE RESEARCH FACILITY

Two men lay helpless before me, one faced the wall blankly – unconscious. The other pulled at his collar in a desperate attempt for air. Mechislav's eyes bulged eerily, a blend of sweat and blood dripping from his forehead.

My hands trembled. Each held a broken strand of wood. I let the pieces fall to the ground to join the other debris.

I stood in shock, in disbelief that I had attacked Chase. The only person in the past month that I had considered a friend lay motionless at my feet. He had been a friend, an ally, but within a matter of minutes I had learned that he was my greatest enemy. He had absorbed the full force of the anger that had been brewing in me for weeks, and it came by a means of a blow to the back of his neck.

I no longer felt hatred for Alexandro, nor fear, nor disgust. I felt nothing towards the host other than contempt. It was Nicholai who was responsible for my abduction, Nicholai who organised my participation within the Trials and Nicholai who allowed members of his organisation to gamble on my outcome.

And Nicholai was on his way to this room.

'Mechislav?' I stepped over Chase's limp body and dropped to my knees beside the man I now put my confidence in. 'We need to go!'

His bloodshot eyes met my own, and he opened his mouth to speak. He let out a painful breath, followed by a heavy cough. His throat swollen, unable to speak, Mechislav looked up at the ceiling and pointed.

'The roof, I know,' I said.

I pulled him to his feet and together we limped for the exit. I couldn't resist a final glance towards Chase's body.

'Do you think he's . . .' Unable to complete the sentence, I turned to face Mechislav, who simply shook his head.

He grabbed my wrist and forced me from the room. Despite my inner conflict, I entrusted my safety to Mechislav, and I followed him down a corridor past the spiral stairs.

We were able to manoeuvre throughout the building undetected. We found no Scouts or members of PSE, but also saw no evidence of any support from the Defiance.

The noises from above us had quietened, and after a few minutes of pacing through doors and corridors we found ourselves in another open space not unlike the foyer downstairs. Silence met us once we entered, and Mechislav put his finger to his lips to hush me.

Following his confident lead, I trailed him through the open area, where he found a long counter to drop his weight onto. His breathing – broken and dense – grew louder.

'Are you okay?' I asked. He gave no response, nor was one needed: it was clear the man was struggling for breath. A tinge of purple remained upon his face, and his neck was thicker than I had seen it before.

I allowed him to rest for half a minute while I marshalled my thoughts. I had trekked the floors of the fifth landing before, but this space was foreign to me. The building was a behemoth, full of curious corridors and doors, and it was possible that much of the fifth floor has escaped me during my scramble.

Empty walls, flickering lights and the heavy breath of a new ally.

Behind me, a door crashing open startled mc. Four Scouts thrust themselves into the foyer like bullets from a barrel. One of them was pointing at us. Without pausing to exchange words, Mechislav and I sprinted towards a door adjacent to the Scouts.

I glimpsed a device in one of the Scout's hands and hoped that it was a walkie-talkie, not something that could activate our bracelets. One spin of the dial in Chase's pocket, or from the Control Room, and both Mechislav and I would be halted.

Passing through an unmarked door, I was yanked to my right by my forearm. Mechislav dragged me from room to room while I focussed on keeping myself from stumbling. The stamping of the Scouts behind us dulled with each door we pushed through, until we fell into a large space which I recognised immediately.

We stopped running. Mechislav dropped my arm.

The room looked exactly as it had on the screens in the Control Room but the being here caused goosebumps to surface on the back of my neck. The room no longer flickered as it had done on the screens; I was standing in the room marked Research Facility. I took in the rows of metallic beds, and the medical components beside each one.

Mechislav limped towards a couple of empty beds and piled them against the door we entered, barricading us from the Scouts who undoubtedly would be approaching at any moment. Some of the beds were not vacant, however. Distracted by the lifeless bodies, I turned to the first bed on my left.

Glassy eyes stared blankly at the ceiling. A gown covered the man's entire body, exposing only his pale face. Strings of wires extended from his body, almost machine-like. He looked familiar, yet so different. I noticed a thick scar stretched diagonally across his face, running past the disfigured ear. Hermes.

I clapped my hand to my mouth instinctively.

The scar remained, but this was an amended version of the man who had worn the number 7 in the

Trials. He was barely recognisable. All pigment was drained from his skin and his frame was considerably thinner. The scar was the only constant, and I wondered whether I would have recognised him without it. Even his hair was several shades lighter than I remembered.

Hermes' empty eyes no longer threatened. I stepped backwards, nudging the frame of the bed behind me. I stepped from the beds, heart pounding, as I thought of the man I had once been intimidated by. The last time I saw Hermes he was beaten almost unconscious by Tallis; perhaps he deserved more sympathy.

I turned to Mechislav, who appeared to have not noticed my absence. He was continuing to pile empty beds and any other objects against the door. The Scouts had arrived on the other side, and Mechislav scrambled to build up his barricade.

I wanted to help, but my eye caught a glistening silver from the edge of Hermes' bed. A metallic tag was attached the frame: Hermes Lombarden, 31 years.

I glanced at the other occupied beds, each with an identical tag. With a surge of horrified curiosity, I crept along.

Naomi Ark, 26 years.

Shy Fisher, 60 years.

I refused to look at each of the lifeless bodies, my focus on one person only. Ignoring the sound of Mechislav building his metallic mountain, I walked to the bed at the end of the row, towards the expressionless face of a boy lying in peace.

Sid was almost unidentifiable; it looked as if his soul had been ripped from his face, leaving a colourless canvas. I leaned over him; his piercing blue eyes stared through me as if I were invisible. It was impossible to confirm whether life existed behind them.

I felt an urge to free him from the prison of wires that punctured his torso and limbs. The maze of tubes extended in all directions across his body and into various pockets of the bed.

Tears welled in me and dropped onto his chest. My knees buckled. I whispered, 'I'm sorry.'

My hands fell onto his chest; Sid offered no acknowledgement of my pain. I felt no heartbeat. My grief transformed into anger, again directed at Chase. How long Sid had been restricted to the bed, I did not know, nor could I understand why, but it clearly was not for Sid's benefit.

I pulled myself up from Sid's body and turned away. I couldn't allow myself to face the same fate. I apologised once more and closed Sid's eyes with the tips of my fingers, telling myself he was now only resting. With a forceful swipe, I ripped the nametag from the bed and stuffed it into my pocket.

Mechislav croaked at me from the other side of the room. Still mute from Chase's attack, he grabbed at his throat after his attempt to call for me. He pointed past me at a door on the opposite side of the room.

Calls beyond the barricaded door grew in aggregation, and the mountain of beds and random objects budged towards us with each heave from the opposite side. The Scouts were coming for us.

In a corner of the room was a mirror-tinted window. It appeared to be an observation room with no notable entrance.

Beside this, the door which Mechislav had pointed to now found his aggressive grasp. He pulled at the handle which caused it to rattle, but refused to open. We were trapped. I swivelled in a panic. There were no other doors. A loud grunt from one of the Scouts followed by an avalanche of beds, side tables and empty drawers suggested they were almost in the room.

Something shone beyond the tinted window, a familiar emerald tinge. The shade of green illuminating in the small room reminded me of the pod I had been confined to over the past month; the exact hue I had spent hours staring at.

I moved to the window for better examination. The cold of the glass kissed my nose gently as I blocked out peripheral light with cupped hands. The green light source was obvious, and within an instant it became our saviour.

'There!' I called to Mechislav. 'That is our way out.'

An illuminated EXIT sign just like the one in my pod nested against a wall inside the smaller room. In the reflection of the glass, I saw a wide smile spread across Mechislav's face. The smile said more than words could have.

Beyond him, I watched as arms pushed the doors ajar, disentangling themselves from the mass of metal. The noises grew louder, empty beds were sent sliding across the floor, crashing into the occupied ones. I saw Naomi's arm slide from her bed as it was hit.

Mechislav matched the sounds of chaos behind us with his own. He had grabbed at a loose metal pole which had rolled towards us, and with a single lunge he forced it through the tinted window. Glass rained down and I turned my face away. The smashing sound was followed by a raucous jangle of falling shards.

Before I could compose myself, Mechislav had already pushed himself through the opening and held his hand out for me to follow.

I carefully stepped across the field of shattered glass and over the low wall to join him in the smaller room. A Scout called aggressively, close now, but I refused to turn. If I didn't see him, then I was safe.

Mechislav kicked at the door beneath the EXIT sign and it opened with ease. A gust of wind slapped across my face. With one hand still grasping his weaponised pole, Mechislav grabbed at my wrist with his other and pulled me from the room.

Together, we had stepped from chaotic warfare onto a narrow balcony that overlooked the serene forest.

34

THE ROOFTOP

The door swung closed behind us and with a swift motion, Mechislav wedged the metal beam between its handle and a nearby metallic hook securing the door against the weight of our pursuers. A breeze tickled my forehead. My fringe danced, and my baggy shirt slapped against my skin.

Treetops extended far into the distance. Somewhere within the forest I imagined the four mascots had previously lain, although there was no beachfront in view.

We only needed to sidestep along the balcony for a few metres before we were met by a ladder, which invited us upwards. Craning my neck, I could identify the edge of the rooftop floating in the clouds. I allowed Mechislav to lead the ascent. I gripped the first rung as Mechislav's foot lifted from it, my blood pumping wildly inside of me.

In the past few weeks I had overcome obstacles I had never dreamed of facing. I had avoided climbing the tree in the forest, but now my fear of heights reignited as I gripped rung after rung. I closed my eyes, instantly visualising the experience in the first Trial. In my head I fell through the clouds towards an open paddock.

I exhaled loudly and followed Mechislav upwards. I knew what had to be done.

Each lunge up distanced me from the thrashing of the door we had blocked from the Scouts, until I only heard the wind against my ears. We climbed for a minute, my arms and legs wobbling with each movement, as the sound of people shouting and loud collisions took over.

Mechislav had reached the summit. His thick head peered over the ledge for a few moments before turning down to meet my eye. Once more, he raised a finger to his lips, followed by a mouth movement that I interpreted as 'be quick'.

In an instant, he disappeared over the ledge, leaving me alone on the ladder. I moved up steadily, unsure of which direction he had thrown himself once atop the roof. I remained too frightened to look down, so I could only assume that the Scouts were either close below me or had given up any attempt to follow us. I took another step up and raised myself high enough to observe the scene before me.

Numerous people patrolled the rooftop with several unconscious bodies sprawled across the canvas. A charcoal-coloured helicopter, much larger than any I had seen before, rested on the far side of the building. Its sides were battered, bullet-sized holes puncturing the frame of the beast, while its propellers spun silently. Several armed figures surrounded it, on guard.

Mechislav crouched a few metres to my left behind an air-conditioning vent, well hidden from the others on the roof. A mass of unmoving bodies lay between his hiding place and the helicopter. Patrolling Scouts stepped over them. It appeared that a hostile stand-off involving both Scouts and members of the Defiance were on the rooftop.

I watched for only a few moments, waiting for an opportunity to break onto the roof. Then it came. A door attached to a small cabin in the centre of the roof swung open and a lone Scout threw himself into the fray. Wielding a handgun, the Scout stole the attention from the others on the rooftop with his erratic shouts. I only caught a glimpse of his weapon as it pointed towards the helicopter before I allowed myself to fall over the railing onto the roof.

Within three strides I had crouched beside Mechislav, panting into my hands and hoping I was not seen.

A gunshot sounded past the vent I hid behind, causing me to dip my neck involuntarily. Was it the newly arrived Scout who had pulled the trigger? I was too afraid to look, too afraid to expose myself.

Sounds of scuffles followed the gunshot until a quivering voice broke through the ruckus: 'It's the kid and the Russian. They've escaped and are going to join their friends on the helicopter!' More scuffles. The sound of a hard object collecting with another, then a body hitting the cement.

I was looking out to the distant trees, straining my ears to hear every detail. I noticed Mechislav facing away from me, focussed.

'What are you looking at?' I asked.

No response. Instead, his fingers were dancing in his lap, his mouth opening and closing as if he were trying to speak. He looked ridiculous.

Looking past him, I saw what he was saw. A couple of metres beyond our vent was another, which hid two more souls from the view of the Scouts. Ruby and Tallis.

Ruby's hands and mouth moved erratically in communication with Mechislav. They were both nodding excessively. Behind her, Tallis poked his head around the edge of the vent to watch the events unfolding between the Scouts. Blood had dried on his cheeks and neck, and one of his legs was exposed through a tear in his jumpsuit.

Before I could comprehend the conversation between Mechislav and Ruby, a new voice silenced the others from the centre of the rooftop. 'What do you think you're doing?'

I found a gap in the vent and crouched lower so I could steal a glance at whoever had spoken. A tall man, as old as Gloria but far better fed, towered over the Scout who had wielded the handgun moments earlier. The gun had vanished, stripping him of authority as he lay upon his back staring at the older gentleman who stood over him.

This man did not wear a Scout's uniform. Instead, his suit was hidden underneath a length cloak that trailed on the concrete behind him. His ivory tie matched his belt and shoes, highlighting the grey hair which hung tidily over his shoulders.

'It's that k– kid and—' the Scout began. His hands pulled him backwards slowly, retreating from the man's glare.

'You imbecile!' the man spat. 'Do you realise that we are not shooting at the helicopter?'

'Yes – I mean, no, sir. B– But the Defiance, they're on that helicopter, sir. And the kid—'

My heart skipped a beat at the thought that my rescuers could be metres from me, awaiting my extraction on the helicopter.

'Do not tell me what I already know.' The man struck his foot out and collected the Scout's ribs. 'But we are not shooting at it. And that's an order!'

The man repeated his final words to the surrounding Scouts who raised their hand to their helmet in acceptance. This man was in charge. He had to be Nicholai. I kept my focus on him as he drifted between the Scouts and gave instructions. His victim remained on the floor, apparently too petrified to remove himself. Eventually Nicholai's cloak disappeared through the door where the Scout had emerged moments earlier. 'Remember, they have one of our own on that helicopter, so anybody caught taking fire at it will have me to answer to.'

I continued to lean on the vent, peering through the gap at the Scouts who returned to patrolling the vicinity. Salvation stared at me with its spinning rotors at the far side of the rooftop. The handful of guards standing before the helicopter must be part of the Defiance, and with the insurance of a hostage on board, they did not appear threatened.

A weight on my forearm caused me to flinch. Mechislav's face was inches from my own; his eyes flickered between me and the helicopter. His lips moved slowly, as he silently mouthed his words: *'Run. Now.'*

Behind him, I saw Tallis and Ruby reveal themselves from behind their vent. Taking alternative routes, they both sprinted towards the opposite side of the rooftop. Mechislav raised himself beside me and vanished over the vent. Through the gap I watched him stride forward towards the Scouts, who noticed him after a few seconds.

I took a deep breath, then exhaled loudly. I might only have one opportunity. I pulled myself from the ground and ran from behind the vent, in the direction where the fewest Scouts were.

There must have only been a dozen of them on the roof, and most of them were distracted by the three contestants who had revealed themselves before me.

A blast from a gun sounded from much closer than the previous shot, but I kept running. A Scout stood before me with his arms outstretched but I sidestepped him towards two others, both of whom turned as they heard me approaching.

Another blast.

'Do not shoot!'

'There's Mechislav!'

A variety of calls blended into one. The roof blurred in front of me; the helicopter was all that remained clear. I could have no way of knowing where the others were, my only focus was stepping past Scouts that continued to materialise from every direction.

'Grab the kid!'

Multiple shots assaulted my ears; this time I caught sight of a Scout beside me falling to the ground. The helicopter edged closer, I could not make out the unfamiliar faces guarding the craft, weapons raised.

I felt pressure on my ankles, and I stumbled forward. Hands clung to my lower legs as the concrete ground raced up to meet me. My head smacked into the rooftop before my hands could shield it.

A Scout lay behind me, holding my ankles. I kicked out at him, but his grip tightened around my legs. I craned my head. The helicopter was so close, the rotors spinning faster than before. The men guarding it had disappeared and I saw Tallis pull himself on board.

'I got one!' the man holding me called.

I couldn't free myself from his grasp. With a groan, he pulled me from the floor and locked my arms behind my back. I scanned the rooftop, but I could see no support; they must all be on board.

Calls from a Scout approaching us were muffled by the helicopter's blades. More bodies sprawled along on the floor as the remaining Scouts either approached me or crouched over their companions.

I closed my eyes, imagining the helicopter lifting itself from the building and retreating. It had saved multiple lives, and even taken a hostage; they could not risk that success for my life. I imagined the grin upon Nicholai's face when he returned to the rooftop and saw me. What would Chase say?

Suddenly, I felt myself topple sideways before colliding with the ground for a second time. The grip behind me loosened and I frantically pulled away from the Scout. The sounds of the rotors grew louder. I crawled from my captor, eventually lifting myself to my feet. Adrenaline pumped through me; a dishevelled Tallis sat atop the Scout's chest, pounding into his exposed face. The helmet was discarded to the side, lost in the mass of bodies. The man who had held me moments earlier was now trying to protect his face from clenched fists. Tallis stopped and turned, his face wet with blood and tears.

I called to him, 'We have to go.' My voice was drowned by the rising helicopter behind us. He pulled himself from his victim and together we turned from the approaching Scouts. Each stride towards our rescue seemed a miracle; I awaited the force from a Scout's tackle.

We reached the foot of the helicopter together; it was hovering a few inches from the ground. Tallis pushed me towards safety first before toppling in on top of me. The metal floor tasted like luxury.

35

VICTOR KNIGHT

My body sank into the hard surface, vibrating to the roll of the door closing behind me. The warfare disappeared, though the blades above continued to wreak havoc in my ears. Afraid to look up, I felt my forehead judder against the metal flooring. I could feel Tallis leave my side, his feet joining the others whose voices I heard indistinctly.

My name was called, once, twice, several times. Gradually, I rolled onto my side to examine the onlooking audience. Unfamiliar faces stared at me, and several hands reached down to heave me to my feet. My body collapsed in their arms.

My name was called again from a distance. This time it was distinct; it had felt like an eternity since I had heard this voice. It could have even been the first voice I had ever heard.

'Dad?'

The arms that held my weight released me and I was pulled in by my father, his sweat stale and his beard itchy against my face. I don't know whose tears came first.

My heart tightened; whether it was the overwhelming emotion or the tightness of his hold on me, I couldn't be certain. Despite all my doubts and concerns, he had finally arrived – alive.

I was finally safe. Nobody else existed at this moment. When he released me, he examined my wounds. 'Get the nurse,' he said calmly, and a woman behind him rushed away.

Before I could speak, he ushered me from the group who had begun clapping and cheering merrily. I could hear Mechislav's loud accent boom over the crowd.

I allowed my father to escort me down a short corridor. This helicopter was far larger inside than it had appeared, seemingly fitted with small rooms off the corridor. The room I was pulled into contained two small beds with a counter between them. I didn't even feel myself fall into one of the beds.

My mind raced, and my curiosity escaped through my lips. 'What's going on?'

My father had already ordered another colleague to fetch water and was adjusting the pillow beneath my head. He did not respond, but he managed a smile before calling for the nurse.

'Dad?'

'Don't worry, son. You're safe now.'

A woman in turquoise scrubs appeared at his shoulder.

'Let's just make sure you're alright first.'

With the nurse's touch on the back of my head, I felt the room spin wildly as my eyes grew heavy. The woman exchanged hushed words with my father, who responded with concern.

Despite my attempts to force my eyes open, my body grew weaker. Sensation left my legs and torso, and with my head nestled gently on the pillow, I allowed my soul to drift.

A cool sensation originated in my forehead and flowed down my body into my limbs. I couldn't move, and my eyes remained closed, but my other senses flexed. The feeling of discomfort beneath me intensified; this was not the bed in my pod.

Droplets of water trickled past my temples from a damp cloth above my brow. The room shook slightly, which forced my body to rattle in the bed. With this, I gathered the faded memories of my expedition from my pod. Memories of the exchange with Chase and the race to the helicopter came to me. I knew where I was.

I allowed my eyes to open and scanned the room. Two people sat on chairs at the foot of my bed, hunched over and babbling intensely. For so long I was uncertain if these two were friend or foe, but for now my heart led me to believe that they were trustworthy.

I exhaled a groan as I shifted in my bed, disrupting their conversation.

'Go get Victor,' Ruby said quickly. Mechislav leaped from his chair and disappeared from the room. Ruby came to my side, her hands covering my own.

'How are you feeling?' she asked.

Horrible. My head ached and my left arm felt as if it was not my own. Looking down at my body, I realised that I had collected several injuries since leaving my pod. Both my arms were bandaged, and my left wrist pulsated irritably.

'I'm okay,' I lied, 'Where's my father?'

'He's on his way. Have some water.'

She poured two cups from a pitcher beside the bed and offered me one, which I did not take. My throat was dry and pleading for water, but my brain insisted I use my mouth for questions.

'Where are we?'

Behind Ruby a circular window showed nothing but darkness. The sun must have set since the battle on the rooftop.

'We are somewhere over the Pacific, and by the time the sun rises, Touhere will be further away than we know,' she answered, adjusting her hair casually. I noticed her wrist was bandaged similarly to mine.

The throbbing beneath the bandage reminded me of the heavy accessory I had become accustomed to. My wrist felt loose beneath the bandage, naked almost. I clutched at it.

'It's gone,' Ruby said simply, noting my movement across my wrist. 'Luckily for us, we have

an amazing technology expert on board who managed
remove the bracelets safely.'

I wouldn't be able to recognise my wrist
without the bracelet; I imagined it appeared foreign
and pale beneath the bandage. I continued to rub at it,
grateful to have control over my body once more.

'But who . . .?' I had everything to ask, but
nothing to say. I wanted answers but I couldn't find
the questions to ask.

Somehow, Ruby understood. 'Who made it?'

I nodded.

'Fortunately, the rescue team did a brilliant
job. They managed to extract both you and me, as
well as Mechislav, Tallis and Gloria.'

'But Chase –?'

Ruby looked perplexed, unsure how to
proceed. My memories were fogged and my feelings
towards Chase were twisted. The puzzle in my mind,
my memory, was missing a piece in the middle – and
that piece was Chase.

Ruby was saved from having to explain more
as Mechislav entered the small room followed by my
father, who beamed from ear to ear.

He embraced me once more as Mechislav
resumed his seat at the foot of my bed. My father
backed himself against the wall and opted to stare out
the blank window before speaking.

'How's your head, son?'

'I'm fine. Tell me what's going on,' I pleaded.
I had not spoken as abruptly in months; the

familiarity of family presence comforted me. I was tired of being lied to or receiving partial, cryptic explanations. It was time to learn the truth.

'Yes, of course. I know that Chase has created a version of events inside his head, and I am led to understand that he has given you his version of the truth. However, despite some elements of accuracy in his story, I am going to explain everything to you.'

I stared at the man I admired above all. His reflection in the window showed a determined figure. A hidden life was ready to be revealed. The secrets he had kept from me for years sat at the edge of his lips, and the look in his eye expressed only one emotion. Relief.

36

THE DEFIANCE

I shuffled upon the stiff plank of a bed, pulling my hips to meet the pillow and forcing my back against the wall behind. My father's eyes glistened in the reflection of the window. Ruby and Mechislav dared not break the silence. Eventually, as if contemplating where to begin, my father exhaled loudly, and then his shallow voice began.

'There is some truth in what Chase has told you, son. There is a government-funded organisation called Harmony Dozen, and for many years Chase and I worked within Private Sector Eleven, along with Mechislav.' I turned to the Russian, who had bowed his head. 'And for years I allowed it to consume my life, oblivious to the damage we were causing.'

He contemplated each word with precision, signing off each sentence with a soft expiration. He paused on the thought of his past trauma. My encouragement to continue was not necessary; rather it was Mechislav who spoke next. 'Zey spread corruption zrew zee vorld.'

Ruby pursed her lips and nodded silently in agreement.

'Yes, they do. Do you have any idea what Harmony Dozen achieves, Tyler?' My father now faced me, a blend of grief, regret and pride swam in his gaze.

'Chase told me that Harmony Dozen has twelve Sectors that exist to protect us,' I replied, 'to create harmony among the different classes of the world.'

'Zat ees vut zey vant yew to zink!' Mechislav spat.

'And that is what we both believed once, Mech,' Victor countered, before turning back to me. 'For many years Chase and I worked beside each other within Private Sector Eleven, thinking we were protecting people. I understand you already know that each Sector is responsible for maintaining relationships within different industries, and that Private Sector Eleven holds relationships with those who affiliate in underground organisations.'

I nodded.

'Very well. It was my understanding that we were to stop the criminals, not work alongside them. I believed that our mission was to eradicate such organisations from existence; however, I came to understand that Private Sector Eleven would rather support them, to coexist with them. It was with this realisation that my relationship with Chase began to deteriorate. Our opinions differed: he believed that there was still good in what we accomplished within our Sector. It took me almost a year to leave. With the knowledge I held, I would be putting myself and my family at risk if I left abruptly. Chase had already developed a professional relationship with you, but I never thought that he would . . .'

Tears overcame him. I could do nothing but watch as he coughed into his hand to settle his emotions.

'It's okay, nobody thought he was capable of this,' Ruby offered softly.

'I allowed him to work with my son. I welcomed him to my house, to my family,' he said to nobody in particular – mainly to himself, perhaps.

For a few heavy moments my father words hung in the air. The room continued to rattle to the insignificant turbulence of the winds outside. Each person in the room kept their head lowered, hesitating to speak next.

It was my father's voice who broke the silence, picking up his story as if there had been no disruption. 'A year it took me to walk away from the Sector. In that time, I had managed to reconnect with Mechislav, my former employer who had resigned a few years prior to myself. There were whispers he was organising a resistance to the Sector, and once I finally made contact, I met the others who accepted me.'

'And we are glad to have you.' Ruby smiled at my father first, then at me.

'You're part of the Defiance?' I asked.

'Of course. Mechislav and I practically established the Defiance along with a few others.' Ruby continued, 'But once Nicholai found out, he attempted to separate us.'

'Yes, we have been disconnected from Ruby for some time now,' Victor added. 'Three months I believe, on that island.'

'Don't know how yew did eet. I vould not have survived zat long,' Mechislav said, clapping Ruby hard on her back. She responded with a shy giggle.

It was strange seeing them out of the jumpsuits I had become accustomed to seeing them in, their furtive whispers replaced with smirks and chuckles. I now understood why Ruby appeared tattered when I first met her: she was exhausted from weeks of isolation before the rest of us arrived.

'Nicholai, the head of Private Sector Eleven, captured five members associated with the Defiance, and threw us in his 'Trials' where he had collected others who had wronged either himself or his associates within the Sector.'

I interrupted, explaining what Chase had told me about Quyén and Naomi's involvement with a narcotics dealer who held a relationship with Nicholai, and how Shy and Hermes also found themselves in the Trials. The trio confirmed the other contestants' unfortunate paths to the Trials, before confirming that it was indeed Nicholai that I had seen on the rooftop who had barked demands at the Scouts.

The puzzle slowly began to form. Pieces joined together, but large blanks remained.

'What about Sid?' I asked quietly. 'How was he involved?'

The air thickened with my question. The three allies exchanged hasty glances. For a moment I thought nobody would acknowledge me.

The eventual response came from my father. 'Sydney was unfortunately caught in the crossfire of war.'

'Like yourself,' Ruby added quickly.

'His mother, Melanie, is part of the Defiance as well,' said my father. 'She has been involved for much longer than I have, and is one of the key members in research and recruitment.'

'But Sid's an orphan. His parents are dead.'

'I have been told that you became close to Sydney in the Trials. The truth is that both his parents were involved with PSE many years ago, until his father was murdered while Melanie was pregnant with Sydney. Since her husband's death, she has committed herself to stopping them. She even entrusted her son to an orphanage and –'

'She left him?' I straightened myself. Images of Sid's lifeless body dominated my mind. He had spent his life believing his mother was dead; instead she had left him for a war.

'Melanie was forced to separate herself from her son in order to protect him. She hates herself every day for leaving him.'

296

I was speechless. I was scared to tell them what I'd seen in the research facility, afraid that they would confirm what I already knew.

My father took my silence as an opportunity to continue his explanation. 'Private Sector Eleven took ten hostages, ten enemies to their cause, and forced them to compete in Trials. However, the Trials only served as a distraction, Tyler. As you know, Private Sector Eleven is responsible for maintaining relationships with underground organisations; however, evidence shows us that Harmony Dozen used at least five other Sectors in the operation of the Trials including Private Sectors Two, Three, Eight and Nine. For example, Private Sector Three is involved with gambling agencies, and Private Sector Two works exclusively on medical research.'

'Victor,' Ruby cut him off. 'Are you sure?'

'He needs to know.'

Hostility sparked within the small room as I watched my father consider how to proceed. He had explained that the Trials were far deeper than I could have imagined, and how Harmony Dozen stretched further than Chase had described.

My desire for information swelled, and words escaped my lips before I could draw them back. 'I want to know. I want to know everything. I lost a friend in the Trials. I want to know what happened to him.'

Mechislav shuffled in his seat. Ruby turned to face the doorway. Beyond the opening, a shadow emerged. The shadow of a human stretched into the room, followed by a bruised and bandaged Tallis. His hands dug into his pockets and dried blood stuck to his face like glue. He looked as horrible as I felt.

'Very well,' My father whispered, ignoring the presence of the newest member to enter the room. 'We have reason to believe that Private Sector Two was engaged in medical testing on the terminated contestants. Gloria managed to evade the examinations; however, the others were not as fortunate.'

'But don't worry, Tyler, we believe that most of them are still alive.'

'Most of them?' Tallis interrupted.

With my words choking in my throat, Tallis had voiced my thoughts. He took another step forward and stood beside Ruby.

'Ah, Tallis. Yes, by our last report most of the terminated still breathe life. However, we have learned that Quyén passed away last night.'

'I don't understand.'

'Quyén was an avid substance user, heavily dependent. Ruby and Mechislav have told me he was displaying all signs of withdrawal throughout the Trials.' My father explained.

'He would have suffered more than any torture imaginable,' Ruby added. 'Do you remember the last Trial?'

I recalled the metallic trolley rolling into my pod, my hands fixed against the wall behind me.

'Can you imagine what was on Quyén's trolley to tempt him?'

'He died within an hour, from an overdose,' Victor confirmed.

I did not feel sorrow for Quyén's passing; rather a shiver trickled through my spine at the thought of seeing a man breathe life in his final days. I cleared my throat, desperate for the courage to ask what I needed to know. I managed two words. 'Who else?'

'By our last report, that's it. The others – including Sydney – are alive. Gloria believes that the medical experiments put the subjects into a state that appears as if they have died; however, they still breathe life.'

I sank into the pit of the stiff mattress. I remained unconvinced of Sid's fate, but I decided to not dwell on it.

Mechislav raised another question about the types of tests they were conducting, and the conversation turned into a debate over whether Private Sector Ten were being used in the process.

I allowed my mind to breeze away from the trembling room and towards piecing together the algorithm of my past few weeks. I now understood that my capture was no coincidence, and that each of the other contestants were as unfortunate as myself, caught up in this invisible war.

Each of the people I'd met had their own agenda, and my true enemy was not Mechislav; it was Chase. Nicholai, not Alexandro, was the puppetmaster. Alexandro's name was mentioned in the muffled debate within the room.

'Daa, Alexandro. Vas a shame vut zey did to him.'

They discussed what substance the host had been unwillingly subjected to. My father reminisced on his experiences with Alexandro before the Trials, at Private Sector Eleven.

'Such a good family man.'

As they discussed Alexandro's loss of control over his body and speculated about his fate, I instead thought of the remaining blanks in the puzzle that was the Oranga Trials. I considered the contestants who I had treated with suspicion, but who had eventually come to my rescue. Tallis saved me on the rooftop, and Gloria could perhaps have been involved in more than I knew.

When asked about how Gloria had managed to avoid the medical experiments, Victor responded with a smirk. 'Let's just say that we are glad she is on our side. Gloria is an extremely intelligent woman with the ability to deceive others that underestimate her. She used the opportunity of being terminated with Naomi to evade the Scouts, and infiltrated the Control Room. Gloria has been a great asset to our cause; she uncovered many of the operations of PSE after her termination and was eventually able to set up communication to orchestrate the rescue.'

I began to make sense of the mysterious openings of my pod over my final days of my capture. I recalled Gloria's surprise at my appearance in the Control Room, and her hasty dismissal of me. *I must have accidentally opened your door instead of Mechislav's.*

The woman dressed in turquoise scrubs reappeared at the foot of the door, unable to enter the already cramped space. She politely asked for clearance. 'The young man needs rest now. You can visit him later.'

At her request, Ruby and Mechislav shuffled towards the doorway. I returned their wave, noticing that they passed a steady-footed Tallis. The nurse made her way towards my father, who began peppering her with questions about my wrist and head. Tallis stepped towards me with his head hanging low and his hands hidden in his pockets.

'You rescued me,' I said to him, unable to meet his eye.

'You saved me first,' he replied quietly. It occurred to me that I had never heard him speak a complete sentence without a grunt before this moment. I couldn't comprehend his response, unable to recall saving his life. 'In the tree. I would have fallen if you didn't help me.'

Remembering the experience as a blur, I reached out and grabbed his bandaged wrist. He had experienced the force of the bracelet on more occasions than any other contestant.

'Don't mention it.'

Tallis remained only for a moment before pulling his wrist away. He was never a wordsmith.

'Tallis, why were you in the Trials?' I asked. It had occurred to me that he was the only contestant whose presence was yet to be explained. He did not appear to be part of the Defiance against PSE, and neither Chase nor my father had confirmed how he had come to be on the plane to Touhere.

Only one word broke through his quivering lips. 'Love.'

Without a farewell, Tallis turned quickly and disappeared from the room. Behind me, I heard my father ask for a minute more, and the nurse's reluctant approval.

He knelt to face me, ignoring the chair beside him. His presence brought comfort; the familiar scent of stale sweat reminding me of a time before the Oranga Trials.

'Tallis is arguably the most unfortunate of all the contestants, Tyler. He had fallen in love with a young woman, and they spent several happy months together until he had the displeasure of meeting her father. The young woman's father is Nicholai, and although we're unclear on the details of what unfolded at their meeting, it is known that she has been distraught since Tallis's disappearance.'

I reflected on my father's words. Tallis had a hidden heart, and I had seen glimpses of it. His resentment towards the Trials sprang from separation from his partner.

'Son, now you need to rest. We'll be landing soon, and you'll need to be fit when we do. There is still a war to be fought.'

'We need to go back and get Sid,' I said firmly.

'I know, and we will. But first, you need rest.' He placed his hand firmly on my shoulder and leaned in close. 'I promise.'

He embraced me a final time before following the others' trail.

'Dad, wait.' He stopped at the door and looked back, one hand on the doorframe. We looked at each other in silence, but no words were spoken. With a sly blink of his eyes, and a nod of his head, he understood all of the words I wanted to express but couldn't. He disappeared around the corner leaving me to the nurse's examining gloves. She pulled at my bandages and applied ointment to my elbow.

After a few minutes, she also withdrew herself from the room.

The room rattled, and the voice inside my head gradually faded. The bed moulded around my body and the pillow wrapped around my neck like dough. The Oranga Trials were over, but something much larger loomed.

Relief and guilt were balanced equally in me as I took comfort in knowing I was finally safe from my captors, and from the tyranny of the bracelet's control. When I closed my eyes, only one face remained. Chase. The man I had put my trust in, the man who had betrayed my father.

For the first time in my life, I knew my purpose, I understood what needed to be done. I had always aspired to be like my father, but never had I felt prouder to be his son. I would complete the work that he and his allies had begun.